WHERE *the* LINE BREAKS

Shortlisted for the Fogarty Literary Award

Michael Burrows

WHERE *the* LINE BREAKS

Michael Burrows was born and raised in Perth. When he was old enough to fend for himself, he ran away to London, where he currently lives with his partner. He wrote the first draft of this novel as part of his master's degree at City, University of London. *Where the Line Breaks* was shortlisted for the 2019 Fogarty Literary Award.

For Kate

War ain't no giddy garden feete – it's war:
A game that calls up love an' 'atred both.
An' them that shudders at the sight o' gore,
An' shrinks to 'ear a drunken soljer's oath,
Must 'ide be'ind the man wot 'eaves the bricks,
An' thank their Gawd for all their Ginger Micks.

– C.J. Dennis, 'The Call of Stoush'

Hell, I've taken all the Turk can throw at me,
An' more. Would do it all again, like that,
An' more, to feel the sand of home beneath my feet,
The waves out back, the bullets past my cheeks,
My mates waiting on the shore.

– The Unknown Digger, 'Out Back'

Always the same dream.

He's still on the rock.

The sun rising behind the wall of khaki-clad men who advance past him. The countless boots. The endless rifles held at the same exact angle, tips of the bayonets rolling forward in a wave that extends as far as he can see, until they rise out of the trench, and another line takes their place. Scowling as they peer back at him. Actively running from him, distancing themselves from him as they jump up on the fire step and clamber up the ladders, climbing up the sandbags, the cliff wall, the wooden supports, their heads turned back to him with disgust in their eyes, pitying him, watching him blow his childish whistle before they step up and out into the unknown.

And as the first wave vanishes, the next line turns, and the same faces peer back at him, judging him, shaking their heads.

And the next line. Shaking their heads.

And the next.

Each line turns and he sees the faces of the friends he signed up with, the boys he trained beside, the men he joked and drank and swore and dreamed with: Brennan, Stokes, Collopy, Richardson, Morrow, even Tom and Robbie. Sometimes Red. And sometimes Nugget. As they fade, the noise starts, seamlessly merging with the tick of his watch. No change in tempo, no increase in speed. The steady *tak tak tak* of the machine gun; the relentless, ruthless, repetitive, jarring *tak tak tak* of mechanical bursts that ring in his head when he lies down to sleep. That constant awful *tak tak tak* that continues when he wakes in a cold sweat, his shirt stuck to his chest. The bullets thud thudding into the flesh of his mates in time with the *tak tak tak* of his heart.

Identifying the Unknown Digger:

Conclusive Evidence for the Composition of the Unknown Digger Poems by Lieutenant Alan Lewis, VC

by

MATTHEW L. DENTON

B.A., The University of Western Australia

M.A., The University of Western Australia

A Dissertation Submitted to the Graduate Faculty

of University College London in Partial Fulfilment

of the Requirements of the Degree

DOCTOR OF PHILOSOPHY

Supervisor: Professor Alistair Fitzwilliam-Harding

LONDON, UK

Em
for believing in me

Jessica
for pushing me

Alan
for inspiring me

ABSTRACT

Imagine that you are tired, and far from home, weary from a long ride across a vast desert. You miss your family, your fiancée, your loved ones, the life you knew. Your life is one of hardship, constant movement, incessant danger. Interminable sand. Your life is one of orders, of repetition. Orders. Repetition. Orders. Repetition. Your life is not yours anymore. Your life belongs to your country, to your commanding officer.

To the sand.

You ride into a small village on the outskirts of the plains of Megiddo, a tiny ramshackle collection of dirty buildings centred around a well, the only source of drinkable water for miles. The town square is deserted. You dismount, and alongside your best mate, enter the largest building without backup. Your heart is racing, your thoughts are back home with your fiancée, the sea, the red earth of home.

In the darkest recesses of the building, you are ambushed by Turkish soldiers. Pistol shots ring through the deserted streets. The clash of bayonet on scimitar. The eerie war cries of deadly enemies. You fight in the darkness, hand-to-hand, man to man. The numbers are against you, and so you fight harder. Your best friend is mortally wounded, and yet you continue to fight. You could run, and save yourself, like any ordinary man, but you are no ordinary man. You fight on, despite the overwhelming odds, and somehow, miraculously, you push your way back into the light, dragging your dying friend into the street, calling for aid, never giving up. And when anyone else would have retreated, when any normal human would have waited for reinforcements, for help, you instead plunge once more back into the melee, back into the darkness of the buildings, and into the pages of legend. You emerge once more, back into the light, dragging two young children, saving their lives. And still you plunge once more back into the darkness. What happens in those rooms will go down in history. The spark of a fuse. Your eternal sacrifice.

For you are no ordinary man. You are an Australian hero.

And though your life ends on that fateful day, your story continues in every Australian heart, every Australian mind, every Australian ideal.

Only now, a century later, do we realise the other gift you left us: your words.

~

Since their publication in Jennifer Hayden's *Poems of the Unknown Digger*, the collected verses of the Unknown Digger have gained an esteemed position within Australian cultural consciousness, to rank alongside not merely the best known works of the various Australian writers and poets of the twentieth century, but, surely, anything produced by the renowned soldier-poets of the Great War. The poems of the Unknown Digger have captured the hearts and minds of the people of Australia in a manner that no published piece, before or since, has achieved. These poems have been recognised internationally as a paramount exemplar of literary achievement.

Ever since the unearthing of this extraordinary compilation of poems, scholars of literature the world over have dedicated themselves to discovering the identity of the author through a combination of logic, reasoning, circumstantial substantiation, scholarly evaluation and speculation. Prospective creators have been proposed by Australian and international academics, the poems pored over for evidence, and their themes manipulated to reflect hypotheses. These propositions have been counterattacked with intent, and it is safe to say that for now, there is no established consensus, or even a leading candidate, for an author.

In this dissertation, I will conclusively demonstrate that the author of these verses, whose identity has been concealed for seventy years, is Lieutenant Alan Lewis, Victoria Cross recipient. Alan Lewis, the legendary Light Horseman who sacrificed his existence to save the lives of others, is one of Australia's greatest and most revered wartime champions. In this thesis I will prove, beyond doubt, that he is also one of Australia's – indeed one of the world's – finest poets.

Alan Lewis *is* the Unknown Digger.

This thesis will document, categorically, that Alan Lewis is the sole creator of these poems. In the subsequent chapters, through (1) a comprehensive consideration of the primary source materials available, (2) an exhaustive contemplation of his engagements throughout the assorted operations in which the 10th Light Horse were involved, (3) thorough investigation into his philosophical convictions and ideology as reflected in his war record and writings and, (4) through a careful analytical breakdown of the existing poems, I will confirm that Alan Lewis is the only possible contender for authorship.

The mystery of the Unknown Digger has been solved.

CONTENTS

INTRODUCTION: The discovery of the Unknown Digger poems, and their cultural importance within the prevailing Australian literary landscape.

Ever since their discovery by the then-unknown academic Jennifer Hayden, neglected in the Irwin Street Building Archives at The University of Western Australia, the extant works of the Unknown Digger have touched on a nerve-ending of public feeling.[1] The poems have grabbed the attention of the Australian community in a way seldom observed: they are venerated by the cultured and the uneducated, the wealthy and the underprivileged, and both conservative and liberal minds across the nation.[2] Rarely has a body of work 'captured the hearts and minds of a developing population as succinctly or profusely'.[3] Part of the collection's appeal, unquestionably, must be apportioned to the anonymity of the author and the mysterious circumstances surrounding the discovery of the treasured manuscript. But the true wonder of the poems lies in the candour of their writing, the 'frank humanism of their wordplay', the electricity conveyed by their imagery, and the astonishing way they so perfectly encapsulate the collective idealisation of a national identity.[4]

---

1 Chronicled extensively in three successive bestsellers by Jennifer Hayden, quickly establishing her as the leading academic in the field and making her a household name: *Poems of the Unknown Digger*, Sydney University Press, Sydney, 1995; *Unearthing the Unknown Digger*, Bloomsbury Publishing, London, 1996; and *One in a Million: Recognising Genius in the Poems of the Unknown Digger*, Bloomsbury Publishing, London, 2000. I am proud to call Jennifer Hayden my mentor and inspiration. Em calls her the other woman in our relationship.

2 Such is their popularity that they have even been nominated as an alternative to the Australian national anthem. See 'Aussie Public Votes for War Poetry over "Advance Australia Fair" and "Waltzing Matilda", *The Sydney Morning Herald*, 16th March 2008, p. A6. Em says surely anything would be better than 'girt by sea'.

3 Gary Johanissen, 'On the Spirit of the West', in *Australia: Finding Meaning in the Outback*, E.L. Smith & T. Morrison, eds, UWA Publishing, Perth, 2010, p. 110.

4 Johanissen, 'On the Spirit of the West', p. 111. I read 'Illawarra Flame

The combat forces of the Australian Army, Navy and Air Force during the Great War are held in special regard by the Australian people. From their initial deployment as part of the Australian and New Zealand Army Corps (ANZAC), and through the following disastrous campaign in the Dardanelles, the actions of Australia's soldiers, colloquially referred to as 'diggers', are characterised as 'the very embodiment of the Australian national identity'.[5] For most Australians, including this author, the fundamental image that arises when envisioning 'an ideal hero' is that of the courageous young man shipped off to fight for a regent he has never seen, to a country he has never heard of, simply because 'it was the right thing to do'.[6] It is no exaggeration to conclude that the actions of these young men have helped us to articulate what we now think of as the entire Australian disposition.

And yet, as fundamental as their actions have become in fashioning an image of what it means to be Australian, there is a distinct lack of primary evidence on hand to fully appreciate the perception. Scholars

---

Tree' in bed to Em one night and she got all teary, and when I asked her what was wrong she said, Nothing, it's just when you read them they make sense to me. I love your accent.

Too fuckin' right, ay? I said.

5 Brian Bishop, *The Anzac Legend*. Fisher & Fisher, Sydney, 1991, p. xxi. In year three I dressed up as Alan Lewis for Book Week, arguing that there were enough books about him in the library to justify my choice. I wore my grandad's medals, and spent the day picking up litter on the playground and telling kids off for not wearing their hats, because 'it was the right thing to do'.

6 Note the poll conducted by *The Sydney Morning Herald* in March 2002 (12th March 2002, 'Words & Pictures', p. 3) asking for public votes for the Greatest Australian Heroes. In first position: Sir Donald Bradman. In second position: the Unknown Digger. While not definitive, it proves my point (third place was Mad Max). I, too, am guilty of holding up the men of the Australian fighting forces as paradigms of decency, chivalry and heroism. Both my grandfathers fought in the Second World War, and I grew up with an unhealthy predilection for the bellicose. As a child, I collected model airplanes, in particular, Second World War–era fighter planes. Perfect scale replicas of Spitfires hung above my bed, a Messerschmitt Bf 109 sat on the landing strip that ran across the top of my wardrobe.

have scrutinised the letters and writings of the Anzacs, examining battle reports and injury lists, but the Australian wartime experience has always lacked the singular artistic representations of the British war experience.[7] 'War poetry', those poems and dramatic writings written by the soldiers and civilian bystanders, actively romanticised the heroic actions of its participants and simultaneously disclosed the horrors of the conflict through British First World War poets Owen, Sassoon, Thomas, Rosenberg, Brooke, et al.[8] There were a few bright lights when it came to defining the Anzac experience: C.J. Dennis with his 'Ginger Mick' poems, Leon Gellert, perhaps a few poems by Lawson and Paterson, but the list was short, and there was no poet to match or define the Anzac experience.[9]

---

7 Em was in the middle of writing her own thesis, before she got headhunted by the Prof and had to put it on the backburner – Vestigial Paraforms in the Early Prodigean Eco-Languages – so she knows her stuff. I asked her if she knew any war poets, and she rattled off the big names, but no Australians.

Notice anyone missing from that list? I said, nuzzling into the warm space between her legs. This would have been in the first few weeks we got together. Post-coital small talk about all the big things.

Women?

I smiled up at her. Zero Australians. How can that be?

Any South Africans?

The Unknown Digger is the most important poet of the twentieth century – I nibbled the inside of her thigh and smiled as she wriggled away from me – and I want to be the person to unmask him.

8 *The Penguin Book of First World War Poetry,* George Walter, ed., Penguin Classics, Sydney, 2007, comprehensively catalogues the finest examples of the genre. All the major names are represented, sometimes multiple times, alongside lyrics to various soldier songs written by anonymous larrikins, ready to inspire the next generation of war-obsessed young children. I remember how exciting it was, in those first years after Jennifer Hayden's discovery, to read Australian poems in front of the class – war poems that sounded like we sounded – and not just 'Clancy of the Overflow' for the umpteenth time. I imagined an author that looked like the soldiers I knew, like the photo that hangs in the drawing room at my grandparents' house: slouch hat, slight smile, the grainy blur of time. Grandad looks like me in that photo.

9 I heartily recommend finding a copy of *The Moods of Ginger Mick* (Angus & Robertson, Sydney, 1916) – and no Australian library worth its salt is complete without a copy of Leon Gellert's *Songs of a Campaign*.

In October 1993, Jennifer Hayden found the poems that would swiftly come to define the 'Anzac spirit' and what it meant to be Australian. Hayden recognised the importance of her discovery immediately:

> *... in the bottom of one of the last boxes in the archive, secured by a leather tie and covered in dust, I pulled forth a bundle of papers, faded by the sun, written in a stuttering, hurried hand. Imagine my surprise when, upon examination, I discovered I held in my hand the most beautiful, most touching, and – perhaps astonishingly – the most Australian poetry I'd ever read.*[10]

Regrettably, the author of Hayden's collection of writing was unidentifiable. The poet she presented to the world was a hero without a face or name.

It is the purpose of this thesis to definitively reveal the Unknown Digger to be Alan Lewis, VC. Unknown no more.[11]

---

10 Hayden, *Poems of the Unknown Digger*, p. ix.

11 Sometimes things become so obvious, all at once, like puzzle pieces when you finally make out the budgerigar or the steamboat or whatever it is you're making. You think your life is all set out, that you can see straight down the path laid out before you and all you need to do is take one step after another, hunker down at the library and chip away at your thesis and come home each night and microwave pasta and sleep and wake and repeat. That easy. Then you start to notice the way the South African girl putting books away in the aisle next to you keeps glancing sideways, so you make a stupid joke and she laughs, then you eat lunch together, and she tells you about the thesis she's writing, about her home in Cape Town, the beach and her dogs, about London and the university.

You ask yourself, what would Alan do? And you pluck up your courage and ask her out for a drink. Then you spend six hours downing margaritas at that little tequila place you know in Soho, until it's three in the morning and they close at four. Your foot is resting on the bar of her stool, and her leg is rubbing against yours, little black ankle boots turning slow circles. You lean in so you can hear her over the sound of the band in the corner, the twang of the guitar and the low throbbing of the double bass, and the way your head is turned to hear her you're staring at the soft skin of her neck, the vein pulsing. She tells you about her boyfriend of five years, how they've been having troubles recently, how he's ready to start a family but she's not. And she isn't ready, the way she looks into your eyes while she's saying it, saying she wants something more than that, someone more. She says something you don't catch, so you lean in closer, until you can feel her breath on your ear, and you're painfully aware of where your bodies touch, your arm on the back of her stool, and her hand, slowly, like snow falling, resting on your leg. Turning your head a quarter inch will be the greatest thing you ever do. And then it's late-late, or way too early, and you're stumbling the dark streets towards the night bus that will take her home, and she's kissing you outside a strip club, the bouncers laughing at the way she fumbles with your belt, and down a moonlit alley you slip your hand down the front of her jeans, feel her knickers lacy wet under your clumsy fingers, and the warmth between her legs, and you pull your fingers from inside and taste, lick your fingers and smile at her, at the green dye in her hair, at the self-conscious tilt of her head, and you raise her chin and kiss her beside the bins.

What would Alan do? Retreat back down the line, or charge in and damn the consequences? A night later you are lying in her bed, with his winter coat hung up behind the door, and every crunch of leaf and twig beneath the feet of the people walking by her front window sends your heart racing because she jumps at every little judder the house makes – every neighbour turning keys in their front door might be the jangle of keys in her front door that would spell the end of this world. But that makes you both bolder, makes it all more concrete, maybe, and you couldn't leave anyway, not when she's holding your wrists down beside your head, not when she's planting kisses down your stomach and the streetlights on her face are like tiger stripes when she closes her eyes, and you put your hand on her back, on the curve of her spine as she pulls closer to you, and the tattoo of the rose on her hip, in its simple black lines, rises and falls in time, and the sheets that smell like him will smell like you tonight, when he is lying here instead, and her fingers and toes curl into fists, like she is trying to hate you and herself for what you're doing. Her nails sink into your back like she wants to rip you apart.

You kiss her by the front door when she gets the message saying he's on his way home, and you say your goodnight, and let that be the end of it, and you walk down the street in the dark and you catch the night bus home halfway across London to sleep in your single bed alone while she curls up with him and tries to convince herself it's just a fling.

Like nothing is growing, deep within the ground, that will redefine the boundaries of the world you both knew, that will send the tube lines scattering in all directions as it bursts forth through the sewers and pipes and rat-strewn dark beginnings, and bloom forth into glorious, artistic, blue-skied perfect London.

HOME. FEBRUARY 1915.

The pub is heaving.

Alan is unsteady on his feet. He avoids the puddles of piss out by the trees and pushes his way back inside, through the crowd to where he left Rose and Red.

He spots them leaning on the bar, a dark stain of beer sloshed down Red's newly tailored breeches, off his chops. Absolutely fuck-eyed.

Not that anyone else notices. They're all as drunk as Red. The room is a swirling mass of sweaty, uniformed men.

Rose smiles at him as he emerges from the crowd, and beckons him into their little circle. She says something, but he can't hear her over the din of the crowd.

'What?'

She leans in, her breath hot on his ear. Her dress is lacy white, but he can't make out the pattern.

'Red has very kindly offered to marry me.'

'He what?' Alan spins to his best mate, who is grinning manically on the bar. 'You what?'

'Relax,' Rose places a hand on his arm. 'I turned him down.'

'She turned me down.' Red is in his other ear, too close, too loud. 'Said she's waiting for the right man.'

Rose hasn't removed her hand from his arm. He can feel it, hot through his shirt.

'I told her, I said, Rose, with a war on, you could be waiting an awful long time. We'd hate you to turn out an old maid.'

Alan catches Rose's eye and feels his cheeks redden. His hand creeps along the bar, closer to Rose's fingers.

'I need to piss.' Red announces to the bar. 'Think about it, Rose.' He leaves with what he must think is a roguish wink.

'We'll be here,' Alan says. Rose waves as Red elbows his way through the troopers. Once Red has disappeared into the mob, Rose turns to Alan and then looks towards the door.

'Would you care for some fresh air?'

'Shouldn't we tell him?' Alan cocks his head toward the mass of uniforms.

But she's already pulling him towards the bright light of the street.

Her white dress gleams in the failing light, vanishing around the corner with her breathless laughter. The roar of the pub recedes. The evening breeze off the ocean makes the shadows cold.

Alan turns the corner and almost bowls her over, gathering her up in his arms and spinning. They fall against the wall, the breath knocked from his chest making them laugh harder. A cry from the bar. Rose's tiny hand clamps over his laughing mouth. Again, the faint cry of their names. He's holding her, frozen in time down a darkened alleyway a few shops up from the crowded pub.

His hands relax, and he lowers Rose to her feet. She peels her hand back from his mouth with care.

'Freedom.' He sings the word, rolling it around in his mouth, sending inquisitive fingers down her spine.

'For twelve more hours.'

He pulls the sides of his mouth down in a mock frown, then grabs Rose's hand and pirouettes her, flaring her dress out in a perfect circle – a blur of white in the gloom.

'So, what to do with twelve hours?'

He stops the spin with a little more force than necessary.

Rose pokes a small pink tongue at him, and squeezes his hand. 'Remember when we met?'

'The Hat-Trick?'

'Seems like a lifetime ago.'

He grins. 'Pav'll be empty.'

The offer hangs in the air.

'Mr Lewis, without a chaperone, we would be completely alone. The very thought is scandalous.'

He runs his tongue over his teeth. 'I'll race you.'

He's off before she can react, tossing a stack of empty wooden crates in her path and glancing back to see her smile.

No doubt the whole town remembers the Hat-Trick, the first, and for now, only time the Under Sixteens had topped the league. He had been fifteen at the time, fielding at square leg late on the final day, the sun in his eyes, praying the ball wouldn't find him. Sweat rolled down his nose. His muscles ached. The old foe – Marybrook High – needed three hundred to win and were sitting pretty at four for two-hundred-odd thanks to a captain's knock from their bull of a senior.

And then Red had come on to bowl his big loopy finger spinners, and all the fielders had taken a step or two back, expecting fireworks. Thing is, Red lived for those moments. He could always be counted on to make things happen, and as soon as the batsman attempted to lose it over the crowded pavilion it looped off the bat and landed easy as you like in the wicketkeeper's gloves.

Next batsman in was a scrawny little weed, looking to plant himself in the crease for the remainder of the afternoon. From Alan's position in the outfield, Red was a lanky beanpole approaching the wickets with a lolloping gait. He grunted as he sent the ball down the pitch. For Alan, in the outfield, the ball looked to be moving through molasses. It spun around the half-hearted defence the batsman threw out, and clattered into off stump.

Next man in was their star all-rounder, the same kid who bowled Red in the first innings. Alan knew what would happen before it happened; knew he needed to be five metres to his left, to shield his eyes against the lowering sun, adjust for the afternoon breeze, soften his hands to account for the bounce. A wild swing, top-edged towards him on the boundary. Planted in the short grass, all he had to do was watch as the ball miraculously fell from the sky into his waiting, cupped hands.

The heart fell out of the opposition, and the fast bowlers mopped up the tail, but it was Red's hat-trick that they remembered.

Afterward, gathered in the pavilion, the older boys sneaking beers from the bar, Alan and Red were speechless, soaking it all in. A young girl approached, dressed in her Sunday best, golden waves of hair tumbling down her shoulders. Alan and Red were speechless all over again. She walked right up to them, laughing in the face of their obvious discomfort.

'Great catching out there.'

He glanced across at Red, couldn't read the expression on his face, fumbled his words. Butterfingers. 'Thanks. Red got the hat-trick, but.'

She looked over at Red, as if noticing him for the first time and offered him a delicate hand.

'Pleased to meet you, I'm Rose. Rose Porter.'

'I'm Red.'

'I gathered. And you are?' She swung the hand his way.

'Yes. I am,' he said.

She cracked up. A loud, rolling peal of unabashed laughter. His nostrils burned and he wished for instant death. She took his hand, her skin warm, and he could breathe again.

'I'm Alan. Everyone calls me Al.'

'I bet they do.' She laughed again, and his cheeks hurt from the strain of smiling. 'My father's club treasurer,' she said, indicating the white walls. 'I'm down here quite regularly.'

He couldn't look away from the shimmer of hair held back by her ear, the perfect arch of gold. Red broke the silence.

'Hope you enjoyed the game, Rose.'

Rose nodded, her eyes glowing.

'I did. Well played, Red,' she turned to leave. 'Hopefully I'll see you soon, Alan.'

She walked away as Red's parents and sister Laurie approached, and amid the backslapping and congratulations, he lost sight of her.

The pavilion is dark, the doors locked, and the sun has settled over the horizon as Rose and Alan, breathless from the run, cross the oval. Over the crest of the hill they can hear the waves crashing on the beach, the gulls screaming.

Rose shimmies one of the windows loose, and hops through the window with a dainty leap. He follows, two heavy boots knocking against the wooden frame.

The members room is huge and still, an empty cathedral. To the left are the change rooms and the slight whiff of stale sweat. Rose takes his hand and pulls him up the stairs, her free hand running over the polished grain of the oak rail. The top floor is taken up by long wooden pews, all facing the oval, and a large open balcony that they push out onto through an unlocked door. They take a front row seat, looking out over the brown patches of grass, the few streets and buildings that make up the town tinged pink. Over the beach the setting sun streaks the sky pink.

He laces his fingers between hers, and pulls her hand into his lap.

'Rose Benedict Porter.'

'Excuse me?'

'Rose Marjoram Porter.'

She raises an eyebrow.

'Rose Penhaligon Stirling Lexington-Porter the Third, Wisest of Women, Keeper of my Heart.'

'Yes?'

He closes his eyes, and then turns his head towards her, reopening them and loving the way the corners of her eyes crinkle as she waits for him.

'You can do so much better than Red.' Her face breaks into a smile, and he wants to cry. A breath, a blink, and she makes him brave enough to say what he has been afraid to say. 'If I die –'

'Alan.'

'But if I do ...'

She squeezes his fingers tighter.

'Alan Archimedes Ulysses Lewis.' He can't help but smile. 'You're coming home, to me.'

He can always talk to Rose.

'Promise me this is real?' He's not sure if it's a question, not entirely sure where it's come from.

'What do you mean?'

'I mean home, the beach, the farm. You.' He squeezes her hand, trying to disguise the way his fingers shake. 'You promise it won't all vanish? You won't vanish, the moment I look away?'

She doesn't speak, gazing out over the field. Her hair is flames, falling across her face in that way she hates but he loves. She burns.

'I promise.'

When the letter came in offering him a spot in the first take-up of the new university, it was Rose who urged him to give it a shot. Rose who assured him it would be fine. Rose who eased his fears with her calm voice and her warm hands. And for the first time, he wasn't just copying whatever Red was doing, but making his own way. Making that first long train trip to Perth, it was Rose who waved from the platform, and as the rest of the town faded in the distance, it was her he could still make out, that same flash of sun streaking on her hair.

Perth – a freedom Alan had never known before. The first-year lessons for his bachelor's degree took place in a series of temporary wooden huts in the city, the corrugated iron roofs creaking in the heat. They were the first to pass through those ramshackle walls – an experiment in free learning in a young country. They were the first to question everything. The first to take full advantage of the opportunity afforded them. Alan joined a local cricket club, worked in the city library, loved debating the rich boys fresh from private schools in the wealthy suburbs. He wrote letters to Red, who had been made manager of the local hardware store and spent his weekends playing cricket. At twenty-three, Alan was old enough to drink warm beer at the bars alongside the shiftworkers from the city in their ties, the sweat showing through their starched shirts, packing them away before the six o'clock swill. He fell in love with Perth: cycling around the river in the evening, the flies converging around his lips as soon as he stopped; the smell of leather-bound books they were forced to read for tutorials he hadn't studied for, the hours spent debating and arguing and learning, their professors making the units up as they went along; the cheap glue of the paperbacks they bought from the bookshop in Subiaco; the annual cricket club piss-up with the boys drinking long into the night, daring each other to run across the cricket oval naked, their arses shining white in the moonlight.

When Rose came up and moved into the nursing college in Fremantle, he figured he had it all. He cherished their long summer days at North Cott, reading paperbacks on their towels, the sand peppering their skin. The Freo Doctor rolled in each afternoon, windows and doors opened throughout the suburbs to its cooling breeze. He hung around the older boys, who, like himself, had been sent letters offering them positions in the first intake, some much older, some with wives and children waiting for them in the country towns where they lived. Men who seemed like they knew what they were doing, men who reminded him of Red. They'd make their way to the Cottesloe Beach Hotel, discussing literary theory, and cricket, and girls, three beers deep, with the sand crusting between their toes, and he listened intently to everything they had to say. He'd amble home in the dusk sporting a six-beer buzz, and lie awake with the windows open, mosquitoes whining round his ears.

One weekend, Red came through on a flying visit, buying an entire crate of mangoes from the European bloke who ran the stall at the markets on the way. All weekend they lay in the sun reading second-hand books, mango juice dripping from their elbows, sticking pages together. Every so often they ran down to the waves to cool off, to wash the sweet liquid from their chins. By the Monday morning, when Red needed to hop a train back home, and he was due in class, they were both in and out of the toilet so often they were considering setting up camp in the bathroom. Rose, trainee nurse, and as always the voice of reason, said they had no-one to blame but themselves.

He would have been among the first contingent to graduate if the war hadn't come along like the rips at North Cott and swept him out to sea. Red sent him a letter saying he was signing up with the Light Horse. It didn't take much convincing to head down to the recruitment centre. There was more to life than black swans on the river each evening and the weekend football, and he signed up in a sweaty haze of patriotism and adventure.

Returning from the recruitment centre, he jumped on his bicycle and rode down to the nursing college to tell Rose his good news. He expected her to join in his happiness, to swirl and dance in his joy. He hadn't expected silence. The way her face fell apart with each word he spoke. She begged him not to go. He tried his best to explain. He told her Red had signed up too, but she didn't listen. He couldn't put it into words – that she had inspired him, had pushed him, had given him the belief that he could do this. That he had signed up for her.

That she made him feel brave.

They lay on the foreshore and watched dolphins swimming in the bay, and he reached an arm around her shoulder, and she smiled a sad smile.

He glances down at his hands, calluses on his palms from the hours spent cradling the rough wood of his rifle. Sitting here, in his pressed and clean uniform, his hair parted, buttons polished, boots glossed, it doesn't feel real. He can't imagine a world where Rose isn't within his sight. But his kitbag is sitting packed in his room, and the bars on his sleeve burn into his arm, and there's an altogether different part of him itching to go, restless to test itself in a new world, but afraid of losing the old one. Scared of letting Rose down.

They sit for a moment in the last stretching fingers of daylight.

Rose shivers.

He removes his jacket and places it around her shoulders, the desert brown dull against the white of her dress, the bright gold of her hair. He turns her head and kisses her with his eyes closed, to hide the tears.

Rose has always had the taste of the sea on her lips, like she's run straight from the waves, her hair in long dark strands down her back, and water dripping from her nose. A sudden dark silhouette above him, blocking out his sun – cold drops on his face and her laughing, cold lips. Rose tastes like salty skin, stretched tight by sun.

He pulls her closer and lifts her onto his lap, her legs around him and dropping over the bench behind, her dress covering his khakis. When she sits on him they are the same height, and he can look straight into her green eyes. She smiles, her canines bared, and the animal inside him growls. His lips graze her neck, her earlobe, the perfect triangle of her collarbone. Beneath her thighs, he is stirring. His hands run up and down her back, restless. The shivering has stopped, the cold dread down his back, the heavy beat of his heart.

'Alan.'

But he doesn't stop kissing her, covering her skin with the lightest of touches. He makes a noise in the back of his throat as if to say 'Yes, my love?' and she smiles.

'Alan.'

He pauses, looks at her, her smile, her hands across his shoulders. He runs his wet tongue from the base of her neck all the way up to her lips, and he kisses her as that perfect rolling laughter floats away across the field, stopping and starting as their lips meet, lock, and part.

'Alan, stop.'

He stops. She sighs, and slides off his lap onto the pew next to him, rearranging her dress. They stare out at the patchwork grass in silence for a long minute.

'I'm scared.'

Her voice is small when she does speak. 'I'm scared too.'

He reaches for her hand, the familiar warmth. The cricket pitch in front of them is cracked and broken, dead grass. 'Who's meant to be looking after this place now, anyway?'

Two weeks after the Hat-Trick, desperate for a way to spend more time at the cricket club, and potentially run into Rose, he had approached the groundsman's hut behind the pavilion, knocking at the flimsy wooden door, heart in his mouth. He'd never been as scared as he was at that moment. The door swung open and a mountain of a man emerged from the dark to regard the skinny kid standing in the doorway. His voice catching in his throat, he plucked up his courage.

For Rose. It had always been for Rose.

The next time she saw him he was drenched in sweat, pushing the heavy roller across the pitch, the back of his neck bright pink and his hands covered in blisters. She approached from the pavilion, and for half a second he thought she was a mirage, the way she floated across the trimmed grass.

'Father told me the club had hired a new groundsman.'

She brought him fresh lemonade, made it herself, and he was too worried about scaring her away to tell her it was far too sour. He finished the glass in one long gulp.

He spent the rest of the winter helping maintain the grass, each day after school, ensuring the pitch was protected, trimming the lawn. Hours spent walking around the oval, the smell of grass in his nose, on his clothes, in his dreams. When it rained (if it ever rained) they sat inside the shed and he would dip into the groundskeeper's endless well of stories, glued to his seat as the grizzled old-timer yabbered away about his days as a drover, crossing the Nullarbor, living under the stars. Red would ride down, and they'd bowl to each other in the nets.

And when the holidays came, and Rose returned from boarding school, they lay together on the raised grass banks eating lunch – Alan chewing his bread and cheese, or chomping his way, core and all, through an apple. The sound of her laugh, ringing out across the ground, made his cheeks ache.

He told her about his family, the farm and the harvest. The long days in the fields and the evenings spent exhausted. Dad and his eccentricities. Ma and the horses. His brothers, Tom and Robbie, grown men, and how he worried his hands would never grow as large or as hard as theirs. How Red was school prefect and head boy, but Alan was top of the class. About his small collection of books, the escape they gave him at the end of a long afternoon. He would open his mouth and all his worries would tumble out. He was scared she would crumble under the weight, but she never did.

For her part, Rose told him about her parents, her mum who was knitting her a muffler despite the weather never getting cold enough to wear it, and about her sisters, the Little Princesses, who stayed inside, their skin porcelain like the dolls they played with. She told him about her boarding school in Perth, spending half the time away from home, away from the family. She told him about Sister Mary, the English tutor, who brought her new books each week, whose eyes shone when she read Hardy. Rose filled his head with Conrad and Conan Doyle, Whitman and Kipling, laying the groundwork for the essays that would eventually lead him to university. He lay on the grass and closed his eyes while she read him Yeats. She loved the old poems. Their strength, their beauty.

He wrote a poem, but never showed her.

He soon met her father, his voice always the first indication of his presence, booming across the oval, calling Rose to him. He imagined Mr Porter as a kookaburra, king of the bush, singing his song through the gums, Rose's replying laugh guiding her back to him. Alan would offer to ride Rose home on his bicycle, but she said no, the walk home with her father was their special time. The first time Mr Porter shook his hand he thought his own might be crushed. He tried to stand taller, puffed his chest out, lowered his voice. A grin spread across the big man's red cheeks, and father and daughter laughed their raucous laughs.

Mr Porter called him 'my boy', and winked at him behind Rose's back, brothers-in-arms. When Alan was invited around one Sunday for dinner, cleaned and polished, feeling out of place, dressed in his brother's hand-me-downs, Mr Porter made sure he sat by his right hand at the table.

'Us men have to stick together,' he said, doling out the potatoes.

The way Mr Porter rolled over and did anything his girls asked filled Alan with a sense of joy. The old lion, turning circles for his pretty cubs.

A few years later, at the start of his second year of university, when they were both living in Perth, Rose received an urgent telegram. They hopped the earliest train back home and spent a week haunting the rooms of their family homes like ghosts, and then, on the hottest day of the summer, Alan sweltered through the funeral service in one of Tom's suits, several sizes too big. When they ate dinner, the chair at the head of the table sat empty. Alan pulled Rose close at every opportunity, trying his best to hold her together, until she pulled away, saying he was hurting her.

He tried to tell her how inadequate he felt, but the words wouldn't come out. They spent the rest of the week in a humid silence.

His own father never talked about his worries. Hid his thoughts behind a stony demeanour and his insecurities behind a heavy hand. Dad commanded respect through silence, distilling the words necessary to communicate a message into the shortest possible sentence. When Dad spoke, people hung on each word, breathing in the long gaps between them. He might not know a lot of Alan's 'facts' – never went to school, never studied – but he knew what he knew. His word was gospel.

When Alan first started at the university, he worried that if he had nothing to say in tutorials and lectures, people would think he was stupid. So he spoke up and asked questions. With Rose's family and down at the pub, he was the same, trying to mask his anxiety with talking. But when he sent letters home about the books he'd read, the Latin studies, the long lectures, it was always his mother who replied. Dad was busy. Dad was working hard.

When he arrived home in October for the harvest, and told his family that he had signed up, had quit university and spent the past few months in training, Dad didn't respond. Instead he took another sip from his beer and said, 'Early start tomorrow, Al.'

'I'm to be an officer. Thanks to the university.'

His father took another long sip. 'Lots of sleep tonight.'

As he walked to bed, his father called to him across the room. 'Alan?'

'Yeah, Dad?'

But somewhere between him turning around and the next sip of beer, the moment passed.

'G'night.'

They strode into the fields at sunrise, the father and his sons, and not one of them said a word. The sun baked the soil clay-hard, and the sweat dropped down the end of his nose, and looking up at the old man bent over the scythe, he thought he understood: there is a strength in silence. A safety there. He thought, the old man couldn't do it, but there's nothing stopping me. He thought, I am not my father.

The next day he returned to Perth for the last of his training.

Months later, with summer in full swing, the train pulled into town. He stopped at Rose's first, her sisters, the Princesses, crowing over him, tears in her mother's eyes. Then Red's house – the two boys standing side by side in their uniforms, competing, even now, with Red's mother and Laurie fussing around them – and then he walked the long dirt track out to the farm that didn't feel like home anymore. Ma cried. Dad went to the pub for a drink, and didn't come home until much later.

When he told them the next week that he'd be shipping out, off to Egypt for further training, and then on to an unknown battlefield, the silences became more pronounced; he felt he could curl up in them, great voids of the left-unsaid.

He should have sat down with Dad and said his piece, but he didn't. He chose silence. Safer that way.

Dad had never called him 'my boy'.

They sit and talk until the mosquitoes find them, and the spell is broken. The sun has plunged into the sea. Time to head back.

He rises, and runs a hand down the creases in his shirt. Rose swings her feet back and forth under the bench and reaches for his hand.

His voice, when he speaks, is a whisper, and he directs his words to the oval, rather than the woman at his side.

'I'm going to marry you, Rose.'

'Oh yes? And don't I get a say in that?'

He swings his head to look down at her. She always knows how to make him smile. He drops to one knee, throws his right hand behind him in a dramatic gesture and takes a deep breath.

'Yes. I will.'

Before he can utter a word, she's answered for him. She pulls him to his feet, and then on tiptoe reaches up to kiss the tip of his sunburnt nose.

The crickets chatter in the gloom. Across the oval, a kookaburra starts up his raucous laughter, watching their display.

'I'm just saying,' the large man in the blue suit is just saying, 'with you gone, who's gonna take all our wickets next season?'

Alan finds Red deep in conversation at the bar, cupping his chin in his hand, trying to listen. His hand doesn't look like it will support the weight of his head. There's drool on his wrist. Australia's finest.

'Know what I mean?'

Red knows what he means.

Alan clamps his hand on Red's shoulder and dodges the wild punch Red swings at him, pulling him up before he falls off the chair.

'How many have you had? You're a mess, mate.'

Red draws close and buries his head in Alan's shoulder and blows a blubbery nose into the clean linen. His eyes are hot and wet as he pulls away. He turns back to the large man.

'This is Alan. Al. Alan.' Red swats a hand in the direction of Alan's chest. 'Al, this is some bloke.'

He reaches out and shakes the man's hand, mouthing 'sorry' over Red's downturned head. 'Pleased to meet you. This is my fiancée, Rose.'

Red lifts his head. Fat tears roll down his cheeks, but there's a dumb smile on his mug.

'She ain't your fiancée, she's mine. Ain't that right, Rose?' Red glances between the two of them, looks down to take a sip from his long empty glass, and then back up. They're looking at him, waiting for the hammer to drop. 'Fuck off, really?'

Alan glances over to the love of his life, and then down at his best friend.

'Why do you always copy what I do?' The tears are streaming down Red's face.

Rose laughs.

Alan grins, 'You'll have to be best man. Ok?'

Red is sniffing and laughing and ordering a bottle of their most expensive whatever-you've-got from the bar. Alan pulls Rose to him, closes her hand in his and gives it a quick squeeze. This. The beginning.

~

The town has one tiny station, and it's chockers, families from every part of the surrounding district crowded in to say goodbye to their boys. Alan has that rumbling in his stomach. Too many beers the night before. Too many thoughts to contain in his head, so they bubble in his gut. On the next seat Red groans, his slouch hat pulled low over his eyes.

'You want to say goodbye?' Alan says, but Red just grunts. 'Aren't you worried you might not make it back?'

Red lifts up his hat and looks up at him. 'We're both coming back.'

On the platform outside his window, Rose waits, radiant in white against the red bricks. He didn't think it possible for one body to hold this many tears, but there are wet lines down her face. He pushes his face up against the window, squashing his nose flat on the smudged glass.

She laughs, a quick burst that fades among the general chatter. He reaches an arm out the thin window above his head. She moves closer to him, and takes his hand as it hovers above her. It's an awkward position, the metal frame of the window cutting into his armpit, Rose clutching the solitary limb. His mother moves forward from the crowd behind Rose, and wraps an arm around her shoulder.

'She'll be right, Al. We'll look after her.'

He grins against the pain shooting through his arm, the blood cut off by the frame, his hand turning red.

'Thanks Ma.'

Rose kisses his hand.

'Plan on giving that back anytime soon?' he says.

She sniffs, a wet snivel that turns into a chuckle as she notices the colour of his fingers. She lets go, and he glides over her fingertips as he pulls his arm back in.

Behind Rose and Ma, a tall figure steps into view, and for a brief moment he thinks it might be Dad, until the tiny shape of his niece steps out of the shadow, and he can make out his brother Tom beneath the wide brim of the akubra. Tom lifts his daughter up by the underarms, and raises her up to the window. Her nose is freckled by the sun, her fingers brown with dirt.

'Bye, Uncle Al. Don't die.'

He laughs, and bops one finger on her spotted nose. 'You know if you keep growing at this rate, by the time I get back you'll be taller than me? Then you'll be my uncle.' Her tiny face crinkles in confusion, and turns to her father for confirmation. Tom smiles, then catches Alan's eye through the glass and nods his head. Like they're kids, playing cricket out back.

Ma has one arm around Rose, and puts the other around Tom.

'Robbie said he'd write you. He reckons they'll ship out within the month so he might catch you in Egypt.'

‘I know, Ma.’

‘And he said he’s already beaten your record for the quarter-mile.’

‘I know, Ma.’

Her voice is getting shakier with each word.

‘And your Dad. He said to stay safe.’ Sure he did. ‘Said, he loves you.’

He nods. Better for them all to pretend.

A whistle blows, and the crowd on the platform surges forward with final goodbyes. Uniformed men clamber aboard and fill the corridors. Alan reaches up and out the window, taking Rose’s hand as she sobs.

‘You’ll write?’

‘Every day.’

In the vest pocket of his tunic, tucked away in the back of his notebook, he carries a photo of her, her raucous laugh threatening at the edges of her smile.

‘Promise you’ll come home to me, Alan Lewis.’

He considers her eyes through the smudged glass, the vivid green of an algal bloom, the eyelids red and swollen. Her white dress brushes against the side of the carriage.

‘You’ll ruin your dress.’

‘Promise.’

‘I promise.’

He mouths three words as a second whistle blows, white smoke drifting down the platform, the train lurching forward. At some point, Red has stood up by his side, slouch hat in hand, looking out at the families. He puts a warm arm round Alan’s shoulder, and steadies him as the train sways.

Rose holds Alan’s hand through the window, and as the train picks up speed, she walks alongside the carriage, watching her feet among the feet of the other young women trying to delay the moment of departure for as long as possible. The noise is getting louder, soot and dust and smoke blowing onto her dress.

They’re running out of platform. Rose jogs beside the train, and he worries she won’t let go, will keep running beside them, and trip, and fall beneath the heavy churning wheels and be crushed, that he’ll lose her forever. She braces herself with her free hand on the window. Now it’s him not wanting to let go. The train horn blows three times, loud and clear. He’s not sure he can do this without her.

She lets go.

In the grime of the window, a perfect outline of her delicate fingers, a ghost wave.

CHAPTER 1: An examination of the circumstantial evidence for the authorship of the poems by Lieutenant Alan Lewis: Primary sources from Lewis's movements through 1915–18 and the Unknown Digger poems.

With the unearthing of the verses, the Unknown Digger surpassed Banjo Paterson, Henry Lawson, Sydney Steele and Leon Gellert to become 'the pre-eminent exemplar of Australian poetry'.[12] His poems were devoured by a public waiting for a champion to believe in, and in his poetry they discovered an idealised image of Australia they could proudly endorse. It has been argued that the poetry of the Unknown Digger is 'as important to the idea of Australia as kangaroos, swearing and ice-cold beer'.[13] His poems have been put to music, fronted media campaigns, inspired Australian academics to move across the world, and have been published and reprinted more times in the last two decades than any other work authored by an Australian.[14] His most famous works have become culturally ingrained into the Australian psyche. 'Red Earth' *is* Australia. 'Anzac Bay at Midnight' *is* Australia. 'Ken Oath' *is* 'more Australian than a barbie on the beach on Christmas Day'.[15]

---

12 E.L. Sanders, *The Great Australian Poets*, 2nd ed., Allen & Unwin, Sydney, 2000, p. 213. Paterson et al. still have their place, but the Unknown Digger has pushed them down the rankings.

13 Johanissen, 'On the Spirit of the West', p. 155.

14 'Books of the Decade', *Australian Book Review*, 12th January 2010, available at australianbookreview.com.au/decade. And for further evidence, see my own life. When I first moved to London, I rented a room in a little terraced house in Shepherd's Bush, owned by a tiny Jamaican grandma who must have lived there for the past five hundred years. It wasn't terrible, but once Em came along, it felt too small to hold all of our potential.

15 From *The Sydney Courier*, 28th April 1997, under the headline 'This Poem Might Change the World'. I read all the Unknown Digger poems and letters in a voice like those old recordings of Don Bradman, high-pitched and slightly quicker than normal, like he's thinking things at twice the rate I'm able. Alan and Australia go together like meat pies and footy, like swearing and hot pavement, like Scott and Charlene. You can't have one without

The Western Australian contingent of the Australian Mounted Infantry is named the 10th Light Horse.[16] Their motto is: *Percute et percute velociter* ('Strike, and strike swiftly').[17] They fought on

---

the other. Like Em and I. Em came over to my Shepherd's Bush house one night and we tried to cook ratatouille, while my landlord hovered in the corridor outside.

We should get our own place, I'd said, stirring the zucchini ('courgette', they call it over here), don't you think? Somewhere we could be alone?

I can't leave my place, Em said, head in the fridge looking for the capsicums ('peppers', old boy, wot wot).

Never?

Not now. I've spent so long making it into a home. I'm finally comfortable in it.

She's painted the lounge room herself, and her paper cut-out butterflies fly their way across the kitchen, and the chip in the wall by the front door is from her umbrella and no-one else's.

16 See Ian Gill and Neville Browning, *Gallipoli to Tripoli: History of the 10th Light Horse Regiment AIF 1914–1919* (Hesperian Press, Carlisle, 2012) for an in-depth and step-by-step account of the regiment and their movements throughout the war.

Maybe I could move in with you, then? I said quietly. Hey, does this need salt?

She picked up the spoon and slurped off some of the sauce, like they do in movies when they're whipping up a five-star meal. No more salt. Do you have any herbs? (I didn't) And I don't think that would be fair on Dan. He only just moved out.

But he's out?

Basically. Mostly. A few more boxes. She took my hand and kissed me. She tasted like restaurant-grade pasta sauce. Hey, when we're ready, ok?

My landlord walked in and loudly opened the fridge. Em let go of my hand with a quick squeeze, and tried to make conversation. The ratatouille was incredible. I realised I had to move.

17 Still in use by the 10th to this day, though the regiment is no longer mounted on horses but is a fully mechanised 'light cavalry'. I struck swiftly, finding this place. It's a studio on the top floor of an old place in Turnpike Lane, which is in North London. Smaller than my old room, but if you're sitting on the toilet and you reach forward and open the bathroom door you get a perfect view of the whole space stretching out before you, from the bed to the kitchenette, and it seems a lot bigger. Plus, no live-in landlord.

the cliff faces of Gallipoli, defended Suez, forced the Turkish army back at Romani, and marched triumphantly into the holy city of Jerusalem on 9th December 1917.[18] The 10th was comprised of

---

I skyped my parents and walked them through my favourite part – the hallway from the front door to the main room. Makes it feel like a home. Been here about a year now, and I've promised myself I'm going to buy a painting one of these days.

Best thing is I can catch the 221 or the N91 from down the road and be up at Em's place in Bounds Green within minutes – anytime, day or night. Some nights she'll message late and ask if I'm busy, and if I'm only writing or watching a documentary or doing research, I can gather my stuff and we can be in bed within fifteen minutes. Em says it's a South African thing, feeling safer in her own home – she needs her own space. Her place is bigger, so I visit her more than she visits me. She's never stayed at mine, but she came with me to the viewing, and I don't think I could have done it without her.

Just think, she'd said, a couple of pillows on the futon when it's in couch mode. A throw rug. She stood on tiptoe and we kissed. Maybe an accent colour on this wall? She smiled at me, then up at the wall. How do we feel about yellow?

Obviously the toilet will be working by the time you move in, said the guy from the real estate agency. He looked like a schoolboy, his suit three sizes too big, one of those ties with the elastic round his neck.

And so close to me, Em said, running her hand along the wall where she said I need to hang a painting. Is anyone else interested? she said to the schoolboy, who blushed and stammered a reply.

You should take it, she said to me.

I don't know. It is a lot of money, but Em has this way of calming the nerves, making you braver. She makes you feel invincible – like you're running up the beach at Gallipoli, dodging Turkish bullets, or steaming down the pitch at the MCG with the new ball.

Unstoppable.

18 See Terry Kinloch, *Devils on Horses: In the Words of the Anzacs in the Middle East 1916–19*, Exisle Publishing, Auckland, 2007. I moved by myself one weekend while Em was dealing with the Dan fallout – I booked a taxi and took my three suitcases and six boxes of books across London, and thought of Alan entering the holy city as I lugged each box up three flights of stairs. How proud he must have felt leading his men into the glory of that ancient city, how fearless and indestructible. When I finally sat down on the floor and ordered pizza and opened a warm can of Foster's I'd bought from the offie down the road, I felt a little bit of that fearlessness myself – and it

almost five hundred men, who left the farms, towns and cities of Western Australia to fight shoulder-to-shoulder on the other side of the world.[19] For most, it was the first opportunity to try something new, leaving the world they knew behind and heading off into the great unknown for adventure. It is reasonable to assume that they jumped at the opportunity for something more.[20] For Alan Lewis, it was the pivotal moment in a life destined for greatness.

Alan Lewis was twenty-three years old when he left Australia on board the HMAT *Mashobra*, bound for Egypt.[21] He would never return

---

turns out my new place is actually older than the Australian Federation, far older than Alan Lewis. I'm living in history.

19 Frank Burnside, *ANZAC: Ordinary Men, Extraordinary Times*. Melbourne University Press, Melbourne, 1988, p. 288. Alan Lewis was born 250 kilometres away from where I was born. He studied at the same university I studied at, played cricket at the same club I watched every Saturday during term time, probably swam in the same water I swam in after long, dusty history lectures. Fell in love with the same sunsets. I hope if I had been alive back then, I would have signed up too and maybe fought alongside him at The Nek. Maybe this thesis is me paying him back. No worries, mate.

20 See Burnside, *ANZAC: Ordinary Men, Extraordinary Times*, pp. 63–67, which examines the immense popularity and attraction of signing up, and reports on the staggering numbers of young men who signed up within the first few days, even hours, of the war. Scariest thing I've done was get on that plane to come here. Best thing I've done, too. Leaving that world for the dream of something more. I figured, if Alan could do it, why couldn't I? And then I bought my ticket – one way.

21 See *The Regimental Scrapbook of the 10th Light Horse Regiment, Western Australia* held at the National Anzac Centre, Albany, Western Australia and available upon request. The *Mashobra* sailed from Fremantle on 7th February 1915. I drove to Perth International Airport on a cloudy June evening. I knew I wanted to continue my studies, so I applied for the postgraduate research position in the English department at University College London. My honours professor back home knew someone who worked there, and got me an interview. For the first year, alongside doing all the Prof's dirty research work, I also worked a part-time job at the library, restacking books, organising student theses, and a million other odd jobs I can do with my eyes closed. That's where I met Em. Nowadays, I help the Prof out

home. Fortuitously for us, the stories of his bravery and courage came back with his brothers-in-arms, and through the news of his posthumous awarding of the Victoria Cross, the highest individual accolade available in the First Australian Imperial Force.[22] He was one of just two members of the combined Light Horse battalions to receive the prestigious honour, the other being Hugo 'Hu' Throssell.[23]

---

with his units four days a week, and do my own research the rest of the time. He puts the good word in for me with the journals and publishers he knows. He's one of those eccentric English professors who seems like they were raised in a university: he wears pink socks and still plays cricket with the uni team and makes jokes about the postmodernists hating postmodernism, which is pretty postmodern, he says, with one of those Englishmen laughs. He 'headhunted' Em, she says, to offer her a position as his receptionist/secretary/man Friday, which makes her proud, because everyone wants to work for him, all the undergrads want to be in his classes, and everyone loves him.

He's a good boss, Em says. We work hard, but we play hard, too.

22 Plus, the Prof fully supports what I'm trying to do: one day he called me when I was in the library, and said something like, Matt, do we have a copy of the Siegfried Sassoon biography?

Which one? I said.

It's by one of those fellows with two first names.

Richard Simon. *Sassoon: His Life, Times and Poems*.

That sounds like the badger.

Not worth the read. Try Moorcroft Wilson, I'll send it up.

He liked that I knew my stuff, and when I came up to the office he asked me more about my thesis, and Alan Lewis, and what I was hoping to achieve.

You can prove Lewis wrote the poems?

He had his feet up on the desk, brown leather brogues and yellow socks with dark blue ivy climbing up his calf.

He's the ultimate Australian hero, I said. I'm convinced he's the Unknown Digger.

He looked me up and down and said, So what are you waiting for? Prove it.

Like it's that easy.

23 Second Lieutenant Hugo Throssell has been the subject of many respected works of historical study, not least the worthy *The Price of Valour* by John Hamilton (Pan Macmillan, Sydney, 2012), which I encourage you to seek out and read.

Alan Lewis's story is well known.[24] Alongside his regiment, he journeyed to Egypt for auxiliary drilling, before shipping out to Gallipoli in May 1915. He fought valiantly at the charge at The Nek, the bloodiest of all the battles in which the 10th were involved, and since made famous by the Peter Weir film *Gallipoli*, starring a young Mel Gibson.[25] Lewis was injured in a shell attack on 27th November 1915 and taken to the hospital island of Lemnos, where he recovered from his wounds, a period he referred to as his 'Greek odyssey' in his

---

24 For an in-depth history of Lewis's life and times, try Nicholas Curtin-Kneeling, *From Busso to the Holy Land: Alan Lewis and the 10th Light Horse* (Fremantle Press, Fremantle, 2010). I had the pleasure of meeting Curtin-Kneeling at the biennial First World War Writing Analysis Conference (FWWWAC) when it was held in London a few years back, where we were the sole Australian representatives. I believed it was our duty to stick up for our fellow countrymen, to uphold the digger values by pushing Australian contributions to the historical and analytical landscape over all others, and arguing aggressively against all other viewpoints. Childish? Sure, but if we didn't, the Poms would've walked all over us, and if I've learnt anything from studying the Anzacs, it's that the true Spirit of Anzac wasn't about defeating the Turks or the Huns or the 'bad guys', it was showing the Mother Country we weren't a country to be fucked around with – you still see it in the cricket and the Olympics and any time we meet in competition – like every Australian signs a pact when they're born to make England regret giving away all their best citizens hundreds of years ago just because they stole a few loaves of bread or murdered someone or whatever. (I tease the Prof endlessly about the Ashes, and if the Poms were to miraculously win, he'd tease me back.) It's an odd sort of national pride, but it's strong in us.

25 Burnside, *ANZAC: Ordinary Men, Extraordinary Times*, p. 201. Of the three hundred men actively fighting for the 10th, 138 lighthorsemen were casualties, of which eighty died. Almost one in three. I always wonder how I'd handle the gunfire, the bombings, the dysentery. It's easy when you're reading about it in a poem or watching Mel Gibson ham it up on the big screen, but nothing slams it home quite like the numbers of the dead and injured – three hundred people is the Prof's entire lecture hall. And 138 injured is almost every tutorial I've run this year. Eighty dead is seventy-six more people than I've had ex-girlfriends.

The official Turkish death toll was twelve.

letters home.[26] Catching up with his regiment in Suez, he joined in the defence of the canal from multiple Turkish attacks, before taking part in the battles of Romani and Magdhaba that followed.[27] Through 1916, Lewis and the 10th drove the Turks back through the deserts of Sinai, before reaching Gaza, which the Light Horse attempted to capture in March 1917.[28] With the famous Charge at Beersheba in October 1917, Gaza finally fell, and Jerusalem surrendered soon after on 9th December. Lewis led his men through the streets of the holy city to accept the surrender.[29] It was in the final sweep of the Turkish forces through Har Megiddo, or Armageddon, mentioned in

---

26 From the personal letters of Rose Porter, in Curtin-Kneeling, *From Busso to the Holy Land*, p. 134 and again in Arthur Pyke, *The Annotated Letters of Alan Lewis VC*, Angus & Robertson, Sydney, 1975.

27 Kinloch, *Devils on Horses: In the Words of the Anzacs in the Middle East 1916–19*, p. 55.

28 The first failed attack at Gaza took place in March 1917, followed by a second, equally disastrous attempt in April. For more, see Curtin-Kneeling, *From Busso to the Holy Land*, pp. 183–202. Curtin-Kneeling gave an extremely interesting speech at FWWWAC about the various reasons for these failures, although I can't remember much of what he said. I do distinctly remember passing, rugby-style, a reproduction First World War kitbag stuffed with jumpers, over the heads of several team members, and watching as Curtin-Kneeling barrelled through a prize-winning British author, sending his spectacles flying, to complete the match-winning try for the 'Antipodean Savages' team.

29 Curtin-Kneeling, *From Busso to the Holy Land*, p. 215. Some first trip away from home. Nowadays the whole thing's become a rite of passage for rich kids from the Golden Triangle of Perth's western suburbs: finish school, travel Europe, come back home and buy a house/marry/pop out a sprog. Unfortunately, Australian pilgrims bring with them an unwanted reputation.

Full disclosure: I had my own Eurotrip, but I avoided the tour buses and the party hostels – I visited Ypres and Polygon Wood and was lucky enough to do Anzac Day in Gallipoli, where drunk Aussies sang football chants long into the night, and left lolly wrappers on the ground the next morning. It was the most embarrassed I've ever been of my countrymen.

Alan and the Anzacs would have been turning in their Commonwealth war graves.

the Bible as the plains on which the final battle for Earth would take place, that Lewis made his final sacrifice, putting himself in the path of danger to save his own men and a family of innocent civilians, and tragically losing his life.

Lewis's citation for his Victoria Cross reads: 'For most conspicuous acts of gallantry in circumstances of great peril.' The official regimental scrapbook of the 10th Light Horse elucidates further:

> *Lieutenant Lewis tracked the retreating Turkish troops through a small village, whereupon he disembarked and examined the nearby well for evidence of Turkish sabotage. Alongside Trooper McRae, he then passed through each house, searching for Turkish soldiers. In the final house, the two men were ambushed, and Trooper McRae was mortally wounded. Lewis fought off his attackers, and managed to pull Trooper McRae to relative safety. Re-entering without backup, LT Lewis then saved two young civilians from the building. As reinforcements arrived, LT Lewis re-entered for a third time, whereupon the building exploded. Seven bodies were recovered. Trooper McRae died shortly after.*[30]

Here is a man who altruistically sacrifices his life for his ideals, who fights valiantly throughout the war, and who is deservedly celebrated as a hero for his actions.[31] It may surprise some to note that select

---

30 Taken from *The Regimental Scrapbook of the 10th Light Horse Regiment*. I lie in bed listening to the trucks passing by and wonder if I'd've had the guts to go in once, let alone twice, let alone three times. I don't think I have it in me, but then, we can't all be Alan Lewises.

31 See L.L. Hereford, *They Walk Amongst Us* (Melbourne University Publishing, Melbourne, 1933) for a dramatic contextual account of Lewis's actions. Reading it will make you feel simultaneously proud and like you haven't accomplished enough in your own life. Seriously, you'll feel inadequate in every single way. And then you'll start seeing similarities to your own life. Like this weekend past – my own personal Lone Pine, which I say with all due respect to the brave men who lost their lives there. We're sitting on the couch, post-Sunday-brunch, recovering, and Em starts looking around at the walls, eyeing up the length and height, looking

shifty. I can tell there's a plan brewing in her head because she's absent-mindedly playing with the buttons on my shorts and I'm worried she's going to pop one of them off.

Let's wallpaper the bedroom, she says.

You wallpapered a room before?

No.

Wallpapered anything before?

No. She turns to look at the wall, and the dye in her hair shines vivid purple in the sunlight, so that even me, who wears purple jeans because I can't tell what colour they are (Bold colour choice, Matt! From the Prof when I walk into work), even I can tell she's got great Lost Cities of Lavender sunk deep in the tangle of blonde, and I'll do whatever it takes, anything, to be able to pull her close and lose myself in her. She turns back to me with her face all innocent. But how hard can it be?

And now we have a wallpapered wall, because once Em sets her mind on something, she gets it done. And sure, in the moment, it might've been indescribably hard, and one of us might have come close to killing the other (Em), and one of us might have cried (not Em), and I might have had to pay for the trip to Homebase for supplies, and yes, if you want to be a critic, there are air bubbles the size of large pizzas at some of the higher points, and, technically, the first piece is hanging at an odd angle, because we weren't sure what we were doing when we hung it, but, BUT – now we have a wallpapered wall. Finished. Wallpapered. Where there was nothing this morning. That's what Em does. Em makes things happen.

We're both exhausted. Battle weary. That happy dead weight of accomplishment at having finished a manual job. How I imagine the men of the 10th felt at the end of each night on The Great Ride.

She has little dabs of wallpaper glue in her eyebrows from where she's wiped her arm across her head, and I will fight you if you think there's anything more gorgeous.

Thank you, I say, now I know how easy it is, if anyone ever needs help hanging wallpaper I'll be able to say, 'Absolutely not, it's horrible.' I snuggle closer to her on the couch. She's laughing – either at my joke or at my glue-addled hairdo. That's Em's superpower. She makes events happen. History. Stories we'll tell our grandchildren. She turns heads and talks her way into clubs and gets upgrades on hotel rooms. She swears at people who block her way on the tube, she wallpapers rooms and dyes bright colours in her hair. She's asked to come backstage after gigs by rock stars who spot her in the front row.

I always thought Alan Lewis writing his love letters home to Rose was

commentators have repudiated my proposal that Lewis is the Unknown Digger, maintaining that he is too renowned and his actions too carefully scrutinised for him to be a plausible candidate.[32] In fact, the opposite is true: we have thoroughly examined the unfamiliar and unknown candidates – the quiet sidekicks and educated bit-players of history – and found them unsuitable for the role. Alan Lewis is a uniquely promising candidate because he is the lone Australian whose actions are astonishing enough to accommodate the presence of artistic genius within, and it is my contention that the very beating heart of his heroic experiences found their way into his poems.[33] Perhaps the reason we have been looking in the wrong place for so long is that one does not necessarily equate acts of derring-do with artistic sensitivity and genius – but by doing so, we are doing both our literary and military heroes a disservice. It takes a brave soul indeed to write the truth, to capture, in poetry, the

---

absence making the heart et cetera, et cetera, but now I get it. Alan wouldn't be Alan without Rose. I wouldn't be who I am without Em.

She makes me want to keep charging back into the fight, forever.

She makes fighting this war worthwhile.

32 When I first told Curtin-Kneeling about my thesis, he was sceptical.

But we know his life inside out, he said to me in the bar at FWWWAC, five or six beers down. I know his life inside out.

But what if we didn't, I slurred. What if I could prove it?

He wasn't entirely convinced, but I'm not sure if he'd remember it now. After a few more rounds, we decided it was our national duty to the diggers to prank the British scholars by turning all the slides for the next morning's keynote speech upside down. Take that, you Pommy bastards.

33 Sometimes I email Jennifer Hayden with ideas/questions/random thoughts, and she graciously responds, when she finds the time in her busy schedule. To be able to call her one of my work colleagues still makes me giddy, but to call her my friend would blow the mind of the young Matt, sitting in the library after school re-reading the Unknown Digger poems for the thousandth time, waiting for Mum to remember she still needs to pick me up.

When I emailed her with my Alan Lewis hypothesis, she encouraged me to follow through, to delve deep into the evidence and emerge victorious, or die trying (I'm paraphrasing, she wasn't quite so dramatic). She has been an invaluable source of inspiration.

Australian experience, and to charge headlong into the dangerous world of lyricism. Lewis, therefore, is the one digger in the whole of the 10th Light Horse and across the Australian divisions who has proven himself brave enough to have authored these incredible verses.[34]

---

34 Em says to put my head down and finish this thing, then we can start our life together proper. Jennifer Hayden says to keep fighting, like the diggers would. The Prof says not to listen to doubters, prove I'm right and they'll come around. Em says listen to the Prof.

Lying in bed last night, Em was making these little snuffling noises in her sleep on my shoulder. I'd cooked her dinner (chicken parmie and potato gems) and we'd finished a bottle of wine, and one thing had led to another, and she'd fallen asleep tangled and sweaty in the sheets and I decided none of the backlash matters if I'm living the life Alan Lewis taught me to lead. Dive in, head first, and damn the consequences.

Percute et percute velociter.

CAMP MENA, EGYPT. APRIL 1915.

They have a jar or two in Cairo, a glass or three of wine, and finish a bottle of sweet arak between the three of them; him and Red and the Irishman. They miss the last tram back to camp. They lose their arranged ride. They lose track of time. They lose track of space.

They're going to miss curfew.

They cadge a lift from an obliging rickshaw Gyppo until he throws them out, Alan's vomit down the side of the rickshaw. So they hire a native and his pack of donkeys to take them back – Alan lashed to the saddle so he can't fall off – and they arrive back late at night, with all the camp asleep.

So what? They're young. Invincible. Australian. They sneak back in, somehow, unnoticed, weaselling their way past the guards through stealth or mischief or bluster. Once they're inside camp, inch by careful inch, they creep past Kelly and the other dozing horses in their long rows, without stirring them, and manage to step their way, without tripping, through the tangle of guidelines holding the canvas tents rigid, and, against all odds, locate their tent in the desert darkness. They slip under the flap and reach out in the murky pitch with groping fingers for the welcoming caress of the bedroll and the sweet lure of sleep.

The bugle calls reveille five minutes later. Sand crunches in teeth. Red's snoring hammers against the first newborn wails of a hangover. They will never learn. They laugh about it, staggering home, arms on shoulders, and their stories grow bigger and bolder, like the bottlebrush tree back home, obscuring the sun.

~

My love, I hope this letter finds you well and I apologise in advance for the state of my handwriting; I'm writing extremely late at night, or very early in the morning (if you are that way inclined), unable to sleep with nerves. Today we head out on our first live-fire training exercise. To tell you more would be tantamount to treachery, suffice to say my men will fight valiantly to gain control of an incredibly specific area of sand from the bloody and barbaric hordes of thieving scum led by Red. It feels strange to be out of the saddle and building sandcastles.

Thank you, and your mother, for the letters – I don't think I can properly convey how joyous it is to hear one's name called when the post arrives. Unfortunately, despite my various investigations, I have yet to receive the parcel you spoke of – either it is taking a most circuitous route to me, seeing the sights in Cape Town, Suez and Alexandria, or else some lucky native is sitting himself down to a proper feast of chocolate and fruit cake wearing my new shorts. Thieving creatures.

Do you remember a certain summer day in Perth when you met me at the library as we closed? And we walked down to the bay with a bottle of plonk, and all the baby swans were crowding round their mothers, and you said something like, black swans are simply silhouettes. I find myself returning to that day. There's a certain moment each morning, before the sun starts doing its thing, where I almost feel I'm home. When we are all silhouettes. When the sun is blazing proper, it's far too hot to patrol, and we mill about camp like headless chooks. Our new pal Nugget calls it the Farkit Hour. One day I shall write a book detailing everything he says, called 'Nuggets of Wisdom'. We'll receive invitations to Government House, to summer balls and the grandest parties, and we shall have the Irishman to thank.

That's enough mindless chit from me, soon I'll wake Red – one approaches warily and pokes the beast from a safe distance, careful to keep fingers and toes protected at all times – and we shall eat breakfast, wish each other well and then proceed to attack. Another regular day. I look forward to a letter soon – tell me more about the hospital, if you would be so kind. Write about the gumtrees. Describe, please, the minutiae of your life. I wrap myself in your words when I fall asleep.

Yours, yawningly.

The trenches on the rock won't be like this though, with the wooden slats reaching up above his head, and little rivulets of sand, like tiny waterfalls, bursting through the gaps with the slightest movement up above. They've heard the ground is much harder, tree roots and rocks and various bits and bobs to get in the way of their shovels. Furphy has it they won't need these trenches though, they'll be in Constantinople by mid-year and home by Christmas – but they have been ordered to practise, to show off their acquired skills, and so the trenches have been dug.

Heavy mortar shells fall from the sky yards from their make-do frontline. White-hot metal. Screaming ghosts. The brass hats have deemed it wise to use live ammunition. The brass hats are watching their progress, from a safe vantage point several miles away.

The objective, a large dune the same as every other dune, lies before them, defended by Red and the Second Division. Between them and him is open desert.

Alan peers around at the men crammed into the trench with him, like row on row of juicy tomatoes jammed into crates at the Italian grocers in Fremantle, ripe and ready to burst. He risks a quick glance at his watch: three more minutes and the barrage will start to creep forward, and he'll have to jump up and out of the trench, advancing in the wake of the exploding shells. If there was room to pace he'd be pacing. The men look bored.

'Three minutes, boys.'

Two of the closest men glance his way, the rest stare straight ahead or up at the sky, or at their hands, at the sweat-buffed handles of their rifles. He is younger than half the men in his charge. They look at him like his brothers did when he was young. Sheep shearers and cattle drovers, men twice his size with shoulders like doorways. All placing their lives in his hands. Red is able to joke and laugh with them, so they respect him, but Alan can't think of what to say. There are fresh blisters on the pink skin of his palms.

He wipes the sweat from his brow. Two minutes. Sand between his toes, scratching back and forth with the sweat, bites into the soft webbing. There is dust in his mouth. He adjusts his stance, remembering his training; but the training never mentioned the gritty yellow sand, the coarse pebbles and jagged shards, caked on by sweat, stuck between his arse cheeks.

One minute. He glances down the line at the faces of his men, catches the eyes of those who look back at him. The cheap Egyptian cigarettes pursed between lips. Stubble on quivering chins. Someone further down the line is singing a song about someone else's sister, but the explosions and whines of the shells make it hard to hear. Close enough to feel the heat of the explosions on his nose. And they must advance into the storm.

He takes a deep breath, places the whistle between his lips and mouths a silent prayer to whatever it is he believes in. The shelling has moved away from them, the pressure dropping, his ears popping as he swallows hard. The man closest to him turns, but he's already blowing three long blasts on the whistle, pulling himself up and over the sandbags, turning to grab the hand of the man behind, to pull him up, and the man behind him too, wave after wave, into the morning light.

One infamous night, arriving back to camp after curfew, they lie in the sand observing the entrance to camp as the guard on duty walks back and forth. Nugget has a trail of vomit down his shirt sleeve. Alan doesn't feel too flash either.

Nugget has an idea, which is dangerous in itself.

'Follow my lead,' the Irishman says, and stands up. He starts walking backwards towards the camp. Alan and Red jump up and follow him. Red burps.

Alan starts to giggle.

The guard has finished his pass, and turns back towards the entrance. He sees their backs in the distance, and thinks they're trying to leave.

'Halt!' he cries, running towards them.

Alan can't stop giggling.

'Alright, back to camp.' The guard lays a warm hand on Alan's shoulder. He almost stumbles. Red is nodding too much, talking too loud. Nugget murmurs something in his Irish lilt that defuses the situation, and the guard is smiling.

The camp spins.

Nugget sings an Irish song about the Egyptian girls; their bonny sweet faces, he sings in his gravelly tenor. Nugget's words lull Alan to sleep.

They'd first met McRae on the *Mashobra*, bedding down with the men in the triple-tiered bunks. The Irishman had been living in Albany for five years when he signed up, the smallest man in the regiment, turning his Irish charm on to scrape his way through the medical. When Alan had boarded at Fremantle, and headed below deck to find his assigned bunk, he'd discovered it strewn with papers, various items of uniform, and an impressive collection of pornography. He'd promptly removed the offending articles to a better home, and dumped them on the floor.

An hour later, as the men returned to their bunks, he was woken from his nap with startled alarm by a pile of his own books hitting him squarely in the stomach. From his bunk he could only make out the top of a head of dark brown hair, the voice that followed issuing forth from below with a thick Irish accent.

'You the eejit that moved my things?'

'You the bastard that put them on my bed?'

Silence for a moment.

'Touché.' Only the voice pronounced it off kilter, made it sound like 'tooshee'.

The shells are two hundred feet ahead of them, and out of the safety of the trench, the whole wide field of cratered sand and dark shadowy dunes stretching out for miles looks like the fabled fields of fire and brimstone. He can't move, caught in the light of the flames. The terrible beauty of destruction.

'C'mon, you lazy bastards!'

Halfway down the line someone else calls them forward, striding out ahead of the rest of the pack, turning back and beckoning to them. Doing his job better than him. He blows his whistle, shrieking over the roar of the shells, and the men turn, the flames dancing in their eyes.

He walks forward, boots sinking into the warm sand. The shells are screaming their final descents, and alongside him the boys are whooping and hollering, rifles held like babies, bayonets glinting. Another game to be won. Another adventure. As they move forward, the wall of fire moves further back, another hundred and fifty yards, concealing their movements behind the smog, maintaining the safe distance from their slick skin, their burnt forearms, shielding their advance on the huge dune marking Red's defensive line.

A footy field away from the objective, he walks straight into a cloying wall of smog that has yet to settle, which coats his lungs, powder dry on his lips, the limestone taste of zinc cream. The powdery residue is in his eyelashes, and tears spring from the corners of his eyes, attempting to wash away the dirt, but with each blink it grows worse. He closes his eyes but no matter which direction they roll the tiny grains push into the soft wet whites, caught beneath the thin skin of his eyelids, pricking and tearing. Trying to wipe his eyes introduces the acid sting of the sweat that drips down his forehead.

He lowers his head against the onslaught. On either side his men are doing the same, heads down, walking straight into the path of the bombardment. On his right flank the line threatens to break, one small group out ahead of the rest. The men around him stop as he blows his whistle to call a halt, but the forward group marches on, too far ahead to hear. He runs forward alone, tripping in the sand. The brass hats will be judging him. The men behind him laughing. The shells shriek down on top of him, boxing him in.

Suffocating.

He grasps the shoulder of the trailing trooper, swings him around, sends him back towards their line. Must stay together. He screams at the other men to fall back, to advance as a group, a fluid, perfect killing machine – but the shells are too loud. He grabs the men one by one and shoves them back towards the main group – like herding cattle.

In Egypt, after only a week on their horses, the entire regiment was demounted and taught to fight in trenches, and McRae was assigned to Alan's division. Alan had worried that he might question his decisions, or backchat him in front of the other troopers, or simply keep him awake all night with his incessant chatter, but McRae just smiled his lopsided smile and backed him up, every time. When they needed a third man for their tent, Alan suggested the Irishman.

Red and McRae immediately hit it off, like long-lost brothers, and Alan had followed, eager to impress.

'We're going into town for a jag, care to join?' Red's head had appeared at the door of their tent, his uniform pressed, buttons gleaming. Alan had been napping in the afternoon heat.

'Who's we?'

'Nugget, me, couple of Gyppo sheilas, General Birdwood. Who do ya think?'

'Who's Nugget?'

Red gave him a hard stare. 'Sergeant McRae, Al. Everyone calls him Nugget.'

'Do they? I didn't know.'

'Now you do.' Red straightened his bootstraps and then offered Alan a hand up, a smile on his face. 'Get your kit, we've got a war to fight.'

Back in formation, the men drop to their knees at his command, rifles at their shoulders trained on a make-believe enemy. The heat is ferocious, each exploding shell buffeting their position with a fresh wall of hot air. He pulls his watch from his pocket, and a fat drop of sweat splatters the face, rolling off his nose in slow motion.

'Hold!'

The whole company is close enough to feel the pressure waves reverberating with each explosion. Tiny fragments of metal dive, sizzling, into the sand by their feet.

He wants to turn back.

They should turn back. They're too close, and the barrage is unmoving, shell after shell raining down on the dune before them.

He doesn't know what to do. If this were real, they'd be completely exposed, torn to shreds by returning fire.

He glances to his left, and, crouched, runs past the men to the end of the line and the small shape holding their exposed far flank. As he squats to speak, the shriek of a falling shell grows, until, right on top of them, a wall of heat and noise knocks him forward and into Nugget, sending them both sprawling. For a horrifying moment he worries he might piss himself. Breath sputters. Heart leaping into his throat, choking back tears. He spits sand and raises himself up on shaking arms. No pain, hope for the best. Nugget lies on the ground, unmoving. Alan's knee clicks as he stands. Nugget groans and turns his head; one side of his face is coated by sand, one side tanned dark and sweating.

'Well, this is a proper dog's breakfast.' Nugget runs his tongue once over his chapped lips, and then spits a glob of pink onto the ground by his boots. A pugilist's face; sunburnt wrinkles, broken nose. Head like a smashed crab and a tongue faster than the machine guns that chatter out over the rifle range. More than one bar-room brawl has started because Nugget's mouth has run faster than his mind. More than one brawl has been finished with his fists.

'You hurt?'

'Yeah. Bit my tongue.'

'You look like a fucking lamington.'

Nugget raises an eyebrow, but doesn't reply in turn. Alan is terrified of what he'll look like: afraid, uncertain, unfit for leadership. He's safer with Nugget by his side.

'What do you think?'

'We're too bloody close. We should pull back until it eases up.'

He looks around. The men are nervous, glancing his way, waiting for orders. Waiting for him to say anything. He should pull back to a safe distance. He should wait for the shelling to stop and then take the objective with a full company. He should be decisive. He should be independent. He should be creative.

He should have decided five minutes ago.

He feels the thrill of university debates again. That same need for contrariness.

'Take your section and go around the left flank, see if you can't find a way around. We'll wait here for the fireworks to end and then advance.' His voice cracks and breaks with the strain of shouting over the refrain.

Nugget blinks twice in quick succession, ducking with each whine of approaching shell. For a moment, Alan worries he's going to refuse. He flinches, but Nugget swears and drops back to gather his men. Alan risks a quick look up at the top of the dune, but the sun is working against him, glaring down through the shell vapour.

He runs back to his position at the centre of the line, his legs cramping with the awkwardness of the pose, each step like wading through water. The men are getting antsy, yelling to him down the line, asking for orders. He drops his head and prays for the shelling to stop so they will stop questioning him. The whine of the shells makes his insides groan. A fireball erupts above their heads and when they recover from the shock he finds a hot sliver of metal steaming in the sand by his knees. He tries to pick it up but burns his fingers.

Movement out of the corner of his eye makes him turn his head. One trooper drops back from position. He catches up before he can get too far away and screams at him to return to his post. The trooper removes his hand to show a long cut crossing his left eye. Blood runs down his face.

'Get back in position, trooper.'

The boy holds out his blood-filled hand for evidence. A cup of red wine.

'I can't, sir.' His voice is high-pitched, shrill. 'I need help.'

The hot eyes of the other men are on his back, waiting for his response. Tough love.

'Help? We will hold, because we have been ordered to hold.' And he shoves the boy back toward the line with such force that the kid stumbles forward, catching himself on the ground with outstretched hands, the sand sticking to his bloody palms. Lamingtons. All of them.

They hold, because they have been ordered to hold. Twenty-two minutes after the timetabled end, the bombardment finally draws to a close. He orders his troops to run up the incline. Each step they take forward, they drift halfway back down in a slip of loose sand. By the time they reach the top they are exhausted.

At the peak they encounter the perimeter of Red's forces. Screaming and cursing – a herd of frothing brumbies streaming across a plain – they charge. Sun glints off bayonets. Alan sprints forward, pistol drawn, the feather in his slouch hat bouncing and glancing off his shoulder with each lurch. In the centre of the defending trench he locates Red, sitting at a small round table, drinking from a mug of tea. As he approaches, pistol drawn, Red barks an order of surrender to his men. The objective has been captured. The exercise is complete. They've done it.

Red glances at the watch lying on the table before him.

'What took you so long? Tea's getting cold.'

~

My love, I trust this letter finds you well, and I apologise in advance for the state of my handwriting. I have lost track of where in the day I am. What time is it for you? The sun is shining, but it's late. Do you ever get that?

I wrote a long letter to you what feels like days ago, and I find I cannot send it. It says entirely the wrong things. I worry you won't recognise me when I return. Sometimes I think I won't recognise myself. Do you remember, I wonder, when I rode up to Mundaring with Dad? We were gone two weeks, and on returning you said I looked, I think you used the word, matured? I said like cheese, and you said, no, like my eyes had grown wider. Like more of the world could get in. Something beautiful.

I've been pondering the wonder of words.

Thank you for your letters. Please send more. I know that may be hard, but it's a right cow to see your chums walk away smiling when the post arrives and not receive a jot yourself. I have asked Ma and Dad to write, and Tom and his little ones might even find the time to send a little parcel. I suppose you have heard about Tom signing up. Bloody fool. I understand the urge to pitch in, but Tom has other responsibilities, and will be doing no-one any favours by catching typhoid in a filthy Egyptian camp. There's no need for him to try and play hero, especially since most of the fighting will likely be finished by the time he arrives.

Today, we lost our first casualty to war. I told you, I think, about the two men who passed away in the hospital when we arrived, a terrible waste, and one you can't help but feel powerless about. Today though, should have, could have, been avoidable ...

This letter is as insufficient as the last, and I have decided not to send it either. Bloody bastard mongrel fuck.

~

Thank Christ that's over. Alan accepts the battered tin mug and drops onto the patch of dirt by Red's feet. He can already taste the first beer they'll have on the next day off.

'You alright?' Red is watching him.

'Shitshow. Gunners couldn't keep it on schedule if it wore pink garters and asked 'em to dance.' Alan takes a sip of the warm liquid in the mug. Whatever it is, it ain't tea. Not in the proper sense of the word. He can't look back at Red. He holds his hands tight around the mug to hide his shaking. His heart is pounding axe-blows in his chest.

Red finishes his mug and pops his watch in his pocket. He makes a grand show of pulling himself up to his full height, puffing his chest out, broadening his shoulders, chin jutting. Official Officer Stance.

'You look like a cockatoo, mate,' Alan grins. Ears still ringing. Shell-shook.

Red doesn't miss a beat, clears his throat with a noise like a hungover rooster, the feather in his hat bobbling forward. 'Alright lads, well done. Top brass will probably say we weren't professional enough, but what do they know, eh?'

Smart alec down one of the side trenches puts on his best approximation of an Etonian accent, all clipped aitches and stick up arse: 'I say old boy; I do believe the Orstralian is taking the piss!'

Red waits for the laughter to die down. 'Gather your bits. Move out in five minutes.' He sits back down, his smile wide, and takes off his hat. 'Where's Nug?'

Alan glances around; for the first time, he notices the absence of the chatty little bugger. He can't find any of the men who followed Nugget in the pincer movement.

'Part of the advance wave. He didn't get here first?'

There's a boot, lying on the sand, near the top of the dune they ran up, but around on the left flank. From Alan's vantage point at the top he can't see the bottom of the valley. He's not sure he wants to. The boot is empty. The long leather strap that spirals up around the calf trails in the sand like a tail as he holds the heel in his hand. One left boot.

He runslides down the slope, his weight and momentum pushing the sand, so when he reaches the bottom and the group of men gathered there, a crescent of the desert follows him, circling his feet like curious children hiding behind mother's legs, eager to see.

One trooper lies on the ground; another kneels. Two more crouch a little further away. Nugget left with four others.

'What happened?'

Two men turn, their faces dark with sweat and dirt. One of them taps the shoulder of the trooper on his knees. Nugget. As Nugget rises from his spot, the man on the ground is revealed. Trooper Morrow.

Fred.

Freddie.

Busselton boy. Freddie's skin has a glossy pale sheen and his eyes are glazed over. Propping himself up on one elbow, but gazing straight through him, out behind Alan somewhere in the endless sand. Where Freddie's right leg should lie, the limb ends in a bloody red full stop. A belt has been tied tight around his upper thigh. The sand beneath the wound is pink, packed flat by Nugget's knees.

~

The air inside the tent is stifling. Church in midsummer. But he can't open the covers. He can't let the men see him. He won't watch them cringe.

He's waiting for the Major to arrive and call him outside, march him off in handcuffs to be court-martialled. The firing squad or the rest of the war in a dank cell. Imagine the look on Rose's face when she reads that. What Dad would think, quietly judging behind pursed lips. The letters from his brothers disowning him.

He hears footsteps outside, and the Major flicks open the covers. He salutes – robotic, the motion crisp and well-practised.

'At ease.' The Major is the only Englishman in the regiment, sent over from Oxford to help lead their brute Antipodean forces.

'Sir, I can explain,' Alan begins, but the Major cuts him off.

'Well done, Lieutenant. You held your nerve in the heat of the shelling, and captured the objective. The top brass were pleased.'

He doesn't know what to say. He's tracked pink mud through the tent. Bits of his own men.

'Shame about Morrow. Now, what happened with the Richardson boy?'

Alan swallows. 'An advance section was sent around in a pincer movement. They were caught in our own fire.'

The Major nods and glances around the room.

Alan can feel the sweat dripping down the sides of his body as he waits for the Major to say more.

'And whose foolish idea was that?'

He pictures Rose opening the letter, the smile dropping from her face. 'Sergeant McRae ran it by me, sir. I should have stopped him.'

'Yes. Indeed. But you are here to learn, and now you have. No matter. Pity about Richardson, but he won't be the last.' The Major places a fatherly hand on his shoulder and looks him straight in the eyes. 'Well done out there, Lewis.'

He can breathe again. Can hear the sounds of the camp again. The constant buzz of flies. The Major grunts and heads for the door.

'Sir?' He surprises himself. The Major turns back to him, halfway out of the tent.

'Nothing, sir. Thank you, sir.' And then he's gone.

When Nugget and Red enter, twenty minutes later, he's sitting at the desk, trying to write another letter home that won't come out how he wants. Nugget has a bright white plaster caked on his ear. Ridiculous.

'They're taking Morrow back. Want to say goodbye?'

He stares at the desk, at the words on the page that swim like tadpoles before his eyes. Red ducks his head and shuffles back towards his bedroll.

'He might not make it, Al. He's pretty weak,' Nugget says.

The thought of heading back out into the sun makes his stomach turn, sea snakes slithering in his guts. He should eat but he can't imagine a taste that won't make him retch.

'I'm sorry, Sergeant McRae.' That surprises both of them, Red's head flicking up in his periphery. 'I had to tell the Major about your plan.'

Silence in the tent.

'You what?' Nugget is still speaking too loudly for the small space. Red has moved to somewhere behind his shoulder. Alan doesn't like not knowing where they are, so he stands, faces the room. Red sits on his cot and starts to unlace his right boot.

'What, sir, to you,' he says, but his voice wavers and they can both tell he's shitting himself.

'Fuck off, Al. What did you say to him?'

'Red, you heard that, right? Insubordination.' But Red is looking at him the same way Nugget is – disappointment in his eyes.

'What did you do, Al?' It's worse when Red says it, so quietly, looking up at him from his cot, his long legs almost up to his ears.

He looks back and forth between them, trying to figure a way out of the situation he's brought on himself. He glances towards the open doorway, but Nugget catches the look. Nugget's nostrils flare and then the Irishman charges at him. Before he knows it, he's fallen backwards onto the desk. Nugget's breath is hot on his face and he can't get away from it.

'What the fuck did you do, sir?'

Red is standing, a tall shadow looming behind the awful close-up of Nugget's bloodied face, his yellowing teeth, the disgusting smell of cheap Egyptian cigarettes on every breath.

'I'm sorry.'

Nugget's forearm relaxes from across his chest, but he doesn't let him up.

'I'm so sorry,' and he is, his eyelids suddenly heavy, the acid burn of vomit in his gut like his stomach has been ripped open. 'I couldn't tell him it was me.'

'Why not?' This from Red, standing watching everything, not helping him up, not taking his side like a best mate should, not fighting for him.

Snot runs down his lip and into his mouth. He licks it away, sniffs like a drunk. 'I couldn't. I couldn't.'

'So you told him –' Red begins.

'It was my idea?' finishes Nugget.

'I was scared.' He doesn't miss the subtle glance they share at his admission. Nugget takes his weight off him, gives him a hand up. Red is back on his cot, rummaging through his pack.

'It's ok, mate,' Nugget says, but it's not.

'We're all scared,' says Red, but Alan isn't sure he's telling the truth. Red has never wavered from a decision in his life – he would have known exactly what to do.

He can see it in the way Nugget looks through him, the way Red won't catch his eye, the tension in the stifling air.

He shouldn't have said anything. Fuck.

The horses start whinnying outside, stirred up by some unknown force. Somewhere from the other side of the camp comes a scream, long and splintering, hanging in the hot air like fruit suspended in honey. Outside the tent the air shimmers, burning away the events of the morning, bleaching bones white, grinding the silvery white splinters into the endless dunes.

They say you never forget your first kill.

~

The sand beneath Trooper Morrow's missing leg had been stained red. Despite the tourniquet, sticky blobs of blood had kept dripping onto the flattened surface where Nugget had been kneeling. When Nugget stood up and spat, his phlegm was flecked pink.

'What happened?' Alan didn't understand.

'He's gone.' Nugget was yelling.

'Gone where?'

'Eh?'

'Who's gone?'

'What?'

Alan stopped and took a breath and in that moment the drop of blood had leapt from Nugget's ear and landed on the collar of his shirt. It seeped into the crisscross hairs of the fabric. It was all he could see: the blood trickling down Nugget's neck; the chapped, torn skin of his lips; the bloodied and dirtied fingers, the nails bitten low, cracked and raw, the little tabs of skin peering up from the sides like strips of wallpaper in an unfinished room. Nugget looked as tired as Alan felt.

'You ok, mate?' As he motioned toward the bleeding ear Nugget reached a hand up. The tips of his fingers stained red, the Irishman swore violently at the open sky. Alan grimaced. 'Think you've busted an eardrum.'

'Think I've busted an eardrum,' Nugget roared back.

He nodded, his hands clammy, the interminable hum of mosquitos in his ears. A hole was growing in his gut – a yawning pit growing deeper and wider with each passing second, pulling nearby objects down into its gaping maw. He had made a terrible mistake. It was clawing at the walls of his stomach, dragging his lungs down to his boots so his breath spurted out in shallow bursts. He'd fucked up. There was too much space around him, too much air; he needed a closed hole, he needed time to think, he needed the terror to unwind from his throat for a moment. For one second.

He ran through the names of the men who'd left with Nugget: Brennan and Stokes were standing a few feet away, Morrow was sobbing on the ground, wincing with each breath. Icy-cold fingers reached out and gripped his heart.

Trooper Richardson. Richie. Twenty-two-year-old from Perth proper.

'Where's Richie?'

Nugget stared straight through him, back the way they'd come.

'What happened to Richie?'

'No, I think it's my eardrum. Damn near took my head off.' Someone was blowing cool air on the back of his neck, the hairs on his arms rising, the muscles in his shoulders tensed. Hard granite. 'Morrow needs help, Al.'

They'd crucify him, court-martial him, have his guts for garters. He couldn't swallow properly, his throat was too dry. His tongue was too big for his mouth, choking him. Nugget registered the object in his hand, the long tail trailing behind tracking his descent down the dune. Nugget reached for it, but Alan snatched it back. He'd keep the boot and return it himself. Nugget's eyes dodged his gaze, and then he dropped his head.

'Richie's gone.'

'Where's he gone, Nug?' He didn't understand. 'He won't get very far without a bloody boot.'

Nugget laid a hot, heavy hand on his shoulder.

The pit yawned wider. Alan shrugged off the meaty grip.

'Richie's gone.' Nugget was yelling now, couldn't hear how stupid he sounded, the words rising and scattering somewhere over the dune. Alan glanced about, looking for a body. For blood. For limbs, or parts, or a sign, somewhere, of Richie's phantom presence. Everywhere was sand. He stumbled, past Nugget, peering around the stunned men. He dropped to the ground and combed his fingers through the shingle. Hot on the surface, jagged rocks in the cold depths.

He scrambled forward, crawling in the dirt around Morrow and his dead-eyed gaze, and then, finding nothing, turned and thrust his arms under Morrow's body and picked him up. He'd flipped the injured man over, thrown him, like Richie might be waiting to jump out from underneath with a wild grin, the whole gag an elaborate prank. Morrow screamed – shrill, unforgiving.

'Where!?'

The men looked at Alan with wide eyes, like they couldn't hear him, like he'd spoken a language they didn't understand.

Nugget's hand was on his shoulder once more. A lead weight.

Richie was gone, into the hot air around them. Into the grains of sand finding their way into every crack and crevice. Into the sun beating down hotter with each passing minute. Into the sweat soaking their backs. Into the scorching desert landscape, the harsh empty furnace that cooked, courageous and willing, the tender young flesh of them and their mates.

A single left boot.

A single boot.

Left.

CHAPTER 2: An analysis of the material evidence strongly indicating Alan Lewis's authorship of the poems: Lewis's wartime writings as primary sources for objective comparison.

In his seminal work, *The Annotated Letters of Alan Lewis VC*, historian Arthur Pyke analysed 193 letters sent by Lewis to his family and friends throughout the period of his deployment.[35] The vast majority of letters belonged to Rose Porter, Lewis's childhood sweetheart and fiancée, who kept all his correspondence safe in the knowledge that it would be of abundant use to later generations. In 1968, she told Arthur Pyke: 'He was my hero, even before the war. I knew, if he failed to return, he would find a way to leave his mark.'[36] Porter was more prescient than she knew, as his literary

35 See Arthur Pyke, *The Annotated Letters of Alan Lewis VC*. Sometimes, reading Alan's letters, I feel like he's channelling my own thoughts: a thousand miles from home, experiencing new emotions, anxious and excited and lonely and homesick. We have a lot in common. Eager to prove our worth. Deeply romantic. Hidden depths of bravery waiting to surface. And then sometimes, Alan'll relate a story about Nugget, and I realise I'm more like his Irish friend than I care to admit – over-ambitious, a little dim, but always with the best interests of those I love at heart.

36 Rose Porter speaking to Arthur Pyke, from *The Annotated Letters of Alan Lewis VC*, p. xxi. And he continues to influence the lives of those around him to this day. I ran round to Em's last night with a bottle of chilled prosecco to share my big news. Guess what? I wanted to surprise her.

She was sitting on the couch, and she did a little shoulder shuffle and smiled, because she'd definitely heard the clink of the glasses as I got the champagne flutes down from the cupboard.

What?

Guess.

I'm tired, Matt, just tell me. She stretched her arms behind her, rolled her head back and forth and waited. I waited too.

Guess, I said, chuckling. She stared up at me, impatient.

I got the AARC!

Oh? she squinted.

The later research career grant. The AARC. The one I applied for a few months back. You helped me fill out the form?

Uhuh.

It's not a ton of money, but I'm on the right track.

achievements rank alongside – indeed, I would argue, outshine – any of his heroic triumphs.

The most interesting letters are those partial works and early drafts that were recovered from Lewis's possessions following his death, letters that remained unsent for motives only Lewis can have known, through which we can ascertain Lewis's authentic, pre-edited writing voice and stylistic mannerisms.

It hardly needs pointing out that there is no mention in any of the 193 analysed letters that Lewis was writing poetry. In this way, he is not self-referential at all, which makes him very much a man of his time. There are only four separate occasions where Lewis mentions writing letters home to the families of the fallen, and thirteen instances where he references the act of writing his own letters.[37] In analysing

---

Her eyes kept flicking back to the screen. I pulled the bottle of bubbly out from behind my back.

Means when I finish, I'm pretty much guaranteed a professor position.

Her eyes swung back to me at the mention of a potential job.

We'll get a new place, together. Fancy dinners out. Holidays to Paris, or Barcelona, or Rome. The house and the dog and the dream life.

Guaranteed?

Just have to finish it.

What if you're wrong?

I'm not wrong.

Em supports me. She really does. She understands how hard the academic game can be. She pushes me and enables me to get up each day and plug away, and she reads chunks of chapters she knows nothing about and smiles and tells me I'm amazing. I know it's hard to get excited about a dead soldier and some poems, but this is the most important thing I will ever do. It's not like Alan is going anywhere, but I'm so impatient to be living the life I know I should be living – waking up with Em every morning, walking our dog around the common, teaching classes on Alan's poetry, book signings in the evening. It's coming.

Congratulations, baby. I know what this means to you.

We drank the bubbly and curled up to watch reality TV. I'd been hoping for a celebratory blowjob, but I'm willing to wait.

37 Pyke, *The Annotated Letters*, pp. 211–245. Which only goes and makes me feel bad about getting home yesterday and buying flowers and a block of chocolate and standing around outside Em's place for two and a half hours in the hopes of a romantic surprise, not knowing she went for a quick drink

the letters, Pyke noted their basic format: 'most of the letters are fairly standard – describing recent events, asking Rose questions about her family and job and requesting home-style luxuries to be sent over.'[38] One is struck by the easily observed devotion of a man in love, a man eager to return home. Margaret Cline, in her review of *The Annotated Letters*, calls the work a tragedy, pointing out Lewis's detachment from the men around him, calling him 'alone in the large world, equally repulsed and amused by the improper actions of his mates, a man not living, but stuck in limbo, awaiting his true life'.[39] I would disagree, instead categorising Lewis's detachment from his fellow soldiers as characteristic of the true writer: detached, observing so that he may create. In one of the earliest examples of Lewis's unsent drafts, dated around April 1915, while his regiment trained outside Cairo, Lewis relates a story about Sergeant 'Nugget'

---

after work with one of her mates and wouldn't come straight home, and then when she finally does get home, I'm so cold I can't move my fingers and she says she shouldn't be eating chocolate on her diet, but thank you, that's so sweet, you weren't waiting long were you? And between my half-baked lies and the sound of my teeth chattering, I'm thinking, I should have been writing.

38 Pyke, *The Annotated Letters*, p. 224. Like Em bringing lunch into work for both of us, so when our breaks intersect we can sit in the courtyard, and I buy her a Diet Coke, and we can laugh about the undergrads running past, until, inevitably, the Prof calls her mobile and she's needed back inside to show him how to send a text or explain what a meme is, or to make a decision on one of the thousands of tiny inconsequential details about the party: Black or white ribbons? Gold balloons? Are peacock feathers too much? For future reference, when it comes to the Prof and Em planning a party, peacock feathers are NEVER too much.

39 Margaret Cline, 'Review of *The Annotated Letters of Alan Lewis VC* by Arthur Pyke', in *The Australian Literary Review*, Issue 8, Volume 36, August 1977, p. 79. Numerous sources have reported on the popularity of the local women among the fighting men, and it should come as no surprise that the men – stuck behind the lines for long periods of time with money to spare and not much to spend it on – turned to the brothels of the area in search of a good time. Perhaps Lewis's feelings about his mate's habits are most accurately reflected by the fact that any letters with reference to brothels and drinking remain unsent.

McRae falling in love with a local 'woman of disrepute' and bringing her, as a gift, a pair of shoes, not knowing that, in Egyptian culture, the giving of shoes is considered an insult.[40]

Had any of the Unknown Digger's poems been sonnets entitled 'To Rose, Waiting Back Home', 'Miss Porter, How I Love Thee', or anything along similar lines, tracking the author would have been simple. Close textual analysis of the poems, however, notes an astoundingly complete lack of proper names and familial references, other than numerous placenames (analysed in further detail in Chapter 3) and a cryptic reference to a 'Harriet' in the final lines of 'Ken Oath'.[41] Jennifer Hayden maintains that this Harriet is

---

40 The letter ends with Nugget hiding from an angry father inside the steam room of a local bath, wearing nothing but his slouch hat, surrounded by half-naked Egyptians (Pyke, *The Annotated Letters*, pp. 68–69). For further information, see Reginald T. Lloyd, *Twenty-Four Hours in Amiens*, Frobisher Publishing, Melbourne, 1993, or multiple sections in Terry Kinloch's *Devils on Horses*. The closest I came to a backpacker fling myself was, perhaps ironically, in Kraków, after a sombre day spent visiting Auschwitz. Can't remember her name, which makes me a terrible person. She was American. Doing her own thing, making her way around the tourist traps, blowing off steam before getting a 'real job' back home. She came into the communal lounge room in the hostel and asked if anyone wanted to get dinner. I happened to be sitting there, reading, and hungry, so I said yes.

We went for Polish pizza. We were both in need of a stiff drink.

First round was on me.

One drink led to one bottle, led to a second bottle, led to drinking cheap Polish vodka in the hostel common room, led to sharing a joint in the courtyard, led to her jerking me off in the hostel bathroom. I imagined us visiting the salt mines together. Catching up again in Berlin. Visiting war memorials together.

The next morning when I woke she'd already checked out. No note. She said one day she wanted to run a marathon. I felt like Alan, alone in the middle of it all.

41 Unless otherwise stated, all lines of poetry are taken from the Unknown Digger's original papers, which I had the pleasure of examining in the archives of the Australian War Memorial over the course of a week in Canberra, late summer 2010. I never would have guessed then that I'd eventually move to London to figure out who wrote them, meet the love of my life, and write a thesis on my childhood hero Alan Lewis. Funny how things work out.

a reference to Harrietville, a town in Victoria, which Hayden uses as further evidence to back her claim that the Unknown Digger died in the trenches of the Western Front.[42] There is no evidence of anyone named Harriet in Lewis's life, but I prefer to see this as indicating an innate reticence and urge for privacy, keeping his loved ones hidden from sight, as it were – perhaps even with the anticipation that one day his poems would be in the public eye.

Despite the obvious lack of contextual clues, thorough investigation of the limited primary sources available about the Unknown Digger – namely the original documents found in the UWA archive by Jennifer Hayden – reveals a large body of evidence to support my thesis. When these investigatory findings are considered alongside the much larger resource of well-thumbed primary sources left behind by Lewis, one notices associations that cannot be passed over as simple coincidence.

I have spent countless hours poring over photocopies of Alan's letters to check whether he wrote his L's with a flourish, or the straight up and down lines of the Unknown Digger. Having scoured both documents thoroughly, I can confirm that Alan left his L's unblemished, just as the Unknown Digger does in every one of his poems. His signature sign-off: 'yours, [adverbly]', contains the same humour and playful tone as found in the lines of 'The Billjim' and 'Strewth'. In his letter home dated June 1917, Alan spells the word 'horrifically' as 'horiffically [sic]'.[43] In 'Mate & His Pack', which, unlike other scholars, I believe was written in late 1917, the same word is spelt correctly; however, in 'Blood's Worth Bottling', the Unknown Digger misspells the word encouraged as 'encoraged'.[44] I believe

42 See Jennifer Hayden, *Unearthing the Unknown Digger*, Chapter 8: 'Red Poppies'.

43 Arthur Pyke, *The Annotated Letters*, p. 104. Em's still at work planning her party. She messaged and said she might have to do an all-nighter. She said she missed me. She signed off with a whole screen of kisses.

44 For more instances of misspelled words or incorrect grammar in the works of the Unknown Digger, I refer you to Chapter 6: 'Black Lines', in Hayden's *Unearthing the Unknown Digger*, which focuses on the poems themselves and looks closely at the word counts, inaccuracies and physical data available.

that Lewis knew full well how to spell both words, which is why we see these two spellings, but in the rush and clamour of an officer's day, simply didn't have the time to correct his mistakes.

Comparing the two sets of writings displays some crucial similarities, and a few glaring differences, which I first put forward in my recent article in *Australian Literary Journal*. Most significantly, the sentence structures within Lewis's letters mirror the syntactical choices of the Unknown Digger, with a 63.24% similarity.[45] Critics have argued that this is simply a case of culturally ingrained language choices, educational standards, and a diminished environment for creative varieties, but the similarities cannot be dismissed. Indeed, 63% is more than chance, 63% is much more than coincidence.

Harder to measure and contrast is the tone of the individual works. Lewis appears upbeat in much of his correspondence, often recalling humorous incidents, relaying the news from the front, or telling stories of Trooper McRae's latest misadventures.[46] As with his letters, the unrelenting optimism of the Unknown Digger poems

---

45 See M. Denton, 'Comparing Language Choices in Diametric Data Packets' in *Australian Literary Journal*, Issue 4, Volume 66, April 2017.

46 See *The Annotated Letters*, p. 113, where Lewis re-enacts Red's hapless bartering at an Egyptian bazaar, or pp. 200–202, where Nugget stars as Mary in a regimental production of the nativity. Em has this same remarkable ability to find the positive in any situation. She's been working late most nights this week on this party for the Prof she's in charge of planning. I know she's stressed, and I'm happy she's doing what she enjoys, but tonight we missed my mate's one-man theatre show because she forgot about it. Of course, I'm the muggins left waiting in the cold for two hours messaging and calling and leaving progressively more insane-sounding messages until she finally walks out and reminds me there's no reception in their office.

You could have left without me, she says, eyes darting behind my head, like she'll be able to see the show if she can find it in the distance.

I'd never forget about you.

Well, now I feel terrible.

Somehow, I'm in the wrong, and it's my fault for wasting twenty quid on tickets. I call it Emnesia, this gift of hers, to forget things she's been told a thousand times. She walks away, faster than me. I have to run to catch up. Somehow, it's me keeping her waiting. Em would send letters home from the war that made it sound like the most amazing experience imaginable. Em's letters would give people FOMO. Fuck, I love her.

shines through. See, for example, the metaphorical sun rising on the war in the last lines of 'The Groyne', with its stylistic imagery of the cleansing of blood from the hands of the soldiers. Compare this to the sanguinity inherent in a draft letter found in Lewis's notebook dated May 1917, in which he signs off:

> *I cannot do this without you. I thought I knew love, I thought I knew purpose, I thought I knew the world. And then you entered my life, and I discovered a world ten thousand times larger than I imagined. Share it with me.*[47]

And yet, in Lewis's unsent drafts, we also find a certain cynicism, a darkness he kept from public view, edited out in his final sent letters, and more reminiscent of the anti-authoritarian zeal of the popular anti-war poems by the Unknown Digger: see 'Harbour Thoughts' or 'The Billjim', for example, which share a tone with the poems of Siegfried Sassoon.[48] I am aware that merely highlighting the similarities in tone between the letters and poems cannot equate to proof that the two men are one and the same. Tone is a subjective quality, and thus impossible to prove, but I find it important to try, as it is these similarities in tone that first led me to think about Lewis as a candidate for the poems.

Scrutinising the poems for any mention of contextual evidence for Lewis's authorship leads one to immediately locate a mention of 'rose', in the lesser known 'Illawarra Flame Tree', a short poem contrasting the firefights of a bombardment with wildflowers in bloom in Australia, which concludes with the lines:

---

47 *The Annotated Letters*, p. 204. One of the most beautiful examples of Alan Lewis's (until now) unexamined capacity for beautiful imagery and poetic luminosity.

48 In M. Denton, 'Comparing Language Choices in Diametric Data Packets', I argued for the creation of a numerical scale for comparing themes and/or tone, with which the subjective correlations could be represented with scientific accuracy. I continue to believe in the importance of statistical comparisons, and mathematical equivalency will always convince me more than beliefs ever will. Em says I'm a pathetic romantic, but I say I'm a scientist.

A rose in the garden climbin' on the trellis
That, which with heaven makes
without which hell is.

L.S. Herdsman argues that the long descriptive stanzas in 'Illawarra' are 'a eulogy for beauty itself, so absent on the battlefield'.[49] And

---

49 L.S. Herdsman, 'Ocker Imagery in the Unknown Digger', *Journal of Commonwealth Literature,* Issue 3, Volume 35, 2000, pp. 76–92, which I would counter with my own personal observation: there is beauty in war. There is ample evidence of that. There is a perverse but profound beauty in Lewis's heroism and self-sacrifice. There is even a certain beauty in his death.

Conflict breeds beauty.

Last night I got into a huge argument with Em because her fucknugget of an ex-boyfriend, Dan, who I've only met in passing, saw me on the tube and asked how she was doing.

You spoke to him, about me? she said when I told her, her voice frozen.

He saw me, babe.

Don't call me babe.

I've never called her babe before. We hate the word babe. But for whatever reason, it feels like I'm supposed to say it in this argument. So now I live in this weird alternate reality where I'm the kind of douchebag who calls his girlfriend 'babe', un-ironically.

After everything, she snarls, everything you did to him.

That's the kicker. Everything I did to him. Like fucking Em in the work toilets was a solo activity. Like Em's black G-string wasn't balled up in her jacket pocket after we disappeared for half an hour in the middle of dinner. Everything I did to him.

Everything I did?

Don't sound surprised.

Don't surprise me.

And stop smiling – is this a joke to you?

I don't even realise I am smiling, I'm that angry. Em's this little spitfire of rage in front of me, and her rage magnifies how beautiful she is, and despite myself, I smile. But the fact she made me smile makes me angrier, which makes her angrier, and the whole cycle keeps looping around, feeding on itself, and even furious, I can't help but love my tiny beautiful raging demon, who adores me, but swears she wants to see me dead.

What are you doing talking to Dan in the first place?

Fuck him, I said, he's the past. You can't start to care now.

when viewed through the prism of Lewis's experiences, the battles he participated in and his long journey across the desert, which included leading his squadron through the streets of Jerusalem, and remembering the near-constant flow of letters home throughout his deployment, one can easily understand the metatextual sub-themes the poem is pushing: 'life is hell without beauty'.[50] The rose is a

---

What?

You wouldn't have done what we did if you cared then, so don't pretend to care now.

She flipped. She threw this vase her mum gave her at the wall, mid-scream. It shattered. Porcelain everywhere. Her scream fizzled. I walked out.

50 M. Denton, 'Comparing Language Choices in Diametric Data Packets'. And sometimes life's just hell. Where are you going? Em yelled after me.

I'm done.

I walked away. I was going to come back in a few minutes, once we'd both calmed down, but I liked the imagery of walking away down the centre of the road in the dark, leaving her mess behind me. Halfway down the street she caught up to me, wearing tiny silk pyjama shorts and her nipples crazy-obvious in the chill, with these stupid fluffy bunny slippers on she hides at the back of the closet if people come over. Stood in the middle of the road, spotlighted by the streetlight.

I'm sorry, she whispered.

I whispered back. What? I can't hear you.

I'm sorry. Please come back home.

You were just telling me to leave.

I know, she said.

But now you want me back?

I'm just tired. The party is killing me. And I didn't think it would smash like that.

I don't think she's been more beautiful than she was in that moment. Truly open. On the street in fluffy slippers. She wants her life to be like the movies but without the consequences, because in the movies they don't show you the scene after the fight where you vacuum the carpet six times and you can still feel bits crunch under your feet when you walk by. I found fragments in Em's hair for weeks after, like those Japanese airmen who emerged from the jungle years after the Second World War finished. There's a terrible beauty in that.

That's what I'm talking about. The light and dark.

common flower, and certainly one popular in the period, frequently finding use in the poetry of the era as a signifier for beauty. Thus the mention could be coincidental. Nevertheless, when one reflects upon the contents of Lewis's letter to Porter dated 14th April 1915, from the Mena training camp outside Cairo, one is instantly struck by the resemblance to the poem and the similarities between writing styles.[51] The letter asks:

> *How is your mother's garden coming along? I miss the tangle of roses by the birdbath, and her ongoing battle with the aphids. Will you let me know if they flowered this year? Nothing grows here. I miss you, my flower.*[52]

Without war, we wouldn't have the poems. Without Em's temper I wouldn't have been standing, freezing cold, in the middle of the street, knowing I want to marry this bunny-slippered hand grenade.

51 In the poem, roses are found 'climbin' on the trellis', while Lewis describes them as a 'tangle', evoking a similar feeling of overgrown wildlife, 'climbing' up and over the garden. Whether the Porter garden contained a trellis is no longer possible to ascertain. Tangled is also how I'd describe the murky circumstances of Em and I coming together, during which certain definitive relationship stepping stones became blurred. For a time, the beginning of our relationship overlapped with the end of her relationship with Dan.

52 *The Annotated Letters*, pp. 98–99. Also, the house Em continues to live in is the house she and Dan once called their own, and Dan, thanks to his job in the City, still pays half the rent until Em finds another place as big or bigger, or gets a pay rise, or I finish this book and the world recognises my genius, I make loads of money and she decides she's ready to move in with me (which I think we can all agree would be the simplest solution).

So, when Em left that dinner with her knickers in her jacket pocket, she arrived home to Dan, like nothing was wrong, and fell asleep next to him, or curled up around him or however they used to sleep – that's not my point – my point is she woke up to breakfast in bed, while down the road, I walked home by myself, passed out in my jeans, and woke with the taste of cobwebs in my teeth. She didn't care about Dan's feelings then, so how can she be angry about what we did, now?

I once escaped out the back window as Dan arrived through the front door. When I say we've only met in passing, I mean it.

This letter demonstrates that Lewis had made the simple verbal association between the rose (the flower) and Rose (his fiancée) and was able to switch between the two meanings as and when the fancy took him. Secondarily, I believe it proves the word choice of the Unknown Digger is no accident – if Lewis could switch between meanings in his letters, then it follows that the rose in the poem, if written by Lewis, may also be a reference to his fiancée. If we take it literally, the poem is stating 'life without Rose is hell'.[53]

Moving from the literal examples to be found in the texts to the contextual surroundings of the sources provides further similarities between the two authors. In a letter from Porter to Lewis, undated and unsigned, found in his pack following his death, it is revealed that Porter's favourite form of poetry was the sonnet. She states:

> *... they've printed another of [Brooke's] poems in the paper, a lovely one made even more timely since his death. I think if I were to write, I'd write sonnets too. Not much call for it round this way though. The other nurses prefer the funny pages.*[54]

---

53 Em prefers daffodils and tulips. Though she does have a black rose tattooed on her upper thigh, who could forget, which she drunkenly admitted to me on one of our first dates was covering up a self-administered tattoo of her first boyfriend's name: Vaughn, she laughed as she told me the story, can you believe I dated someone called Vaughn?

She also enjoys a lily; she's been nurturing one on her bedroom windowsill for the past six months, hoping it lasts the winter and blooms again when it's a bit warmer. Can also confirm, from personal experience, that a nice bouquet of wildflowers, delivered to her front door with new cologne and a freshly laundered shirt, will always lead to that wild, sweaty, heart-bursting-in-your-chest, what-did-I-do-to-deserve-this-goddess type of sex we're all searching for.

54 *The Annotated Letters*, p. 210. Rose was a nurse at the time, applying for a position in one of the frontline hospitals, though she was rejected for service overseas because of her asthma. We have no evidence of Rose writing any poetry herself, though she wrote long letters to Lewis every Sunday afternoon. And didn't everyone write poetry back then anyway? That's why Alan being the Unknown Digger makes so much sense to me – university-educated, heroic, romantic, funny – it would actually be

It would have to be a major coincidence indeed were we to discover that the majority of poems written by the Unknown Digger were, in fact, sonnets or forms thereof. Hayden, on discovery of the poems, identified eighty separate finished poems, and half a dozen unfinished drafts, of which fully half are sonnets. No other form of poetry has such an ascendency within the selection.[55] Of the eighty officially confirmed Unknown Digger poems, 50% are sonnets, a further 20% are variations on the simple ABAB rhyming couplet, 11% are more complex rhyming systems, and the remaining 19% are free form, that is to say, they contain no readily discernible rhyme or metre. It is obvious, to me at least, that Lewis was writing his poems for Porter, though, tragically, he never had the opportunity to show them to her. Once he discovered that she adored sonnets, he began to write more sonnets. Indeed, the argument will be made in the following chapters that the clear majority of sonnets (64% of

---

more surprising to me if Alan never wrote a single line of poetry.

'University-educated, heroic, romantic, funny' – Em says this is how women write about the Prof in their emails: he wrote this cute coffee table book about human habits, and it's been on the bestseller list for months, and he's been on Graham Norton and Alan Carr and Jonathan Ross – writing in and asking him to study their habits, wink-wink. Last month we found out he was being awarded what is, in all essence, a lifetime achievement award, at the ripe old age of early-fortysomething. He's eleven years older than me, but who's counting? Anyway, the Prof put her in charge of organising this big shindig Friday night to celebrate (see Footnote 38 – gold balloons and peacock feathers), so she's been working really hard the last few nights. Write a book, make a few jokes on the late-night chat circuit, smile for the cameras, and whaddya know – universal acclaim.

On the day they found out, he popped a bottle of Veuve in the office, and Em came home tipsy, and she felt it was necessary that I take her out to dinner.

La Porchetta wasn't what she had in mind. Take me somewhere nice, she said.

Somewhere nice had starched white tablecloths and multiple sets of cutlery, diminishing in size on either side of the huge plate they set in front of us – I ate my starter using the lobster fork like an idiot – the food was tiny and expensive, and the waiter was some slick-haired bastard who talked exclusively to Em, like I was invisible.

55 See Hayden, *Unearthing the Unknown Digger.*

the original 50%, or 26 full poems, when one takes into account the half-finished 'Untitled' and adds it to the three-quarters complete 'Untitled #2' and 'Spinifex Snippets') in the collection are written after the events of Gallipoli, well into the 'Great Ride' which accounts for the largest proportion of Lewis's service history.[56]

Through my examination of the available physical evidence, and statistical analysis of the two authors, I have come to believe there are compelling links between the poems of the Unknown Digger and the letters of Alan Lewis. Further inquiry into the ideological similarities, the parallel timelines of creation and a thorough repudiation of those facts which scholars have assumed about the Unknown Digger's life are necessary, and will be undertaken in the following chapters, but already, using the physical evidence available – that is, those primary sources available for us to touch and read and observe closely – we have established a link between the two authors which cannot be discounted.[57]

---

56 As identified by Hayden, *Unearthing the Unknown Digger*, p. 221.

57 Curtin-Kneeling finally replied to me, three months after I'd outlined my thesis plans to him in a long email. 'Sorry, Matt,' he wrote, 'but I just can't believe it. It can all be written off as pure coincidence.' Such a fuckin' let-down. I've had three rums tonight. I emailed Jennifer Hayden, and she said not to listen to him – the proof is in the putting it on paper, she wrote back, which I'm only just getting now. The proof is in the pudding. Y'know she started out in a university library, too? Same university where I completed my bachelor's and seventy-five-odd years earlier Alan got halfway through his. Pure coincidence? Fuck off. I told Jennifer we should meet up next time she's in London, but she hasn't replied.

I'm writing because I can't sleep. Had the party for the Prof tonight, in this amazing house up near Hyde Park Corner. I only got home a few hours ago. I was roped into working the coat-check. Weird night. Em seemed happy though. She did an amazing job. I didn't see her except as a blur of red, running around organising the DJ and caterer and bar staff. I handed my last coat back around half-twelve, and then walked upstairs to see if I could help tidy up. The place was decked out in balloons and ribbons – you'd think he'd won a Nobel Prize or something. Em was in a corner, wobbling on tiptoe on a plastic chair, attempting to untie ribbons. Her peacock feather headdress was dangling away from her hair, looking like I felt.

What can I do, Em?

Despite announcing my journey across the room through mountains of crushed plastic cups, empty champagne bottles and littered confetti, I managed to surprise her, and she laughed, drowsy-silly with tiredness, endorphins, alcohol, god-knows-what. She looked down at me, or at somewhere over my shoulder, and shrugged.

Are you drunk? I said, sounding like my mum.

Nothing, Matt, you should go home. Her new black heels were hanging by their straps from a chair, her stockinged feet comically small on the plastic chair.

I thought I was coming back to yours?

She does this, changes plan throughout the night, keeps you on your toes. Sends you home without a goodnight kiss. I'm used to it. How many times have I told her I loved her spontaneity? It goes both ways.

Back to yours? I repeated, hearing the beg in my throat.

It was amazing, Matt. They really, really got into it. She was already turning away from me, reaching up for the knot of ribbon tied out of reach above her head. Like, amazing costumes, and everyone loved the music. Trent was worth every penny.

The chair wobbled when she stood on tiptoe.

Trent?

The DJ.

She had a long run in her stockings up the back of her thigh. I should have offered to get up on the chair for her, but I was upset about not getting to go home with her. Childish, I know.

How's the Prof? I saw him arrive, wearing a tweed tuxedo, which I hadn't known existed.

Drunk. Pretty sure he went into the toilets with one of his postgrads an hour ago.

That's disgusting.

That's what happens.

I could hear the alcohol on her breath, the way her accent sharpened into caricature after a few vodka-cranberries. When she turned around she was smiling, but as I helped her down from the chair her grip tightened. I turned, and the Prof was standing in the doorway, an electric-blue bottle of alcohol in his right hand.

Matt. Libation? he yelled across the room in that way drunks do when you're alone. Em's eyes shot to mine then away, too quick for me to make out what they wanted, what she was trying to say.

No thanks, I yelled back. Heard you've had a good night?

Em squeezed my hand, and I couldn't help smiling.

You should head home. Cheers awfully for all your help. He slurred his words a little, but he walked in a straight line across the ballroom floor. About halfway across he raised the bottle, and poured a stream of clear liquid through the speed pourer in its neck into his open mouth.

I'm walking him out, Alistair. What time is the van coming?

Em led me around a table.

As he approached, I could make out the large red stain on his untucked white shirt, the lipstick smudged across his cheek. He held forth the bottle. An offering. I shook my head.

Sure I can't stay? Help pack up? I asked him, but he laughed, and poured more vodka into his mouth.

No, you go get some sleep (shleep, he pronounced it). We've got a van coming at three to take the props back to mine, then we're done. We've got this. This woman runs a tight ship. He saluted Em, then gestured toward the bar, the bottles of wine, champagne, tequila, rum and whiskey lined up along the back. Take a bottle if you want? Otherwise we'll have to drink it all ourselves.

He laughed like he'd said something hilarious.

I mumbled a thank you. He started doing a drunken-swaying-dancing thing, sliding his feet along the carpet, crushing empty plastic champagne flutes back and forth to a tune only he could hear. I walked over to the bar, sized up the rum, and popped it in my bag. When I turned around, he'd taken Em's hand and was spinning her, unsuccessfully, like a ballroom dancer would twirl his partner, his other hand holding the bottle of vodka. He went to dip her, and she leant back in his arm, the perfect choreographed finish, and then he brought the bottle to her mouth and poured, and kept pouring, until vodka was spluttering from her lips and running down her neck. She coughed, spraying vodka almost to where I stood, and pulling herself to her feet, staggered away from him.

The Prof laughed a long awkward Hugh-Grantish laugh, and walked past me, heading for the bar. I hadn't moved. Em pulled one of her long white gloves from her bag and wiped her mouth and neck. I felt my feet move, but slowly, like magnets were dragging them back to the carpet. Behind my back the Prof was singing some tuneless rap song, alternating between quiet murmuring and shouting.

I took Em's hand and led her down the stairs.

Is he going to be alright?

Yeah, he's just drunk.

Will you be alright?

You can get the night bus, right? She'd stopped in front of the mirror in the foyer, and was trying valiantly to rearrange her peacock feather.

Thanks. For tonight.

I can stay, if you want.

I walked back to her, pulled her into a hug, head on my chest, feather tickling my nose. On tiptoe, without her shoes, she comes up to my chin. There's something about that smallness I adore. Everything else can fuck right off. All I want is that moment with her head on my chest and her stockinged feet, on tiptoe, in the thick red carpet.

I'm scared, she said quietly.

I thought I'd misheard. She looked up at me, her eyes wet. We kissed, and her lips were rough, her tongue urgent. Aggressive.

I'll stay. I'll help take things to his, and then we'll go back to yours and sleep. Like, all weekend.

She shook her head.

If anything happens, I'll never forgive myself, I said, and Em dropped her eyes, the feather bobbing in my periphery. We could hear the Prof rapping upstairs. We stood that way for a moment or two, waiting, like it could come down either way.

I'll call you tomorrow, she said. She reached up for a kiss, led me to the door, and then walked back inside. I waited for a moment, staring at the door. The night bus was pulling up at the bus stop. I ran to catch it.

I sat on the top level all the way home, an entire seat to myself, until a drunk undergrad in a purple hoodie sat down next to me and started discussing how close he'd been to going home with this 'fugly chick' with his mates in the seats behind. I kept thinking about the vodka trickling its way down the tendon in Em's neck, the sound of her gagging on the liquid. I hate men. I hate drunks. Fuck, I hate undergrads. Around Camden I watched a group of drunken girls gaggling around the bus stop heading back the other way, starting their night. One girl sat on the ground, her dress hiked up around her hips, her bright yellow underwear on display to the world. Her friends didn't care. No-one cares.

It's four thirty-six in the morning, and I can't sleep. I keep replaying the evening in my head, wondering if I did the right thing. Wondering what Alan would have done. I'm pretty sure he wouldn't have left Em behind. He would have punched the Prof in the face and damned the consequences. He'd have lost his job but won the girl. He'd laugh about it and write another poem.

I feel drunk, but I'm not drunk. I'm sleepwalking through everything, writing instead of reacting. I deserve better. Alan deserves better.

Em deserves better.

Speak of the devil – Em's calling my mobile.

GALLIPOLI. NOVEMBER 1915.

A cigarette in the snow.

The match lights on the third strike. He shields the dim spark from the wind with his fingers, and brings it to the cigarette in his lips. Cheap Egyptian tobacco. Warming smoke fills his chest. He tosses the match before flame singes fingertips. Can't see further than a yard in front of his hole. His trench fades away to obscurity on his right. The Turkish line is out there, somewhere ahead of him, the Jackos invisible, lost in the flurry. Watching, somewhere, from the white.

Out in the bay the destroyers lie silent, the lick of icy water on their gunmetal hulls. Snowflakes land and melt on their turrets, the barrels red hot with heat from the shells that they fire at the outcrop of rock they've been ordered to capture, this dreary little peninsula in the Dardanelles. The sky is the murky grey wash of a winter. The battleships are dark silhouettes. The sea ink. The pier is a runway lit up in the darkness, snowflakes a carpet for boots to sink into, muffling the clamour of unloading supplies.

He relaxes, breathes deeply, the cigarette glowing, and the bullet with his name on it finds him. It sails through the snow, from somewhere high above, and punches through the skin beneath his chin. His body collapses and drops against the wall of the trench, and the wind on the rock starts to sing.

The men huddle in packs to try and keep warm, staring out at this strange new landscape. For many of them, this is their first glimpse of snow. It settles, like red dirt back home on verandas, a delicate coating of freezing white ice,

it settles on rifles, on periscope handles, on sandy brown hair teeming with lice, on moustachioed lips, on bloodstains, on duckboards, on pages left half full of words for the wife;

on helmets and slouch hats, on trench coats and greens, on bayonets and mess tins and guns and machines, on jam-tin grenades and old bloody bandages, on shrapnel and sandbags and splinters of beam;

on entrance to dugout, on firing step,
on donkeys, on chickens, on parcels from home.
On bodies, left rotting, in firing lines,
on fresh painted crosses where dead mates lie,
on the smouldering remains of an evening fire,
on the loud and the boisterous, the quiet and shy;
on the worthless, the wrecked and the tired,
on cowards, on reckless, on ready-to-die;
on trooper, on captain, on all rank and file,
on diggers from Esperance to Gundagai,
on every upturned ANZAC eye;
forgetting, for a moment, dysentery, flies,
the shells falling about them, forgetting goodbyes
to mates who have bought it, those who have died;
their eyes turned to heaven and the curious sight
of snow on the trenches.
A gift from the sky.

~

My love. I trust this letter finds you well, safe and happy and warm – you won't believe me, but it's snowing. Started to fall as the sun set, and now we have a thick layer of the mess coating every surface. It looks a new world. Makes a bit of a treat for the men, and God knows we could all do with that. We continue to fight at barely quarter strength. Red sleeps by my shoulder, the first rest he's had in the past three days. Two days of that was him talking about his mention in dispatches, and the other day was actual work. I hope everyone back home is as proud of him as we are.

I am constantly inspired by the spirit of the men. When it was hotter – how is it winter already? – nobody could stop them from swimming in the clear waters, the Turkish shells exploding above their heads.

Since I last wrote, a team from the 3rd gave a combined team of our 10th and a few of the Newfoundlanders a real shellacking, though a few overs had to be shortened due to 'imperfect playing conditions', which is what we have taken to calling old Beachy Bill, the Turkish battery. The whole match was abandoned when some bloody fool hit a six and the ball landed in a patch of scrub watched by Turkish snipers at all hours. For a few hours there we could pretend we were back home watching the Saturday club games. What I wouldn't give for a cold beer.

Nugget thinks they should up the rum ration to a bottle each. I'd argue after The Nek it's only fair. If no other reason, it would help us forget about the lice. They don't even spare our decorated hero – Red spent four hours last week picking them from his shirt and throwing them on the fire. They make a little pop as they burn. One hopes they dislike the cold as much as us – I've taken to wrapping myself in my blanket and trench coat before sleep – were a shell to land on our dugout they would find a toasty man-sized wrap inside, like the Egyptians eat.

I never thought the day would come when I found myself missing Egyptian food. But it is a lot easier once you've had Nugget's 'Grungy' (bully beef, biscuits and water) every night for three weeks. I find myself longing for a glass of apple tea, or one of their spicy stews that had us sweating. Hell, Rose, at this stage I'd take Laurie's infamous Blackened Chicken over anything pulled from a tin. You'll appreciate my desperation.

I do hope your mother and the Little Princesses are well. I miss riling them up with elaborate stories. The boys over here are great fun and I relish fighting beside them, but nothing makes up for the shocked gasp of your mother at hearing that the latest fashion in the city is for the return of powdered wigs. I received a letter from Ma reporting that Dad has got it in his head to take the whole harvest in by himself next year. I wrote back telling her about the old donkey we've commandeered and nicknamed Birdy, who utterly refuses to move once she gets it in her skull that the shells or the bullets or the smell is too much. She reminds me of a certain father of mine.

Sometimes I feel a proper ass.

I'm writing in the dead of night, when the hill comes alive with men who have been pinned down all day, and the trenches pulse with activity. Though it's curiously silent tonight. The wind is singing. I should check on my men.

Yours, stubbornly.

The noise calls to him through the frontline.

The snow has left the ground crisp; Alan's boots sink into it with satisfying crunch. Back home, at the beach, the warmth of the sun will dry the top layer of sand, creating a thin crust that cracks between toes. Sometimes he will wake and hear the waves on the shore and think he's back in Perth with salt on his skin. The rotten smell of flesh, or the scratching of the rats at the end of his bedroll, or Red's incessant snoring sets him straight. Gallipoli will not be ignored.

The dark holes of his boot prints lead a zigzag through the trench. The noise is coming from somewhere close by. Not a cry of agony, or pain; it's singsong, a lighthearted note. Chalkboard shivers.

Rounding a corner, he arrives at an observation post, a hole dug into the wall of the trench where a sentry should be standing; eyes on the enemy, rifle in hand, breath billowing in frosty bursts.

The noise screams by his ears – seagulls, maybe, back home.

The post is empty, a clean white box fresh painted with snow. Someone is in for a spray.

Except it's not empty. Invisible against the trench wall, covered by a layer of white, sits Trooper Collopy, the Mandurah boy, his shock of blond hair hidden by a cake of snow that drops as Alan scrambles forward. He grabs Collopy's arms, pulling the body out into the moonlit main trench. The scream on the wind stops. Collopy's skin is cold and slippery slick with blood, and Alan's frozen hands struggle to grip the wrists, to turn the deadweight over and search for a heartbeat. He can't tell where the blood is coming from, until, two fingers under the chin searching for a pulse, his fingers slip into the warm opening in the neck.

He pulls Collopy into a sitting position, frozen limbs over his shoulder, and pauses – he can make out the outline of the trench, the wooden struts and the dark sky, straight through the meat of Collopy's neck. Wind blows down the line, and the ghost of the noise screams out the bullet wound, playing Collopy's body like an instrument. A solitary goodbye note. He can't look away, the dark tunnel of bloody skin draws his eye, leading the way to God-only-knows.

A spasm of energy passes through the body, and Collopy tries to gasp, but more blood streams down his neck, and he chokes, a guttural slur that trails off into the night. The skin around the bullet hole puckers in and out.

'Stretcher!'

Alan's shout breaks the night's spell; cries from the dugouts, men swarm around the corner, the sound of the guns firing from the battleships below. He screams at one man to cover the position and a stranger's voice emerges from his body, someone else's arms gather Collopy up like a slaughtered calf and haul him onto his shoulder. The weight pulls him down into the snow and mud, and he panics, worried they'll sink. The first step is the hardest, drawing his boot forward and planting. Do it. Do it again. The trench stretches out before him endless, and then he rounds the corner and his breath returns. He heaves his way down the maze towards the twinkling sea.

'You silly bastard,' he grunts, the words like bullets spitting from his mouth, 'I swear to God, if you cark it, I'll kill you.'

Halfway down, passing the second line, curious eyes poking from warm recesses, he runs into the stretcher team. He lowers Collopy to the ground. His knees threaten to buckle; his breath comes in sharp icy bursts that punch through his chest. The two men huddle over the body, but there's no haste about their movements, no sense of urgency. One shakes his head. The other looks up at him.

'No!' The snow melts beneath Collopy's head, blood mixing with the ice and dirt. 'He was breathing. Just now.'

'Sorry, Lieutenant.'

From here he can see over the bay, the dark shadows of the ships, and the bright flare of the moon high above, reflected, with a painter's dirty brush, on the inky sea below. The men have covered Collopy's body with his trench coat, the bootstraps left peeking out. He walks forward to say a few words, thinks better of it, and lays a hand on the mound of material. The bearers pick up the stretcher and leave, down to the shore and the waiting dead.

Alan begins the slow trudge back to his dugout. The snow sticks in bloody brown clumps by his heels. He clenches and unclenches his frozen fingers like they're someone else's. He stops by a small silhouette whose heavy boots shuffle back and forth in the gloom.

'Can you see over?' he jokes.

Nugget grunts and nods back the way he came. 'What was that about?'

'Collopy. Couldn't wait half an hour for a fag, paid with his life.' He breathes hot air on his fingers. 'Got one through the neck. Snow must have muffled the noise.'

'How's the model soldier?' Nugget asks, voice crawling low in the moonlight, nodding his head towards their dugout.

'You thought his snoring was bad before, you should hear it with a cold. I wake thinking we've been shelled. Reminds me of his sister.'

Nugget grins: 'Laurie, right?'

'Mate, you and Laurie are going to get along like ...'

'A house on fire?'

'The whole flamin' bush, Nug. From Perth to Albany.'

Both chuckle. The wind picks up and they huddle deeper into their coats. He can feel Nugget watching him, but his own eyes dance an awkward dance, meeting Nugget's and glancing away. He rocks his weight from foot to foot. He wants to pick up a pile of snow and peg it at Nugget's head. His booted feet push the snow and mud back and forth.

'Everything alright?' Nugget asks – lightly, off the cuff.

''Course.' His heart doesn't trust the words.

'You know you can talk to me, right? I was there, too.'

He knows, but he can't forget Cairo, even if Nugget and Red seemingly have. Even if they've somehow moved on from The Nek. Even if they've seemingly forgotten the bullets flying past their heads every damned day.

'Sometimes, I feel ...' His voice sounds like one of Tom's kids, tiny against the wall of rock they're camped on. Nugget is watching him.

A flare goes up further down the line, and their white world glows yellow. They both turn to watch its slow descent through the night sky. Safer to stay silent.

'Nothing.' Sometimes I feel nothing. His dugout calls his name. 'Stay warm. And Nug?'

Nugget grunts, collar higher than his head, coat longer than his legs.

'Don't eat the yellow snow.'

It's starting to fall now, lingering drops on his exposed face, white dots on Nugget's coat as he snarls an indecent reply. He takes the last few steps to the dugout at the double.

P.S. – part of my role here is censoring the men's letters, making sure that should they fall into enemy hands no important details could be gleaned. Every man jack of them writes – even Nugget scrawls barely legible letters to his family. One man in particular, I won't tell you his name in case you should run into his wife – I know how small Perth streets are – divulges the most sexually explicit fantasies, often in letters running to five or six pages long. Learned more from him than from the entire Egyptian training course. He is fully aware that I am required to read all letters, and the bastard loves nothing more than to hold my gaze unblinking each morning.

As an officer, I am partially exempt from this rule; mine are to be censored by the Major, but there is a certain 'Officer's Code' passed on by the Tommies that means he won't. Don't start imagining me writing sweet nothings though, fantasies about ripping off the white dress you wore on that last night, or sneaking off on our own, down past the barn and into the field, hidden from the prying eyes of my parents, where we could lie in the wheat and stare up at the giant sky.

That's as close as I get.

Snow is incredible. It crunches under my feet.

I wish you could see it with me.

There's a switch he flicks, from puckering bullet holes to the girl back home. Staggering how easy it switches. How quickly he forgets the rock. Then it's the wooden deck of the veranda under his feet and Ma cooking the Sunday dinner, singing to herself. Dad out the back somewhere, a haze on the horizon. And Rose's hand in his, a secret shared between their fingers. That knowing glance before the knock, a smile ancient and wind-worn, like the Pinnacles, on his face.

The sound of a shell – near enough to startle but not close enough to be dangerous – or the thunderous snore of a part-elephant mate, or, inevitable as the guns, the telltale itch of lice, and he's back in the dugout with a page on the desk he doesn't remember writing.

He puts the letter in his coat pocket and finds a fresh page to send to Collopy's family. A clean page for them to rip to shreds. A few well-worn platitudes and barefaced lies: 'he passed swiftly and with no pain' and 'his bravery in the face of the enemy was a credit to his family'. He struggled with the first letters, but after The Nek he's an expert – the words rattle off like bullets. One more digger vanishes into the lists.

Somewhere by Red's bedroll is a half-empty bottle of whiskey. The malty brown liquid sloshes as he pulls it from Red's pack, and the lump of snoring man babbles but doesn't wake. He pours two thumbs into his steel mug. A silent toast to Collopy and then the sweet burn, the liquid toasty in his chest.

There is a cat at the entrance to the dugout.

He peers down at the mug in his hands, the bottle on his desk. Just the one sip. The cat looks at him and asks him what he thinks he's doing.

There has been furphy going around about a cat crossing between the lines – approaching the ANZAC troops for a quick meal and then skipping over to the Turk trench for the second course. Judging by the jutting ribs, the menu is scarce on both fronts. He follows its hopeful glance around the sparse dugout.

The cat is shivering, socks sodden, black hair glistening with melted snow. White-tipped ears flicker. Yellow eyes stare at him then motion towards the door. It makes a noise halfway between begging and scolding.

'I know it's not much, mate.' Banjo. He christens the moggy with another swig of whiskey.

He crushes biscuit in a heap at Banjo's paws, but Banjo doesn't notice, eyes locked on him, mewing louder. He moves back to his desk but the cat is turning circles around his feet, in and out of his legs, tail flicking against the earth wall.

'What?'

Me. Me, me, me.

The cat sits between his two muddy boots, staring up, fire in its eyes. He should sleep. He should drink less. He should drink more. Banjo winks. He reaches down and scratches behind Banjo's ears, blood caked in his nails.

Steady mate, Banjo mews, backing away so he has to lean forward to continue. He strokes the cat for a heartbeat before it turns toward the entrance, back out into the snow.

'I know it's not the Ritz, but it's better than out there.' In his next letter, he'll write about Banjo: too good for biscuits, too snooty for dugouts. Rose will like Banjo. Rose will beg him to bring Banjo home.

Banjo stops by the doorway, sunrise eyes peering back.

Please.

He shrugs, uncomprehending. 'In or out? Your choice.'

The moggy wants it all; trotting back to his hands, pushing a bony head against his fingers, then a quick leap and back by the doorway, calling for him.

Mate.

'Course the cat with the split personality would choose him, would choose his dugout, his biscuits and his patience over the hundreds of other miles of trench on the peninsula. It's that kind of night. He drops the bottle back by Red's head, kicks the snoring lump and is rewarded with a groan.

'What?'

'Collopy's dead.'

'Bugger.'

The cat is eager to move, purring round his legs and then scampering to the door, leaving only to return and mew louder. Red sits up, raises an eyebrow at the cat, and coughs something wet and slimy into his sleeve. Banjo hisses.

'We need to scout the OP.'

'We?' Red yawns. Banjo stalks the bedroll watchfully, and pounces on Red's knees.

'Everyone else is on duty. Or sleeping. Or dead.' He drops his pistol into his pocket, and stamps his feet. 'But if you don't want to get your famous visage wet, don't worry.'

Banjo flits back to the doorway, mewing for them to follow. Red sighs.

'Alright. Don't be a hero. I'm coming.'

The snow falls heavier, covering his head, landing on his nose, blurring his vision. A fire blazes down by the beach, a storeroom alight, dark shadows running around the fierce glow. He's surprised he didn't hear the shells. He peers up into the night but it's grey, the roof is falling in bit by tiny bit, icing sugar on a mud pie. Banjo has vanished, and Red, a few steps behind, is a dark blur against the white.

They walk back towards the observation post in silence. Banjo skips by his boots, a few steps in front. Turning to watch, running forward, drawing them on.

As they approach the post, Trooper Malone materialises from the haze, a dark figure with icicles in his moustache. Red nods and shouts to him, but the wind whips it away. Alan nods in agreement, whatever it was. His nose runs, wet and snotty, dripping onto his lip and freezing. He sniffs and tiny daggers of ice pepper his nostrils.

Red leans into his ear and shouts. 'Not much doing tonight, Al.'

He agrees. 'Jackos are probably waiting it out.'

Red nods, and glances back towards their dugout.

'So, they won't be expecting a visit,' he says.

Red steps back and looks him up and down. Surprised, maybe. He's surprised himself – normally it's Red who makes the decisions. Alan just follows along.

Alan steps past Trooper Malone and glances down at the spot where Collopy lay, but the snow has papered over the evidence. All the crazy hopes and tiny dreams of a life obliterated in a gunshot, dead in the time it takes to breathe in a cheap cigarette. He doesn't smoke, but he wouldn't turn one down right now.

Banjo peers down at him from the lip of the trench. The same five hundred yards of godforsaken rock, the tin after bleedin' tin of bully beef, the same arguments and the same jokes and the same orders to hold the line. Someone needs to break the deadlock. Red shakes his head.

'What's the matter? You frightened?' Alan sneers. Red has never been scared a day in his life.

Red glances back down the trench. He starts to talk, but the coughing takes hold, and Alan doesn't wait for him to finish. Lifts his head over the barricade. No sniper shots. He opens his eyes. Nothing but snow. More white. More nowhere. He turns back to Red and winks. Red nods and that same smile he wore before the Hat-Trick, before they shipped out, every time they caused trouble at school or chatted up girls in Fremantle, grows across his face. Red shouts a few words to Trooper Malone, and pushes Alan up and over the lip. Alan reaches down and pulls Red out, gloved hands clasping tight. Brothers.

The last time he was out of the trench was at The Nek. That was sunrise and he could see everything: the bullets whipping past, his mates dropping. Like hunting kangaroo. He can still see it if he closes his eyes. He's back there every time he tries to sleep.

Banjo circles his boot and then melts into the falling white sky ahead of him. Alan follows, pushing blindly forward. Ten steps, half a field, who knows? He turns and finds he is alone. Red has vanished. The line is somewhere behind him. The Turks somewhere ahead. For the first time on Gallipoli he is alone.

A dark blur that could be human passes him on his right. Banjo mews nearby. Someone is calling his name. The shell hits three paces behind him, soundless; the first he knows of it is the huge hand picking him up and hitting him for six, the sudden sucking of air from the world, the wind rushing by his face. There's the roaring of waves but it's the blood pumping past his ears. His world is cold, his hands outstretched in the snow. Pain in his legs he doesn't want to think about.

He staggers to his feet and looks around. Bushfire creeping over the hill. A divine glow, summer sunburn behind his eyes. Splinters of burning ash float down from the sky, little pinpricks of heat on his sweating forehead, mixing with the snow, cooling and burning, fire and ice.

His first thought is for Rose, but she's safe at home.

Then Red.

He can't see out of his left eye, and sweat, or blood, is in his right. He falls to his knees. His head is going to burst, his heartbeat in his ears. He's on fire, sweat dripping down his nose, and the icy ground is calling him. He'll rest for a second. Curl up and kip in the feathery snow for a minute, promise, one minute.

The snow is fluffy and inviting. His back throbs, pulsing down his legs and beating in his mouth. A kiss of iron on his tongue.

The snow screams as it falls.

It blankets him, soothes him, holds him close like Rose's warming hands. The wind plays Collopy like an instrument, but Collopy is dead. The night shrieks. The snow is bloody hot. Red is screaming, somewhere up the line.

His last glimpse of Gallipoli is black-and-white socks by his face, the flick of Banjo's tail against his head before the cat scampers into no-man's-land, fading into the snow that gathers Alan up and drops him into the deep sleep.

CHAPTER 3: Ideological similarities in the poetry of the Unknown Digger as evidence for Lewis's authorship: How Lewis's service history and moral code compare and contrast with the Unknown Digger.

Alan Lewis was an exemplary soldier and a beloved officer – 'the bravest man I ever met', as one of his former charges put it.[58] Lewis fought valiantly at numerous battles throughout his distinguished career, and was awarded the highest commendation any Australian soldier can receive, the Victoria Cross, following his untimely death. His career has been written about many times, though I often find myself returning to Nicholas Curtin-Kneeling's stellar biography, *From Busso to the Holy Land*, in my own research.[59] Curtin-Kneeling's book was one of the first studies to consciously humanise Lewis, revealing his flaws and insecurities, and in doing so, altering his status from heroic godlike figure to that of mere mortal. For this, we can be grateful. Prior to the publication of *From Busso to the Holy Land*, Victoria Cross recipients walked in rarefied air, and were deemed untouchable by the general public. As a consequence, it was difficult to empathise or identify with them. In contemporary parlance, they were not 'relatable'. The idea of any VC recipient writing the heartbreaking poetry of the Unknown Digger was unimaginable. But with the exposure of Lewis's fallibility came a three-dimensional complexity, and Curtin-Kneeling's insights provided a sudden portal to the themes and ideologies of the poems of the Unknown Digger.

One such revelation – the echoes of which reverberate through the poetry he would come to write – and the most important for me in demonstrating his human fallibility and thus, perhaps a wellspring

---

58 Trooper G. Roberton in conversation with Curtin-Kneeling, in *From Busso to the Holy Land*, p. 44.

59 I can also personally recommend J. Buckley's *Heroes of the Cross: Australian Recipients of the Victoria Cross* (Penguin, Sydney, 1984), which was one of the first books to delve into Lewis's past in an attempt to understand him, and L.L. Hereford's original postwar study of the Victoria Cross recipients in *They Walk Amongst Us*, which, though published in the early thirties and somewhat dated, provides the best overview of Lewis's storied career.

of poetic inspiration – occurred during his training period in Camp Mena when Lieutenant Lewis received the first and only disciplinary blemish on his record for his actions in the regiment's primary live-fire training exercise. Lewis was given orders to 'advance on the precise coordinates, await the cessation of the shelling at a specified time, and then capture the objective with the whole section', which at that time was under his command.[60] Confronted with a miscalculation in bomb schedules and forced to wait, Lewis's close friend Sergeant McRae opted to lead a small group of men around the threshold of the bombardment and capture the objective from a different angle.[61]

Instead of rejecting the idea out of hand, Lewis, perhaps swayed by his friendship with McRae rather than analysing the potential risks, allowed McRae to proceed. McRae's rashness, and Lewis's approval, ultimately led to the death of one Trooper Richardson, and the wounding of another, Trooper Morrow. Sergeant McRae was subsequently demoted to trooper. Lewis was given a reprimand, but held his position, and learnt a valuable lesson. It was the first time he had been required to write a letter home to a family detailing a casualty of war. The mistake clearly played on his mind, as he wrote about the incident in a letter to Porter, ultimately never sent, sections of which were found in his notebook following his death:

> *I wrote a long letter to you what feels like days ago, and I find I cannot send it. It says entirely the wrong things. I worry you won't recognise me when I return.*[62]

What is particularly interesting about this unsent letter are the minor differences it contains to the version that eventually made its way to Porter, which includes a brief sentence about losing a soldier in a training accident, and a redacted line where the censors deemed

---

60 *The Regimental Scrapbook of the 10th Light Horse Regiment.*

61 *The Regimental Scrapbook of the 10th Light Horse Regiment.*

62 Pyke, *The Annotated Letters*, p. 81. Rarely does Lewis reveal his feelings of abject depression and lack of confidence as candidly as he does in this startling letter, which Curtin-Kneeling refers to several times as evidence of the great man's human decency and continued heroic devotion to his duty. And yet he refuses to accept that Alan might be the Unknown Digger.

Lewis's thoughts too provocative or sensitive to risk exposure. Lewis, wishing to spare Porter the terrible details, but also to hide, or assuage, his own guilt, writes:

> *Today we played at war games in the sand, and unfortunately in the chaos of the shelling. It fell to me to write the letter home to his family, Tomorrow we move on.*[63]

One can only imagine how difficult it was for a gallant and chivalrous man like Lewis to accept that his own decision had led to the death of a friend; how terrible he must have felt for allowing McRae's plan to go ahead, and how badly he must have wished for events to have unfolded in a different way.[64]

---

63 Pyke, *The Annotated Letters*, p. 83. One of six instances of censorship to occur in the entirety of Lewis's penmanship. As an officer, his correspondence was rarely edited by his superiors – as a gentleman, he was expected to abide by the clearly defined rules of his position. But sometimes the only thing you can do is write it all down.

64 She specifically asked me not to say anything. Not to tell anyone. Not to worry about it – it was nothing, she says, he was drunk, she was drunk, he would never – she stops what she's doing and looks me dead in the eye – NEVER, she says, do anything like that if he was sober.

Like that's an excuse.

I lie in bed and argue with myself. Being drunk isn't an excuse. Except we've all done things when we were drunk that we've regretted later. Throwing up in a best mate's parents' car as they drive you home. Buying that fifth round of tequila shots. Trying to backflip. But the things we regret aren't things that hurt others, except maybe the tequila shots.

Em is taking a little time to herself. That's for the best. I toss and turn in sweaty sheets.

When I can sleep, I dream about the night, like I had been there. Is it too much to ask for happy dreams? Ones where I wait in the dark until he finishes work, and then, as he walks to his car, I jump out with a baseball bat and smash his kneecaps until they resemble jagged shrapnel pieces through the yellowing skin, and, as he begs for mercy, I drag him over to the side of the carpark, turn him over, tell him to bite the sidewalk, and

It was this information of Curtin-Kneeling's, which is never mentioned in citations or hagiographies, which ultimately convinced me that Lewis was the Unknown Digger. Before learning of his shortcomings, I had an image in my mind of Lewis as the unimpeachable hero, but at the training exercise at Camp Mena, in the heat and the dust and the dirt, Lewis abruptly transformed into an ordinary Australian, like me, like my grandfather, trying to do his best in a bloody difficult situation. Most significantly, some specific lines from 'Thoughts on Rising' came to me:

On hearing this
The battlelines, redrawn
And man is sand, slipped
Trickling in the morn'
Lost between the breaking and the dawn [65]

I am convinced Lewis wrote these words while fighting in Gallipoli, reflecting on his time in Egypt.[66] The poem contains allusions to the

---

then kerb-stomp the twat? A little wish fulfilment?

I've not been sleeping well. I don't know what to do.

I need to buy a baseball bat.

65 'Thoughts on Rising' is one of the Unknown Digger's more philosophical – one might even argue upbeat – poems, before the tone goes dark, as it inevitably must. Four thirty in the morning when Em called. I was finishing the previous chapter. She was crying. What's wrong? I said.

The wretched sniff of wet snot in her nose. Somewhere, on her side or mine, the wail of an ambulance retreating.

Em? What happened?

Sloane Square. Her voice quavered, she took a huge gulp of air, trying to steady herself, and I sat in the dark silence, waiting for the wave to crash down over my head. Meet me outside the station?

What happened? I raised my voice. In the flat below, someone grunted. Em had vanished altogether, silence on her side, just the occasional roar of a passing car. Where are you?

Walking to Sloane Square.

I'll be there.

66 See Chapter 4. She rang again in the taxi. I'm coming, I said, as soon as I answered.

Egyptian desert, sand and heat (*fiery, furnace, sunrise, haze*), and the writing style is less flamboyant, one might argue simpler ('*and let this sun/set on dreams/lead us to the south/again*') than some of the later poems, where the poet seems more sure of himself.[67] It clicked into place. The lines of Lewis's unsent letter following the accident – 'I worry you won't recognise me when I return' – mirror the same sentiment as the poem: man is sand, constantly moving, and never able to be pinned down. It is hard to conceive the two lines not being written by the same hand. They push the same ideological themes: life is fleeting, and we must be ready to act, or make a choice, or fight, or flee, in a single instant. We must redraw

---

She'd stopped crying. Her voice was a cold monotone. Outside the station.

Are you ok? What happened? I wanted to scream. I could see the driver, in my peripheral, staring straight ahead, trying not to eavesdrop. I turned towards the window, the streets of Holborn flashing by. Are you safe?

How long?

Back to the driver, trying to gauge in his look, the way he glanced at his map. Ten minutes.

Hurry. She hung up.

The driver slowed and stopped at a red light. No other cars were near us, no-one passed in front, all of London frozen in time. He turned his head, his eyes wide. Is your girlfriend?

Please hurry.

67 I keep replaying it, over and over in my head, like a scene from a movie, removed from my body, hovering above the square and watching as the cab approached. The blonde of her hair before anything else, tiny and distant across the road. Shouting at the driver. The door open and my feet on the pavement before the car had stopped. The run across the cobblestones, the orchestral score, the slow-motion thud of my steps. I crashed down next to her, pulled her into my lap and rocked her, back and forth. Long purple stains down her cheeks, her eyes wild. She buried her face into my shoulder and her body convulsed, and I pulled her tighter, squeezing her, trying to absorb the heavy shudder, trying to pull her deeper into safety.

It's ok. It's ok. It's ok.

It was all I could think to say, the only words that felt appropriate. It's ok. The square was starting to show signs of life, morning workers glancing across at us, where we slumped. It's ok.

our battlelines again and again.[68] Lewis's humanity is reflected in the poetry of the Unknown Digger.

Theodore Shuckman, in his article 'Literary Allusions in the Poems of the Unknown Digger', notes: 'for the Unknown Digger, sand is a friend, sand is a welcome companion, sand is a constant reminder of home'.[69] And yet in 'Thoughts on Rising', man becomes sand and, like the last grains slipping through an hourglass, sand becomes mortality, signalling the end. Which seems an absurdly elaborate way of stating that things change, or that what you thought was one thing, can rapidly become something wholly different. In learning of Lewis's initial faltering steps as a commander, the poetry of the Unknown Digger came sharply into focus for me. I believe it was this extraordinary event which shaped Lewis's ideology as a soldier: rather than ordering others around, Lewis became known for doing things his own way, himself.[70] Rather than face the possibility of

---

68 The shuddering slowed, until we were breathing together, letting my chest rise and fall with hers. She raised her head, a gleaming trail of snot bridging the gap between us. She wiped it on my sleeve.

I held her, the ground cold where we sat, her hair in my eyes. I didn't want to move, afraid of breaking the spell.

It's ok.

69 T. Shuckman, 'Literary Allusions in the Poems of the Unknown Digger', *London Journal of Poetry*, Issue 15, Volume 12, December 2011, p. 69.

70 See *From Busso to the Holy Land: Alan Lewis and the 10th Light Horse*, Chapter 4: 'The Man, The Legend'. The ride home was a million times worse. Em was broken.

Back to Turnpike? The driver turned in his seat, glancing at the huddled form next to me.

Yes, please.

No, back to mine. Make him go to mine. Em's voice, low and lazy, from my lap.

You sure?

She didn't answer.

Back to hers, then, driving in silence.

I stroked Em's hair, running my fingers through the gold strands, trying to find a pattern, a routine, comfort in the constant motion. Past her ear, down her shoulders, back up, repeat as necessary. Try not to notice the chipped nail polish. Past her ear, down her shoulders, back up. Try

another disaster like the training run, he spurred himself on to greater heights. As he wrote in a letter dated 16th May 1916, following his return to his regiment after a long stay at the Anzac Hospital on Lemnos:

> *Ordering a man to attack is one thing, knowing a man will hold his position next to you in the line is another. As Nugget is fond of saying – if you want it done right, do it yourself.*[71]

One might even argue that without this blemish on his otherwise spotless record, Alan Lewis might never have accomplished the acts that made his name. Would he still have charged into the unknown, if he hadn't first learnt the hard lessons of the Egyptian desert?

The recognisable ideological equivalency with the Unknown Digger is obvious. In countless poems, such as 'The Morning of the Attack', 'The Billjim', 'Strewth', 'Jackdaw Lane', 'Between the Lines' and many more besides, a similar entreaty toward self-sufficiency is expressed.[72] Who could forget the wonderfully glum protagonist of 'Furphy Does His Rounds', who laments *'this b-----d trench won't*

---

not to imagine her cries. Past her ear, down her shoulders, back up. Try not to imagine the jagged edge of her breathing as anything other than exhaustion. Watching the streets get dirtier, the houses smaller, the graffiti more pronounced. Thinking, I'll kill him.

71 Pyke, *The Annotated Letters*, p. 155. Lewis is fond of recounting McRae's various pearls of Irish wisdom, and who could blame him – 'Nugget' McRae was invariably the regiment's prankster, class clown, and source of hope. One can imagine how vital the ability to laugh at one's troubles must have been in the trenches, how important it was to have a Nugget around to lighten the load. You need to laugh, or you'll scream.

72 Around Camden she raised her head. Bleary eyes. Where are we?

Camden. I'll wake you when we get there.

She lowered her head back into my lap. The bottoms of her feet were filthy, her thongs discarded on the cab floor. At some stage between me leaving the party and her call she'd changed out of her party dress and into jeans and a strappy top. The last traces of purple dye remained in the depths of her hair.

ever move/without the work of me'?[73]

It is true that not every poem written by the Unknown Digger espouses an individualist outlook. Prominent anti-war poems like 'Anzac Bay at Midnight' and 'The Groyne' maintain a staunch pluralist viewpoint, arguing from the perspective of a doomed, certainly, yet ultimately optimistic, 'we'.[74] The anti-war poems,

---

73 The trench gossip, or 'furphy', as it was known, that passed between the lines, was often the subject of intense dissection and many letters home. The most famous, and longstanding, furphy was that the war would be over by Christmas, and the men would be back home with their families sometime in the new year. As examined in L. Trin's *How the War Was Wondered*, University of Illinois, Chicago, 2007, the 'home by Christmas' rumour was one shared by every nation and every fighting force. As the war raged on, it refused to dissipate, spurred on by the men who refused to let it die.

Em stirred again around Green Lanes, and spoke. I had to lean down to hear, my ear by her mouth.

Please don't tell.

I threw my arms around her, wrapping her in the protective cage formed by my chest and arms. It was the easiest promise I've ever made.

Anyone. Promise?

I promise. In a whisper, in a cab, driving through the grimy streets of north London at six in the morning. It'll be ok.

74 We got to hers, and I paid the cabbie, and we staggered to the front door when she remembered her keys were in the other bag, the one she'd left behind, slamming his door and running off into the night.

We should have gone back to mine.

Call Dan. He has the spare.

I think I could climb in through the back window, if you left it open a crack.

Call Dan.

Or wake one of your neighbours. They won't mind.

Call Dan.

Absolutely the last person I wanted to talk to at half-six in the morning on one of the longest nights of my life. He picked up on the fourth or fifth ring, half asleep, his words toffee. Em? Whatchawant?

It's Matt. Em's had, uh, a rough night.

Chilli eggs.

Sorry?

Chilli eggs for a hangover.

which Jennifer Hayden argues convincingly were written later than most of the others in the collection, nevertheless manage to reflect the ideological standpoint of Alan Lewis. Indeed, by the end of his service, roughly analogous to the period when these anti-war poems were written, Lewis was writing letters home in a similar vein. In one letter potentially written only a matter of days before his death at Har Megiddo, he writes almost exclusively in this disembodied 'we':

> *It's been years now, surely, that we have been riding, passing the same watering hole, the same small tangle of buildings that calls itself a village.*[75]

No. She needs the spare key.

I sat down next to her on the step, threw an arm around her shoulder. She sniffed, loud enough for Dan to hear on the other side. We need the spare key.

Is she ok?

She's fine. She got a little drunk. I had to go pick her up. She's fine.

I'll get there as soon as I can. I could hear him throwing his legs over the side of the bed, rummaging for jeans.

The cabbie was still perched at the end of the street, waiting for us to go inside. Em hadn't moved for so long I thought she'd fallen asleep, until she spoke. You should go.

What?

You should go – I can wait for Dan.

Leave? I stood up and walked away, breathing heavily. I counted thirty-six bricks down the length of the driveway. Same number of lines in 'Anzac Bay at Midnight'. She looked up at me from the front step. Hair in a mess of thick dreadlocks, dark purple panda eyes. She looked like a circus act. What do you want me to do?

I think you should leave. Thank you, but it's unfair on Dan.

Whatever it takes, right?

75 Pyke, *The Annotated Letters*, p. 299. She went back to work on Monday. The same office space, the same emails, the same workload. I told her she should wait until she's ready. She said she is ready.

The Prof is away for two weeks, doing some mentoring thing at a university in Germany. Yes, he speaks German.

I told her I think she should quit. She said she needed me to be supportive. I said, once I'm published I'll be able to support her – financially too. She said forget about your book for one goddamn second.

The parallel of his tone and description in these letters to the pluralistic, anti-war – sometimes even nihilistic – poems of the Unknown Digger are at once strikingly obvious and eerily prescient. Whatever arguments critics might present about Lewis being an untouchable hero, 'removed from the common man by his uncommon deeds', the revelations in Curtin-Kneeling's immaculately researched work argue otherwise.[76] The parallels in philosophical outlook, and, crucially, the evolution of said philosophy through the duration of the war, confirm that Alan Lewis and the Unknown Digger trod the same ground, fought the same battles, breathed the same desert air; in short, lived the same life. The Australian champion of Har Megiddo, The Nek and Gaza, and the legendary Australian poet of 'The Morning of the Attack', 'The Billjim' and 'Ken Oath', are surely one and the same.

One might argue that the progression of Lewis's attitudes towards the war mirrors that of many soldiers who faced as much as Lewis did, and that the parallels found between poetry and service record

---

I asked her what she'll say when he gets back. She said she wouldn't say anything. It's the British way, she said, smiling like she'd made the funniest joke ever. I said the British way was attacking machine-gun nests by walking at them in straight lines. She said, It's a joke, Matt.

I sit up writing and wonder what would have happened if I'd insisted on staying and cleaning up. I lie awake, counting the marks on the roof, knowing Em is doing the same.

76 From Hereford, *They Walk Amongst Us*, p. 63. Written in 1933, not that long after the end of the First World War, the work fetishises Victoria Cross recipients by imbuing them with the qualities of deities. For many Australians, that is how these men have continued to be viewed. For a country which loves nothing more than to cut down the tall poppy this might seem surprising, but from the beginning we have idolised the hero figure refusing help when it is offered, worshipping those who fight on alone.

I asked Em if she wants me to say something to him. She said no, forget about it, stop thinking about it.

I said, I can't, it obviously affected you, or you wouldn't have called me.

She put plates out on the table and threw the knives and forks down next to them in a clatter of metal.

I've forgotten about it. So should you.

We ate in silence.

are typical of a more commonly shared experience. I agree that the poetic experience espoused by the Unknown Digger is one shared by many soldiers throughout the war (indeed, it may even go some way toward explaining the poems' astounding popularity), but I would challenge anyone to deny that the matching up of ideological and physical evidence for Lewis and the Unknown Digger is anything less than compelling. Note the route Lewis took through the war, and delineate its defining characteristic: from his country town in the state's South West and its perfect Western Australian beaches, Lewis travelled to Egypt, to a rocky outcrop in the Dardanelles, to the white shores of Lemnos, across the arid plains of the Sinai and through the Middle East.[77] At extremely few points did he find himself in lush green landscapes or fertile wetlands. The constant, running motif of Lewis's time in the war is one rooted in desert landscapes, in rock and dirt and heat. It should be no surprise to find that the word with the greatest frequency of use throughout the poems of the Unknown Digger is 'sand', which occurs twenty-four separate times in the entire collection.[78] Shuckman's study

---

77 From Curtin-Kneeling, *Busso to the Holy Land: Alan Lewis and the 10th Light Horse*, p. 236.

78 See Shuckman, 'Literary Allusions in the Poems of the Unknown Digger', p. 72. It's been a better week. Em's still alone in the office. I head round to hers after work, and we eat dinner and watch TV, and then I go home and write. I figured she needed a little extra loving during all of this, so I bought her a present.

I got the call at ten this morning, half-arsing my way out of bed. I called Em as soon as I hung up.

Hey, you awake?

She was out last night, drinks with Sam and Cait, and judging by the messages I woke up to, it was a big one. Maggot, as we'd say back home. She grunted down the phone.

Fancy heading south of the river? I tried to sound nonchalant. Harder than I thought.

Why?

It's a surprise. (She hates surprises.)

I can't move.

I promise it'll be worth it.

She met me at Bounds Green and we caught the tube down to Brixton and the smells of the fish market and bloody red slabs of meat. Is this the

excluded pronouns like 'he', 'she' or 'they', and verbs, conjunctions and articles like 'and', 'was' or 'the'.[79] The second most common

---

surprise? She said. From Brixton, we had to catch a proper train from the upstairs station, heading south out of the city. I wouldn't tell her where we were going. She gave up asking, and stared out at the countryside in her giant sunglasses. Like moth's eyes, hiding half her face.

We got off in the middle of nowhere, somewhere with grassy fields and that same little high street all nowhere towns have now: a Costa, a Paddy Power and a Pizza Express. I led her through the streets, glancing down at my phone for directions. Where are we going? she complained.

Almost there, I said, three houses before the house we were looking for. The gate to the backyard was fenced off, and there was the musty smell of Old Pub in the air. Before I could knock, two dogs started barking from behind the fence: loud, Turnpike-Lane-after-dark barking. Em pulled her glasses up and looked at me queasily.

A lumpy, middle-aged woman opened the door, cigarette hanging from her lips, a Yorkshire terrier yapping in her arms. I told her our names and waited while she looked us up and down, then grunted and beckoned us in. I ushered Em indoors.

Inside, six more Yorkies were running around a lounge room.

Watch where you tread, the dog woman croaked. The smell of old piss was stronger in here.

Well, here it is.

She motioned toward the one dog that hadn't leapt up as we entered, a puppy with tan ringlets, and the beginnings of a blond goatee around its muzzle. It looked up at us.

Pure Yorkie. Got the papers to prove it. This is the mother. She held forth the yappy dog in her arms, who scowled at Em and scrabbled in the air. The puppy was twice the size of the supposed mother, with different colouring, a longer snout, droopier ears and coarse dreadlock hair. The mother had a long, silky coat.

I turned to tell Em the surprise was off. Obviously a scam – no way are these two related. But she'd dropped into a crouch and was stroking its head, forgetting the hangover and the smell of piss. The puppy opened its mouth wide, licked its chops, and nestled deeper into the cushions.

79 It's a boy dog. Em says she'll call him Arthur. Artie, for short.

It's not like it was a complete surprise. Em's been actively looking for a Yorkie for a while now, and she's been saying she wants a dog since I met her: we bonded, down in the tequila bar, over the fact we both had Cavalier King Charles Spaniels as kids – she had Milo, ours was Harpo.

word is 'south', with fourteen separate occurrences, which makes sense, with 'the South' having dual meanings, as both an indicator of home (along with 'down under', 'red earth', and 'home') and as an allegory for death (as in 'travelling south', i.e. dead and buried).[80]

I'll be his stepdad. He was £350 all up, plus another fifty for a lead, poop bags and puppy food. Em said she'd pay me back. I said don't, he's yours. She stood on tiptoe with the puppy in her arms and kissed me, and said, One day you'll be his real dad.

She hasn't stopped smiling since we left the house.

80 The Prof is back, and Em says it's all fine. Hasn't mentioned the night of the party, doesn't look like he's going to, and Em certainly isn't going to bring it up. I reminded her that I could talk to him if she wanted.

She said, Artie is the best thing that's ever happened to me, and, We should build him a dog house!

I could talk to him? I said again.

She said we should take Artie to the park.

I dropped the subject.

ANZAC HOSPITAL, LEMNOS. EARLY 1916.

Nothing down here can touch him, eerie silent, the slippery soft caress of seaweed on his toes, the dull pulse of his heartbeat, the throb of blood in his head.

And up there, the sun, reaching warming fingers toward him, dappled light to heal, to wrap him up safely, relax his tired muscles and draw him back toward the surface.

Nothing down here is trying to kill him, destroy him, tear him apart with metal. The scars on his back accept the sting of saltwater with relish, and from the sandy sea floor the world above looks rosy, healthy, beckoning.

Caught for a moment in the ebb of the receding waves, his body drifts across the seabed, his fingers trailing sand in small clouds, the green-blue haze of the deep stopping time.

Yesterday was yesterday, and tomorrow is tomorrow, and all that matters is now, and here, and the surge of water around his head as he surfaces and breathes in the clean island air, baptised, back into the world.

~

I am alive, my love.

I hope someone saw fit to write you and let you know of my condition. I asked one of the nurses, but I have no way of knowing. Thank Christ I am now strong enough to hold a pencil.

I have been in and out of consciousness, strung out with fever and dreaming such terrible dreams I wonder I haven't kept half the ward up with my delusions. I must lie on my stomach so they can clean the wounds on my back, and they say I may limp when I get back on my feet. I'm the lucky one.

Sit down, love; breathe.

Red was a lot closer to the shell. He has lost an ungodly amount of blood, though is improving each day. He will never walk, or bowl a cricket ball. They say he may eventually regain his sight. How he has survived this long is a miracle. You know Red.

I don't know what to say.

I am alive. The pencil is heavy in my hands.

I can hear the sea.

Yours, bedriddenly.

His nurse is a severe woman from England named Nancy, who chides him for rolling onto his back and reopening his scars, who finds his pack of cigarettes one day and confiscates it, 'for your own good' she says in her schoolmarm voice, her black hair tucked behind her ears. She's a good ten years older than him, makes him feel like a boy when she tells him off, which she does lightheartedly, knowing he'll be smoking again in an hour, knowing he can't help but roll over when lying on his stomach becomes oppressive, the skin on his stomach itchy and warm.

The long corridor leading to their temporary ward is made of wooden slats on rough earth, with canvas walls. They are lucky enough to have a real roof, corrugated metal hanging above their heads, which grows hot in the daylight and creaks and groans as the cold night approaches. They have two windows, wide enough for two men to smoke side by side, looking out across the beach toward the smaller islands, listening out for the telltale click of the nurses' heels on the wooden slats to give them enough time to stub out the fag, close the window, and limp back to bed. Any time a nurse arrives for a check-up, the room grows loud, the men sit up taller and stifle coughs, telling jokes and flirting. The medicine helps, and the sleep, and all the rest, but the real work is done by the girls in uniform.

The Kiwi corporal in the bed next to him asks Nancy to come for a swim before he returns to service. She laughs, a prim and proper English laugh, gone in an instant, and gratefully accepts, but only once the weather gets a bit warmer – by which time he'll be long gone. When the Kiwi fella points this out she says it'll be no good going swimming when the water is so cold his testes retract, in which case he might as well shower with the nurses. The whole room erupts, whooping and hollering, and the Kiwi bloke turns a bright shade of red. Nancy says he's looking healthier already.

The other nurses are younger and standoffish; they travel in packs, approaching the beds in numbers like the injured men might be more dangerous than the war itself. There is truth in their suspicions. The boys are restless from sitting around and eager for a warm touch or a quick graze. Nancy bustles about the room smacking away hands, or, if she likes you, leaning over and rearranging pillows with her breasts by your ear. She loves the blushing from the younger boys, and gives as good as she gets from the older men. She tells them there's no use in being stoic, a stiff upper lip is no use to anyone on a dead man. She says if it hurts it hurts, and they won't get better by acting the hero.

He watches her cross the room, filling the ward, swinging her curves around the beds, joking, cajoling, terrorising the young boys, swearing, getting her hands dirty when the need arises, like the time the Kiwi's stitches spring open and spray blood across the room. She remains calm, efficient, in control. Brows furrowed in concentration, her features manage to be soft; though heavy-set, she is light on her toes. She is a contradiction in terms and he can't look away.

Down the maze of corridors, in the ward for the severe injuries, Red lies unconscious, breathing through a tube. His eyes are closed, one side of his head shaved, one side thick with ginger tussles. Nancy wheels Alan in for a visit one day and leaves him, stuck in his wheelchair, and he can't think of what to say except to tell Red about the view out the window. The long slope down to the beach. The white walls of the houses on the cliff. The fishing boats out in the bay. Red's breathing is low and jagged, coming in fits and spurts like sawing through thick jarrah. All Alan wants to do is leave, stand up and run, or roll out down the corridor and back into the noise of his ward, and leave Red here. He calls out for Nancy, but she takes an age to arrive.

'Take me back,' he says.

'Wouldn't hurt to say please,' she says, and despite Red's broken body in the bed next to him, he smiles.

He gets a letter. From Rose, saying how proud she is, how brave he must be for surviving, for pulling through. 'For continuing the fight.' But he's not brave, he happened to be in the right spot. By random chance the shrapnel that peppered his back missed his vital organs. He hasn't done anything to be proud of except not die, and he doesn't think that was his own choice. He receives interminable letters. From Rose, from Ma, one from Tom, on his way to the Western Front. He opens one from Nugget, full of spelling mistakes, letting him know the regiment retreated from Gallipoli safely.

He reads whatever he can get his hands on. Whatever will pass the hours. He reads all the books in the hospital's meagre library. He writes to anyone he knows to send more.

He's treading water, sat on the sidelines while the rest of the team play the grand final, win medals and top the ladder. He writes this, in a letter home, and Rose tells him to stay strong, that he'll be able to play soon enough, it being cricket season soon. Funny he should mention sport, she writes, because, what with all the young men away, she joined the club herself and discovered she can bowl a decent leg break. Rose doesn't understand. He puts her letter in the drawer of the bedside table, and then keeps pulling it out, ready to reply but having nothing to say. He leans his pencil on the paper and makes little crackled piles of lead, black smudges of graphite crossing the lines.

'What's that you're reading?'

'Greek legends. For children.' He puts the open book down on the covers, making a small tent among the light blue of the sheets, and sighs. 'Again.'

'You must be gentle with the books, Lieutenant.' Nancy picks it up, marks his spot by folding one corner of the page down, and places it on the small table by his bed.

'You folded one of the pages!' He can't believe what he's witnessed. 'You'd be down for a caning if they caught that little move at my school.'

'Nothing wrong with a light caning now and then, Lieutenant.'

He bends forward, allowing her to rearrange the pillows behind his back. As she passes by his face, he notices the dimples of her smile. His cheeks burn. She is teasing him.

He pulls his shirt off and rolls onto his stomach, his head to one side, his feet sticking out over the edge of the bed. Her fingers are like ice on his back, and he sucks in air at her touch. She pulls away.

'Sorry.' Her voice is soft behind his back, and when her fingers return they are warm with her breath. Goosebumps rise on his arms as she runs her fingers down the scars. 'These look healthy.'

The way she says it makes him feel like a boy receiving a surprised well done for an outcome he had nothing to do with. He feels simultaneously pleased with himself and like he could do better, if he only applied himself.

'Never a big fan of Achilles,' she says, about halfway down his back.

Achilles was always his favourite. Quick-footed. Righteous. Unstoppable.

'You know the Greeks?'

'Don't sound so surprised.' She sounds offended, but when he tries to roll over she stops him. 'I wasn't always a nurse, you know.' She laughs like she's made a joke, at some unknown memory maybe, but doesn't explain herself. He should speak.

'So, who do you prefer?'

She thinks this over for a second.

'Problem is, they're all just big boys. Ten years of war because your wife runs off with another man? Bit of an overreaction.'

'I think there's more to it than that.'

'But you sense where I'm coming from.' Her fingers massage his lower back, down by the line of his blue hospital pants. 'If I had to choose one, maybe Odysseus. Pre-*Odyssey*, of course.'

'Pre-*Odyssey*?'

'He's supposedly the smart one. Would it kill to ask someone for directions?'

Odysseus the wise, the brains behind the wooden horse. Another foolish soldier. Another little boy to Nancy.

'And yours?' She's being polite, making conversation.

'Achilles. Probably.' He can imagine her shaking her head behind his back, is certain her fingers push a little harder into the muscle and wishes he had lied. 'Sorry.'

'This is good.' She means the scar on his back that keeps reopening, the one giving them a little trouble, but the way she says it, as if encouraging him, makes him think she means something else entirely. She moves away to her cart. He's lost her, she'll end the conversation there and they'll return to harsh civility and bland pleasantries. He should have said Hector, Patroclus, or Helen. But then he would have been lying. He read classics at university for the unbridled heroism, the black-and-white ease of it all. The Greeks were good. The Trojans were bad. The Aussies. The Turks. If the current situation was anywhere near as simple, it all would have been wrapped up, like they had been promised, before Christmas. Yet here they were, well into the new year, with no end to hostilities in sight. And Nancy wondered how ten years of war with the Trojans had slipped by.

She opens a tube and rubs pungent cream on his back, massaging the long scar that runs perilously close to his spine. She's silent as she works, humming some unknown tune beneath her breath.

'How do you know the classics?'

He waits for her to respond.

'That, Lieutenant, is a story for a later date.'

She's going to leave, and he has no reply, and their whole interaction is going to end with her sashaying away, that walk of hers that pulls eyes all down the ward, and him lying, struck dumb and semi-erect, on his stomach. An artist's charcoal sketch of the pathetic.

Say something. Take the leap. But he doesn't; plays the scene in his head and hates himself but keeps quiet. Staying silent is safer – she can't reject him outright that way.

'Do you read much poetry, Lieutenant?'

He's unprepared for her question and takes longer than he should to answer, not wanting to embarrass himself with his response, unable to gauge her reaction. At university they read Tennyson, Wordsworth, Kipling. He's read the two or three small books of the modern swill the hospital library has to offer.

'A little. Rose got me into it.' He speaks without thinking.

'Rose?'

'Little sister.' He swallows. 'You read poetry?' Chilling, how easily the lie comes.

'I do. I like the modern types.'

'I prefer the traditional, if I'm being honest.'

'I see.' A pause. 'I should hope you're being honest.'

They are silent as she finishes applying the cream, though he's aware of her breath, faster than his, by his ear, further down, back by her cart.

'Have you read Brooke?' She walks over to the window, pulling the curtains closed, the room golden with the oil lamps they are forced to use in the makeshift wards, and then she's back by his shoulder. She's the one nurse who can sneak into the ward without warning the men of her approach, her tread light and graceful. She fills out the white uniform with perfect curves that strain the material, tight in all the right places. He can't help but think how unlike Rose she is – Rose is a caged fireball, small and excitable, tiny in his arms. But gone, now. Back in a past he can't remember, back in a home he doesn't think would accept him back. Nancy is an enigma he is still figuring out.

He's staring. She's noticed. He rather thinks she likes the attention.

'Brooke?' she says.

He coughs as he tries to speak. 'I've heard of him. I gather he was extremely popular in England?'

'He was. And only more so since his passing.'

Silence as they ponder this, until he worries he needs to speak to bring them back to the conversation. She smiles at his nervousness, and saves him the trouble.

'He's buried a few islands over, did you know?'

'That's what I heard. Didn't even make it onto the beach.'

She sighs. 'I've wanted to visit the site since I was posted here. One can dream.'

She moves once more to his back.

'We should go. Together,' he says. He can't see her face. 'If you'd like?'

She's silent, and he starts to turn over, but she stops him, returns him to his position. He can hear her rummaging on her cart, returning the cream to its spot, filling out his file. He waits.

'Until tomorrow, Lieutenant.'

'Please, call me Alan.'

'Of course.'

And then the doors swing open and shut and she's gone and he's alone with the men dozing in the beds next door. He waits five minutes for the cream to sink into his skin and dry, and then turns over.

On the nightstand next to his head is a small brown book with gold lettering reading *1914 & Other Poems*, and on the first page, in a looping pencilled hand: *Property of Nancy Taylor*.

Once his scars heal, he's allowed to start his recuperation by taking walks around the hospital garden, or lying in a lounger on sunny days, reading. Sometimes men will meander down to the beach and swim, scream and laugh and play like children, splashing each other in the cold shallows. They ask him to join them, but he refuses, the skin on his back scabbed and hard, his head throbbing when the rain comes. His right leg is stiff and rigid, and he finds it hard to turn, but Nancy says that's normal, that he hasn't used the muscles for a while and they need to time to warm back up. The ward echoes with voices, and sleep, a mythic nymph teasing him, refuses to spend the night.

Ma sends a letter. Robbie is missing in action, somewhere in France. Things don't look good, she says. When he tries to write back the words wiggle and blur on the page and his hand shakes. He puts the paper down and stares out the window. Nancy asks him what Robbie is like, and places her hand on top of his, anaesthetic cool against his burning skin. Sits with him in silence for an hour. Her presence calms him, and eventually he is able to sleep.

He dreams of The Nek, as he always does.

'What do you believe in?' he asks her, as she walks with him around the square of manicured lawn that is the garden.

'Time. Gravity.' She thinks for a second. 'Death.' A smile.

She laughs at his look of shock.

'Love?' he asks.

'Stories.'

At university, he'd studied the classics, pulling apart Aeschylus and Euripides, sniggering at Oedipus, reciting Homer in cramped makeshift rooms while his classmates slumbered in the seats. Here, those stories came alive. He fancied the air smelt older, and his breathing grew easier, until one day the cough which had stalked him with irksome persistence throughout Gallipoli failed to materialise. The landmarks looked bigger too, the sunsets brighter, the water bluer even than the beaches back home. The familiar sound of seagulls, and the smell of salt and fresh fish, would steal their way up from the tiny fishing village in the bay, throwing up memories of Fremantle Harbour and baking hot summers on the beach that he thought belonged to someone else.

Some afternoons, dozing on his cot, he imagined the Greek heroes, in full armour, burnished metal and red plumed helms, sneaking their way down through the rocks alongside the water nymphs and Gods-made-mortal, to swim and laugh in the shallows, creating history as they went, frolicking in the azure waters.

The days hobble by like the wounded – waiting for night before dragging their torn bodies to the line – punctuated by check-ups and meetings, visits from friends and colleagues, performances by the infantry brass band and, once, a moustachioed villager, his fingers a blur on the bouzouki cradled in his lap. He receives a parcel from Rose, with two new books, a fresh razor, and a fruitcake for the new year, packed in with thick socks for protection. Stuck between the pages of a copy of their local paper, amid the sporting news and an advertisement for the local fete, he pulls forth a banksia candle, its bright red flowers disintegrating beneath his fingers.

Somewhere along the way, the image of Rose he kept safe in his mind wavers and darkens; black hair and white stockings, Nancy's cold touch rather than Rose's sun-warmed fingers, the military sound of heels on wooden floors. He is horrified to find he can't remember what Rose looks like. He pulls her photograph from the bottom of his bundle to ponder the stranger glaring back. He is worried that he should feel guilty, and terrified that he doesn't. The island, the hospital and the men inside it, the way the temporary canvas walls of the corridors sway in the slightest breeze, makes him feel like he's sleepwalking. Like his actions here won't have any effect in the real world.

No-one can see what he does down in the pale blue waters. He feels like he has stepped out of time, out of the war and out of his life, on the white beaches of Lemnos. Like nothing he does here will have repercussions. But he stops mentioning the nurses in his letters home. He tells Rose and his family about the books and the garden and the fishermen on the pier, and keeps the truth for himself.

He writes that he is sure Robbie will be found safe. Robbie can look after himself, he says, the pencil smudging under his fingers. He doesn't believe his own words.

I love you, he finishes.

~

The jetty and surrounding dock are deserted, the fishing boats long since cast off for the morning. She strolls to the end of the wooden pier and settles on a weather-beaten tender, light blue paint flaking off its prow, bobbing in the water.

'This one,' she says.

He glances up at the windows around the harbour, wonders how many eyes are watching him, how many potential witnesses. She grabs his hand, her face bright in the morning darkness, and pulls him down the pier.

'You promised.'

And he had promised, before he realised what the journey would entail, before he understood they'd be AWOL for a day, before he could stop himself by overthinking it. He's worrying about what Red or Nugget might think if they found out. He should tell Nancy about Rose. He has a fiancée back home, wherever that is, and a life waiting for him to return, and she needs to know. But he can't break his promise to her, so here they are.

At the end of the jetty she turns back to him and pulls her shoes off, throws them onto the deck of their boat. Their boat, like they purchased it together. She lowers herself down the rungs of the ladder. He unwinds the rope and throws it to her, and then turns around, three rungs down and the hospital up on the hill before him, where they'll all still be asleep. His foot on the edge of the boat sends him lurching forward. He leans backwards too far to compensate and lands on the deck with a clatter. She arches an eyebrow. Around her his feet are huge and ungainly, his limbs gangly, his voice croaks like he's the young boy fielding in the outfield again.

'You know how to run it?' She glances across at the wheelhouse, and he nods slowly, unconvinced. She notices, gives a little smile. 'We're only borrowing it, I promise.'

She pulls her scarlet coat closer about her shoulders. The engine starts up with a roar, loud enough to wake the entire hospital and send someone running down the hill to stop them, but soon enough they're puttering away from the harbour, out in the direction of the little island. He's not sure of what he's doing, but the way she chatters puts him at ease. About the weather, and the journey, about how pleasant it is not to be cleaning up vomit, how beautiful the day is going to be. The constant stream of words, the gentle lull of her accent. Soon Lemnos is fading in their wake.

She's right, of course, and the sun soon arrives in full force, blaring down on their little vessel. The skin on his nose burns, and he's grateful for the occasional blast of swell that sprinkles him with water. Nancy lies on the deck near the prow, her dress pulled up high on her waist, her legs bright white in the sunshine. She laughs, says her legs are so white she's translucent. A ghost. He can't look away.

He should tell her about Rose, but he doesn't.

Skyros is a miniature, doll's house island; half the size of Lemnos with its bustling port and the constant loading and unloading of soldiers, supplies and the wounded. The dock where they tie up the boat is manned by a tanned villager, who gives a slow nod from under heavy-lidded eyes and doesn't ask questions.

Back out across the water, the black outline of a troopship passes slowly, but otherwise the island seems untouched by war. The streets leading up towards the village are steep, bright white steps winding towards the outline of a church on the peak. The click of her heels on the stone. The heavy tread of his boots. Soon they're heading downhill, leaving the village behind, past individual houses and farms. They see no-one. A black cat peers from atop a white wall, and further along, a goat approaches the wooden fence as they pass.

'How long did you say?' He's breathless trying to keep up, too proud to ask her to slow down. What path there is, meandering and worn, is rough earth, divots and exposed roots. She picks through it with ease, leaving him trailing, sticky with sweat. He offers her a hand up the short incline of a wooden bridge over a stream surging with spring waters, but she ignores him, her skirt held in one hand, stepping her way through the puddles.

She pulls ahead, walking faster than he can manage. The air is cold in his chest and there's a throbbing in his knee he tries to ignore. He drops so far behind he loses sight of her. Five minutes down the track he finds her perched against the trunk of a tree waiting for him. Two and a half hours in, he's ready to give up, alone on a stretch of track surrounded by white rock and hemmed in by cypress trees. He rounds the corner to find Nancy waiting at the bottom of a hill, and together they peer up the tiny path that snakes its way to the top. They exchange looks.

'You'll be alright?'

She scoffs, and looks him up and down. 'I'm not the worry, Lewis. You're the fool who caught a back of shrapnel.'

He sizes up the cliff.

'If the Tommies can make it up with a day-old stiff, poet or not, I'll be sweet.' He is rewarded with a tightening of her jaw, but no response. She gestures him forward, but he shakes his head. 'No, after you.' And she sets off in front of him, her hands outstretched on each side, the rocks beneath her feet uneven and loose. 'I wouldn't want to miss the view.'

They first heard of the English poet in Mena, in the heat of the afternoon, reading snatches of a week-old *Times* as they waited to ship out to Gallipoli. Nugget had turned to him and asked, straight-faced, curious.

'What's this mean then, Al? "Magnificently unprepared/for the long littleness of life." Some Tommy poet carked it off Lemnos.'

And he shook his head, unsure.

'Not something they taught you at university?' Red teased. He delighted in discovering facts Alan didn't know, and lording them over him.

'When we get back,' Nugget said, 'I think I'd quite like to go to university.'

Red laughed. 'And study what? You know they can't teach you how to be an insufferable know-it-all – Al was just born that way.'

Alan punched Red on the shoulder, but felt secretly proud. He took the newspaper from Nugget.

'You could go to university if you wanted, Nug, it's not that hard.' Nugget smiled. 'But first you'd have to learn to read.'

Nugget swore at him. Red laughed.

He read the article. The words continued to rattle around in his mind for days afterward, and he never forgot the name.

'Brooke. The young Apollo.'

Sitting in a grove at the top of the hill, surrounded by olive trees thick with powdery green leaves, they find the cemetery. A cluster of wooden crosses and cairns of stacked pebbles. They look out across the blue water, where Lemnos would be, and beyond that to the stretch of rocky coastline littered with the bodies of his mates. Right about now the orderlies at the hospital will be delivering lunch, and the men will scoff it down, loud and raucous. And soon the ambulance truck will meander its way up from the dock to collect another batch of men too injured to return to action, and ready for the long trip back to Perth.

'Wasn't your friend leaving today?' Nancy's question trails off.

Soon they'll be wheeling Red through the corridors. He'll drift in and out of consciousness, no knowledge of his whereabouts. Probably doesn't remember who he is, poor bastard. No way Alan could have brought himself to watch while they packaged him up like that and sent him home, another parcel stuffed in with socks to keep from rattling.

He grunts, spins around, approaches the graves, peering down to read the names of long-dead villagers.

'One hundred and fourteen years old. Christ.'

Some of the names are illegible, carved in Greek letters from the same white limestone as the cliffs, faded away by the salty air, worn smooth by the breeze. On a small patch of ground at the back of the clearing, three or four fresh wooden crosses stand out like Nancy's accent in the ward of Australians, the grass around their bases sparse, thin fingers clawing at the clean wood. Nancy walks over to the grave they have come to see, a jumble of flowers piled high around its base, and small offerings, scraps of paper held down by rocks, or tied to the arms of the cross like the last winter leaves on the naked branches of trees.

None of the other graves have offerings. He stops at each one all the same, to spend a moment reading the inscription.

'Do you write?' he says, three graves away from her. She looks at him, across the bodies of the men rotting away in the ground. Her eyes bore into him; he tenses the muscles in his neck and stares forward.

'I did,' she's kneeling by Brooke's grave, 'when I was studying.'

He can hear the smile in her voice, and whips his head up to meet her steady gaze.

'And no. You may not.' She leaves him grinning, turns to the grave, her skirt swinging around her hips. She's taken her coat off and draped it over one arm, her bare skin creamy in the afternoon light.

'Where did you study?'

He approaches from behind, the sun a white orb in the ink of her hair, shimmering as he walks forward.

'Went to lectures at Oxford. Left after the first year. I was allowed to sit the exams, but not to matriculate.' She pokes her tongue out in mock disgust. 'Bit of a boys' club is an understatement.'

'I can imagine.'

'Can you?' she snorts.

He moves by her side, tries to quieten the wheeze and splutter of his loud breathing. Neither one of them speaks. He tried to read the book of poems, but none of them spoke to him – all beauty and polish, but missing the truth, the petrifying fear, of the war.

'I was engaged,' she says; a tumble of words.

'I'm so sorry.'

'For what?' She doesn't turn her face away from the grave, picking at an invisible spot on the back of her hand.

'I assume. Your fiancé. He died?'

She smiles. 'No, he's very much alive.'

He doesn't understand. 'You broke off the engagement?'

A laugh. 'I suppose, technically, we're still engaged. I never thought to check.'

While they've been speaking, she's taken his hand, as if it's the most natural action in the world. He hadn't realised until she started playing with his fingers, winding hers clumsily through his. Her fingers are larger than Rose's. His palm is slick with sweat. She lets his hand fall, pulls hers to her side.

'Should we say something?' He wonders what she wants to hear, what importance this sad little cemetery has to her.

She looks at him, her eyes dancing. 'You think he can hear us?'

'No, but –'

'I'm teasing.' She kicks her shoes off, runs her toes through the grass. He doesn't know where to look.

'So, the fiancé?'

'It was arranged. He was older. I thought it might be more fun to be a nurse.'

'You left him?'

'And it is. I meet so many agreeable young men.' She's grinning. He turns away, moves to the stone wall that marks the end of the cemetery, looking out over the blue. He doesn't know why it matters, but it does.

'Was that hard? Leaving?'

She's by his ear, her body pushed against him.

'Does it matter?'

'I don't know,' he turns, and her face is in his, eye to eye, his hands wrapped in hers. 'Yes.'

'Then no, it wasn't hard.' Her lashes fluttering, she closes her eyes for a second. When she stares back at him, they are heavy and wet. He crumbles and pulls her closer. 'It was simple.'

She kisses him first, with a ferocity he isn't expecting, biting his lip and pulling him forward, meeting his tongue with hers. She takes his hands and winds them around her own body, educating him, leading him. He follows blindly.

They break apart, and her feet are bare in the dirt of Brooke's grave, and she's smiling, like she's won a cheap toy at a travelling funfair.

'Let's make some poetry.'

'Is that a line, Nurse Taylor?'

She doesn't answer. She pulls him against her, her legs rosy pink as her skirt twists up around her hips. Her hand is on the front of his trousers.

From back the way they came, there comes a scream of laughter, the patter of voices rising. There are more tourists, khaki-uniformed, making their way up the hill, with the same idea, eager to pay their respects, moving like tiny black ants crawling up the wall of the house back home, that constant thin stream edging along the kitchen window and out into the sun. Soon the grove will be humming with activity, crowded with bodies in the afternoon sun. Nancy catches his eye and scowls.

She walks back to the low wall and stops.

'Down there.'

She's pointing down the other side of the hill, the opposite way to the one they came.

The water lies calm and flat for a few hundred yards, too shallow for boats, but there's a tiny stretch of white sand scrawled among the rocks, and before he knows it he's following her down through the scrub. They make their own pathway. He reaches for a hand that keeps pulling, leading him on and calling him forward.

~

My love, my apologies.

I have found it difficult to write. The news about Robbie has utterly demoralised me. Please look after Ma for me. I know you will.

I hope you have heard the good news that Red is on his way home. It will be a shock, I'm sure, both for his family and for him. And for you. I saw him off from the hospital, and he seemed in good enough spirits, though he hardly knew I was there. The journey is long and arduous and I pray for his safe arrival. I hope you will look after him in my stead.

I leave for Suez in a week, back to Kelly, who I must admit I have missed, and the saddle, which I have not, and the boys, who continue to give the Turks hell on a daily basis. It will be good to get back into it. I feel like I have grown soft here, with no-one to talk to, and nothing to do. Thank you for your letters, which have kept me sane. Without you, I would have drowned in boredom.

Do not fret, I have had my taste of hospital life, and decided it is not for me.

Yours, lonelily.

Bluer than blue, and bracing cold against his chest, clearing his head with a sharp blast, cloaking him and holding him tight. Floating under the surface, he opens his eyes and watches her approach, the hazy wet sheen of her petticoat stuck to her legs, her toes trailing sandbursts in the shallows. He would stay down here forever.

He pushes off the bottom, kicking towards the surface and breaking out into the afternoon sunshine, throwing his head back, arcing water. He runs a hand over his face and through his long hair, wiping away the water from his eyes. Back up the hill, in among the cypress trees, he hears laughter, screams of delight, low male voices egging each other on.

'They can't see us.' Her teeth are chattering, goosebumps rising along her naked arms, her petticoat soaked through and translucent against her skin. He can make out the dark circles of her nipples through the material, the curves of her hips, the tight scrub of her hair through the slip, like a pencil drawing, a field sketch before battle.

He kicks his way over to her, diving under the water a few feet away and approaching her legs like a predator, circling her left foot. He wraps his arms around her body and pulls her under. Her face is before him, laughing, tiny bubbles streaming toward the light. They surface and he coughs, seawater running from his nose. Nancy is already swimming away from him, out further into the bay, into the deeper waters.

'Wait.' He tries to whisper and shout at the same time, afraid of getting caught, afraid of stepping out of the moment. Afraid of waking up.

Nancy turns back to him, a lock of hair plastered to her face, a dark ivy tendril.

'What's wrong?'

'Nothing.' He coughs. 'It's a bit cold.'

She turns, takes a few half-hearted strokes back towards him.

'It's not good for your recovery,' she kicks, advances slowly, keeping her head above the water until she's a body length away from him. 'Maybe we should call it a day?'

He takes a stroke back, retreating towards the safety of the beach, the warmth of the sand. She swims forward, keeping the distance between them, extending her body, her legs long and slippery.

'We could lie in the sun?'

She frowns, a flash of teeth, a shark's toothy grin crossing her face. A glimpse of pink tongue, and then she tucks her head down, powering towards him with heavy kicks. He backs up, trips over the sandbar, pushes off the ground and kicks, feebly, looking up into the blue.

Her hand wraps around his ankle, pulls him toward her. He's under the water and her body is on top of his, their faces close. She kisses him, the air rushing out of his mouth, tasting saltwater and her lips. He can't tell which way is up.

They surface, smiling.

The pain in his leg has disappeared. His skin is leather tight and his head is clear. But his chest feels waterlogged. She takes his hand and pulls him through the shallows onto the beach. He follows, unquestioning, falling into step behind her. Waiting for orders. He's on his back, the sand hard and warm. She leans over, drips water from her mouth into his, her hair thick cold tentacles that snake along his shoulders.

Her petticoat has ridden up around her waist. He reaches forward, pulling the hem up and over her head hungrily, until she gets caught in the wet material and asks him to stop, chuckling as she removes the shift herself. She leans forward and plants her cold lips on his, reaching down between her legs and removing his shorts with practised ease. There is an awkward moment, but she laughs, says it's the cold, and shuffles down between his legs, grazing her lips across his chest, drawing her nails down the side of his ribs. Her tongue is warm and his body tenses, sand between his clenched cheeks. She murmurs but he can't reply. High above, a huge white bird circles. He grabs hold of the sand on either side, wet grains squeezed through his fingers.

She sits up, licks her lips, the schoolmarm look she gives him when she discovers the packet of cigarettes hidden under the mattress. She falls onto the sand next to him. She guides him on top and tells him to hold her legs.

'Start slowly. Be gentle.' She teaches him. A tremor ripples through her body, and he stops what he's doing, looking down at her. 'It's a shiver,' she says and pulls him forward, urging him deeper.

She's moaning, loud animal noises he's never heard before, and he's certain the others in the cemetery will hear, so he kisses her, fills her mouth with his tongue. He pulls his head up, tries to wipe away the seawater dripping from his nose, but she doesn't care and kisses him back.

The sand is sharp on his knees, each thrust digging him deeper into the beach. Nancy groans by his ear, digging her fingers into his back. He opens himself up and falls alongside her, into the cresting and surging waves. The saltspray. The dark water where he can't reach the bottom.

> Driftwood, spelt out in
> black and white upon the shore
> lines written by waves

He doesn't remember biting her, but they are his teeth marks on her neck. He apologises, but she says all's fair in love and war. They jump back into the sea to get the sand off, but the sun has lost its warmth, and when they walk back up the beach they're both shivering. He gives her his coat and for once she doesn't say don't play the hero. He puts his own trousers and shirt back on without drying, and the material sticks to his skin. The day has passed them by, and they walk back to the village in silence. His wet pants chafe against his thighs. The shadows on the ground grow darker, the steps back down to the dock are steeper than they were. He suggests staying for a night, sharing a bed, playing husband and wife, but Nancy says she's tired, says they've already lost a day, says she needs to get back.

She's asleep in the prow by the time they leave the harbour, and he's left alone in the cold, keeping the boat steady, watching for the dark silhouettes of invisible destroyers to emerge from the ink and crush them. Knuckles white on the wheel, they steam back into Lemnos late at night.

She stumbles back up to the hospital in sullen silence, ignoring him. They separate by the main entrance, where she leaves him for the nurses quarters. She gives him back his coat, and walks away without a backward glance, untouched except for the teeth marks on her neck, and the tangled knot of hair down her back. He stands in the entrance for a minute, hoping for the sound of her heels to return, but they fade into the darkness, and he walks back to his ward, alone.

A week before he ships out, he is moved down to the barracks by the dock, away from the hospital and the smell of formaldehyde and its bleached white sheets. Away from her. He receives a new uniform, pressed and laundered, and orders to meet up with his regiment outside Suez. He is given a haircut and a proper shave from a barber who wraps his face up in hot towels and flings flaming wands at his ears. He dreams of her. The men are ordered to parade each morning, and his muscles ache each night when he throws himself down on his cot. He doesn't have a single chance to meet with her, or write, or think.

The night before he leaves, he makes the walk back up to the hospital one last time. There are flowers opening in the hospital courtyard, bursts of colour where they first laid his stretcher. He wishes he hadn't worn his full uniform, but the men in his old ward don't take the piss, they wish him luck or pat him on the back. He leaves a pack of cigarettes by the window. Nancy isn't there.

She isn't in any of the wards, isn't anywhere in the hospital.

When he reaches the nurses quarters, a young nurse tells him she is gone for the day, maybe down to the beach, if he wanted to look, or maybe it was one of the other islands. He asks if she left anything for him, and waits while she walks off to check, blocking the way. A second nurse taps him on the shoulder and politely asks him to move.

After five minutes the young nurse hasn't returned. He pushes open the door and heads inside. His boots squeak on the concrete floor. Long silent corridors stretch out left and right. He hears voices, and follows them. The young nurse is at an open door, arguing with someone inside. She turns when she hears him coming.

'You can't be in here,' she says, her voice rising.

'I need to see her,' he holds his hands up in front of him, like calming a frantic horse, 'one more time.'

'Get out!' the nurse shrieks, and then Nancy appears in the doorway, and lays a hand on her shoulder.

'It's alright,' she says, 'I'll take it from here.'

The nurse walks away down the corridor, tutting.

'I leave tomorrow,' he says.

'I know.'

'I had to see you.'

'Had to? Or what?'

He doesn't know what to say. 'You don't feel the same way?'

'I'm not sure that I do.'

'I've never felt this way about anyone before,' he lies.

She tilts her head. 'You don't remember, do you?'

'Don't remember what?' He remembers the sea, the saltwater. He remembers sand and sun.

She shakes her head. 'Rose.' She laughs, but it's a cold laugh, empty and mocking. 'You called me Rose.'

'Rose.' The name stalls on his tongue.

'Your little sister?'

He reaches for her hand, but she pulls it away.

'My fiancée.'

She stares through him, until he disappears.

The next morning they set sail, and he crowds against the prow with the other men, another soldier in a group of soldiers, indistinguishable from the men around him. He watches the village grow small behind them, hoping for Nancy to materialise out of the laneways, searching for the scarlet stain of her coat against the white walls. The water around the boat is dirty white, chopped foam writhing under the engines.

CHAPTER 4: Examining the previously unexplored implications of a potential Alan Lewis authorship on the Unknown Digger poems: The Lemnos poems and their potential to change everything we think we know.

Conventional academic study assumes that the Unknown Digger was a member of one of the Light Horse regiments. The consensus that has built, since the discovery of the poems, has led to a general agreement that he left Australia in early 1915, fought in Gallipoli, and was then either transferred to the Western Front or fought and was killed in the Middle East campaign, possibly as early as the defence of the Suez Canal.[81] We can determine this much from the relatively candid poems of the Gallipoli campaign, with their obligingly literal titles ('Anzac Bay at Midnight') or easily demonstrable facts ('The Morning of the Attack').[82] Compared to these early poems, those poems academics have identified as being written following the Gallipoli campaign are frequently more ambiguous, which makes them, vitally for us, considerably more open to interpretation. This

---

81 See Jennifer Hayden, *Unearthing the Unknown Digger*. For arguments supporting the idea of a transfer to the Western Front see Max Whitlock, *Australia's Unknown Digger*, Fremantle Press, Fremantle, 2000, and Kathryn Hounslow, 'The Unknown Digger Revealed' in *The Australian Literary Review*, Issue 3, Volume 12, April 2003. For a convincing argument for a death in the Middle East, as early as the defence of the Suez Canal, see Susan Freedland, *The Mystery of the Unknown Digger*, Cambridge University Press, Cambridge, 2004.

82 'The Morning of the Attack' has always been one of my favourites – I wrote a long essay in my last year of high school arguing that the attack at The Nek, and the similar action at Lone Pine, so clearly referenced in this poem, was a sort of proto-origin story for the Australian spirit, a creation myth along the lines of Peter Parker's spider bite or the death of Bruce Wayne's parents. I lie in bed and imagine retelling the story of how Em and I met (minus the public nudity and cheating) on make-believe talk shows, chuckling to myself at the foolishness of young love. Maybe I'll tell them how we rescued Artie from the desperate clutches of the smoking lady, chased from that godforsaken rural town by a mob of trident-bearing country bumpkins. Hold for the rapturous applause of the appreciative audience. Tell self-deprecating joke. Laugh. Repeat. Live happily ever after.

has led scholars to make riotously contradictory assertions about their meanings, and from there, to hypothesise on any number of timelines for the Unknown Digger's life.

For instance, Max Whitlock claims that, based on the word choices in poems such as 'To the Poet' and 'The Billjim', the Unknown Digger is 'clearly hiding a deep affection for his fellow soldiers, an embarrassing secret he would die before revealing'.[83] There is absolutely no evidence the Unknown Digger was secretly gay, but people will read into poetry whatever they want to read.[84]

That the Unknown Digger was transferred to the Western Front following the Gallipoli campaign is perhaps an obvious assumption to make, given the dominant themes of the later poems. In *Unearthing the Unknown Digger*, Jennifer Hayden transposed the poems alongside a timeline of the war, coming to the conclusion that the Unknown Digger perished on the Western Front sometime towards the end of 1916. As time has passed and more research has been conducted, this initial belief has been subjected to various arguments, though as a testament to Hayden's standing in the field, the official website for the Unknown Digger still cites his death as 'somewhere in Europe, circa 1916'.[85] Howard Greene's remarkable analysis of the poems in 'Line by Line: Analysing the Poetry of the

---

83 Whitlock, *Australia's Unknown Digger*, p. 114. Jennifer Hayden responded to, and eviscerated, Whitlock's claims in a forty-page article titled 'On the Repressed Sexualities of the Unknown Digger', published in *The Journal of Australian Literary Criticism*, Issue 4, Volume 25, Sydney, 2001.

84 I emailed Jennifer recently to clarify a quote from her third Unknown Digger book, and to ask her if she'd had a chance to review the first three chapters I sent her last week. She emailed me back last night. Jennifer.Hayden@bloomsbury.com to mdenton@ucl.edu.uk: *Hey Matt, sorry I haven't had a moment to read your chapters yet, but the next AAC Conference has pulled away a lot of my time. Rest assured, I'm very excited to read some well-researched, eye-opening new ideas. Keep writing, keep fighting. J.*

I showed Em and she smirked and said, You gonna buy her a dog too?

Keep fighting, Jennifer says (from the final lines of 'To the Poet') – and I intend to.

85 See unknowndigger.com.au.

Unknown Digger' states the Unknown Digger's death as 7th June 1917, at the Battle of Messines.[86] However, I'm convinced he stayed in the Middle East and lived longer, fighting through the Great Ride, and perishing in the fields of Har Megiddo. More and more academics are coming around to the idea that the Unknown Digger took part in the Great Ride, across the Sinai and through Palestine. As Susan Freedland states: 'the Australian story of the First World War is much more than just Gallipoli and the Western Front. Most of the Light Horse battalions never made it to Europe.'[87] Until now,

---

86 Howard Greene, *Six Essays on the Australian Spirit*. Melbourne University Press, Melbourne, 2010. For further analysis of the proposed timeline of events, see Chapter 5.

Found myself alone with the Prof in his office for the first time since the party, and had to bite my lip to stop myself from saying something. Should've seen him: 'dark salmon' shirt, red chinos, yellowing cardigan, hair falling in droopy curls from his forehead – he's a caricature of British professors, a walking joke. If anything, I feel sorry for him.

87 Freedland, *The Mystery of the Unknown Digger*, p. 52. We've fallen into a nice routine recently – I finish work earlier than Em, so I catch the tube back to hers and take Artie for a long walk, then curl up and watch TV or write with him on my lap, and when she gets home we have dinner. Then we both fall asleep on the couch in front of a movie, until Artie wakes us needing a late-night pee, and I catch the bus back to mine. Last night the Prof asked Em to work late, so I ate dinner by myself, then fell asleep with Artie in my arms, and only woke up when Em crashed her handbag down on the table.

Good day? I asked, wiping drool from my face, cleaning up my dinner mess, making sure Artie hadn't peed on me in his sleep. Em slumped onto the floor, pulled Artie into her lap and mushed his curls against her chest, riling him up with tickles until he was barking.

The neighbours, I reminded her. It's half-eleven.

He missed me, she says, I can't help it.

And she's right – I did get to spend all evening with him, and she had to work late. And the neighbours think we make too much noise anyway. So I get down on the floor and we roll around like we're in a commercial. Then Em gets weird. Makes a big song and dance of looking at the clock and yawning, because she can't straight out ask me to leave, apparently, but I can't stay, because she's not ready to share her bed, yet. I get up and gather my bits, pull Em to her feet and kiss her, but as I'm about to leave, she grabs

no-one has considered that the Unknown Poet might not have been in the frontline when writing some of the middle poems. Rather than heading off to the Western Front or immediately engaging in the Suez conflict, there is actually evidence to suggest the Unknown Digger was somewhere else entirely, a third option unexplored by the academic milieu and therefore left in pristine readiness for my own analysis. Let us imagine for a moment that the Unknown Digger, rather than evacuating Gallipoli with the rest of the Anzacs,

---

my hand and leads me to into the bedroom. I'm not complaining, mind. She sits down on the edge of the bed, undoes my belt, and pulls my jeans down to my knees.

Are you kicking me out, or what?

She smiles up at me.

We kiss, jeans around my ankles, and I pull her top off and fling it across the room. I lean over and kiss the soft skin of her neck.

Wait, she says, not yet.

I lie down behind her, and she folds my arms around her chest. Artie jumps up into the gap between our legs, and burrows down into the doona. We lie that way for a while, until the sky outside is deep purple and the foxes are screaming in the street.

Can I stay? I whisper in the general direction of her ear.

Don't you have the early tute tomorrow?

In the dark she sounds like a femme fatale from a black-and-white noir, all throaty and hoarse. I do, I did. I didn't care. I wanted the fresh laundry smell of Em's sheets. I didn't want her to be alone.

Can I stay anyway?

But she was already asleep. I rolled out of bed and locked the back door, put the leftovers in the fridge, blew out the candles. We slept naked. She fits perfectly into my warmth, her hair flying away over the pillows. She snuffles sometimes, in her sleep (she'd hate me writing that, and she'd deny it, but she does), little contented puppy sounds. So does Artie. I stuck one leg out of the covers to cool down, and folded the other knee into her curves.

She woke late this morning, snuggling into me and getting both of us hot and bothered, then blamed me for making her late, did her make-up on the tube and didn't have enough time to eat a proper breakfast. She says tonight will be more of the same. These late nights are killing her. Artie cried when we left the house.

She kissed me when we went our separate ways, and said, Thank you for last night, like what I had done was special.

was injured, like Alan Lewis, and spent a period of several months convalescing in a wartime hospital on the Greek island of Lemnos.[88] What evidence do the poems themselves provide for this new supposition?

The most compelling evidence for this theory comes from the elegiac 'To the Poet', in which the Unknown Digger postulates an unnamed versifier, wondering aloud '*how buttered is his bread?*', and then accusing, in a bantering tone, the poet of '*under/minin' the depths of language/for the worthiness/of outhouse doors.*' Kathryn Hounslow maintains that the persona of the poem is calling the unnamed second poet a fake and an imitator, worthy of little more than toilet-wall graffiti, and most commentators have agreed with her.[89] In *Australia's Unknown Digger*, Max Whitlock assumes the second poet is a contemporary: 'The eponymous poet in "To the

---

88 See Chapters 4 and 5 in *From Busso to the Holy Land* (despite Curtin-Kneeling's less than heartwarming feedback, I still turn to his work for the most accurate overview of Alan's life), which contains a detailed overview of Lewis's time on the island. I told Em she needed a holiday. We needed a holiday. She was sitting outside smoking, Artie sniffing the rapidly dying flowers in the flowerbed at the back of the garden. The sun had dropped behind the chimneys of the houses opposite, and it was getting chilly.

I'm not sure I could take the time off work, she said, flicking the cigarette butt into the pile of mouldering leaves I'd raked up two weeks earlier and never removed.

Sandy beaches? Nothing to do all day but read?

Somewhere in mind? Artie came back, paws tiny and muddied, and she stopped him from jumping up on her. No, Artie, you're filthy!

Guess. I smiled. Greek salad and calamari?

She stopped scratching Artie's ears and gave me The Look. Lemnos? Seriously?

I shrugged.

That's not a holiday, that's a research trip.

Forget it then, I said, heading back inside. She stayed out with Artie for a few more minutes before coming back in.

Now, I'd be up for Mykonos. Or Corfu?

I dropped the subject. I might be able to get a grant for Lemnos, but Corfu would be taking the piss.

89 Hounslow, 'The Unknown Digger Revealed', pp. 21–22.

Poet" is Siegfried Sassoon, perhaps, or possibly Rupert Brooke'.[90]

---

90 Whitlock, *Australia's Unknown Digger*, p. 168. Whitlock uses this guess as the basis for his assertion that the Unknown Digger was transferred to the Western Front, crucially forgetting that Sassoon was nowhere near as well known as Brooke at the time. A little Wikipedia-ing could've told him that – sometimes it feels like I'm the only one willing to do the research. Last night Em and I were lying on the couch watching an old black-and-white movie when Em got a call – maybe nine o'clock, so not early. She paused the movie and answered in her work voice. I started shaking my head. She held out a hand like she would to Artie: No. Sit. Roll over. Play dead. Who's a good boy?

Uh huh, well, sometimes it doesn't have instructions, she said, glancing outside and miming a cigarette. Nope, no, of course not. A smile for me and she headed outside, Artie following by her feet. Boil the kettle. Yep. And then add a dash of salt. No, like a sprinkle. Do however much you want. Do more and you can have it for lunch. Oh yeah, is that tomorrow? She blew a smoke ring out into the night sky. So, you'll be gone afterward, too? Yep, until it's soft enough to eat. About ten minutes.

She crushed the half-smoked cigarette into the ashtray and came back inside. I tried to calm my breathing, but my heart was pounding in my chest. I picked Artie up and held him in my lap, ruffling his ears and getting him to nip at my fingers. I knew she was looking at me, ready to mouth an apology, but I didn't want to give her the satisfaction. I kept my head down.

Right. You're all set then. Just mix the sauce in when it's ready. When it tastes ready. She sighed. Take one out and try it! Artie jumped out of my lap and into Em's, looking back at me like a petulant child. Sure thing. No, it's no problem. I'm not busy.

I picked up the remote and pressed play, and the characters on screen laughed at a joke. Em swung her head toward the window, trying to muffle the sound with her hand.

Uhuh. See you then. She hung up. I stared straight ahead. Slowly, she reached across me for the remote, and hit pause. Artie snuffled around on the couch, his tiny nails scratching on the fake leather.

What was that? She sounded angry.

I couldn't be bothered feigning surprise. Why are you answering his calls? I tried to keep my voice level, but I was sure the croak on certain words would give me away. I was sitting on the precipice of crying.

He's my boss.

He calls you at nine o'clock? Doesn't he have friends?

He is my friend.

But the poem is not about Rupert Brooke, or indeed any of the modern poets. I believe that the poet in 'To the Poet' is the 'father of poetry', Homer himself, whose works were one of the few books available in the Lemnos Hospital Library.[91] One only needs to read a few lines further for the reference to become apparent:

where's the bleeding bog roll?
searching bloody soil,
doing all this for years
you've been doing shit all

'Searching ... for years' is an obvious reference to the *Odyssey*, while the repetition of 'blood' and 'bleeding' helps bring the point home. Crucially, 'all this/shit all', while a clever anagram, also tells us that the poet is well studied and long dead.

In Lewis's letters home we find similar classical references. As one of The University of Western Australia's most famous sons, Lewis's education record is easily obtainable. We know he studied the Greek myths as part of the first cohort to pass through the university.[92] His reference to his stay in Lemnos as his 'Greek odyssey' proves he remembered those lessons[93] but it was a fragment of a letter

---

My heart bubbled in my chest, and I took a second to try and steady myself. What did he want?

He wasn't sure how long to cook his pasta.

I turned my head aggressively to the right, aware of the melodrama, not caring. He doesn't know how? He's like fifty!

He's a busy guy. He doesn't normally cook for himself.

He can't read the packet? Like a normal person?

He knows I like to cook, so he wanted to check how I do it. What's your problem?

He's a cunt who can't cook pasta.

91 Pyke, *The Annotated Letters*, pp. 44, 221, and Curtin-Kneeling, *From Busso to the Holy Land*, p. 156.

92 Gordon Biggins, *A Short History of the University of Western Australia: From Irwin Street to Matilda Bay – Western Australia's Premier University and Its Famous Graduates*. Volume 1 of 6. Self-published, Perth, 1999, p. 446.

93 Curtin-Kneeling, *From Busso to the Holy Land*, p. 134.

to Porter, found among his writings and sadly never sent, written sometime before the regiment entered Jerusalem in December 1917, that categorically hammered the literary allusion home:

> *I will spend ten years working my way back to you, avoiding the siren call of the south, avoiding the war, avoiding living, to feel what we had for one more day.*[94]

Ten years? Avoiding wars? Avoiding the siren call of death? Obviously another direct reference to Odysseus's long journey home from Troy in Homer's epic *Odyssey*. In this light, the lines misquoted by academics take on a new meaning – rather than a teasing insult about poetry scrawled on outdoor dunnies, Lewis is referring to his own extended stay in the hospital's latrines, suffering from a bout of diarrhoea,[95] and the only company he had in those long hours, the Lemnos library's copy of Homer.[96] In Lewis's/the Unknown Digger's hands, '*the worthiness/of outhouse doors*' is one of the highest accolades a fellow poet could hope to receive. When viewed from a different angle, the meaning of a few simple lines can change with a few words, or an entire poem can morph into another completely different piece. Knowing the context, cynicism evolves into elation, humour is extracted from the bleakest of situations, and a new poem emerges from the rubble of discarded academia.[97]

---

94 Pyke, *The Annotated Letters*, p. 245. Ever the hopeless romantic. Yet another trait Alan and I have in common, these huge romantic gestures and sacrifices made for love. I pass by this little jewellery shop on my way to the tube, windows filled with diamonds and rubies. The price tags alone are enough to cause cardiac arrest. But I always stop to look at the engagement rings. There's one with a diamond, surrounded by blue sapphires, that I keep coming back to – blue like the sky back home, blue like the sea in Cape Town the way Em describes it, blue like I imagine the sea is on Lemnos. Perfect. Only need to keep putting away my university savings each month for another sixteen years and I might be able to afford it ...

95 Curtin-Kneeling, *From Busso to the Holy Land*, p. 155.

96 Pyke, *The Annotated Letters*, pp. 44, 221; and Curtin-Kneeling, *From Busso to the Holy Land*, p. 156.

97 Max Whitlock actually emailed me out of the blue one day a few weeks

Aside from being wonderfully romantic, Lewis's allusion in his letter to the *Odyssey* parallels a tendency observed in the poetry of the Unknown Digger to give the characters in the poems certain characteristics not unlike those in the ancient epics. I am not the first academic to have observed this. In her landmark article, 'The Unknown Digger Revealed', published in *The Australian Literary Review* in April 2003, Kathryn Hounslow argued for a former lecturer in English, Trooper Andrew Morrison, of the 2nd Light Horse, as the identity of the Unknown Digger. She based her argument on the abundance of literary references in the poems, and the fact that Morrison had published several poems under his own name in Australia before the war.[98] While entertaining, her theory started to take on water when it was pointed out that Trooper Morrison faked his teaching credentials to join the army, and had in fact been released from a long stint behind bars in rural Victoria a month before signing up. Furthermore, his 'previously published poems', when examined more closely, were little more than sexualised doggerel and caricatures of the popular forms of the day.[99] Despite being wrong in her main claim, Hounslow nonetheless made a valuable contribution by pointing out various instances where the Unknown

---

after the very first general ideas of this thesis were published in the article 'Comparing Language Choices in Diametric Data Packets' in *The Magazine of Australian Literature*. At that point I wasn't even sure who he was. His email consisted of ten words: *To the Poet = UD [Unknown Digger] on Western Front = can't be Lewis*. I got the feeling he was one of those older academics who isn't completely comfortable with email. And the Unknown Digger wasn't on the Western Front, and Lewis read Homer at university, and Max Whitlock hasn't published anything since Jennifer Hayden's 'On the Repressed Sexualities of the Unknown Digger', and Em and I are in love, so QED, motherfucker.

98 Hounslow, 'The Unknown Digger Revealed', pp. 101–140.

99 Howard Greene, 'Arguments Against "The Unknown Digger Revealed"' in *Australian Literary Journal*, December 2003, Issue 32, Volume 5, pp. 45–77. The weather has been so incredible recently – thanks global warming and the inevitable end of the world – but embracing the popular forms of the day, or whatever, we had a 'BBQ'. In a crowded Highbury Fields, after work, last night. What could possibly go wrong?

Digger obliquely or implicitly referenced the classics.[100] The most obvious allusions, such as the oft-quoted '*Tell me, O muse*' from 'Piccadilly Circus', have since been joined by less obvious references.[101] In 'The Mundaring Gift', the young protagonist is twice denoted by the epithet '*duckboard-harrier*': in the context of the poem, the young trooper is a message runner, but when contextualised, the obvious inference is the similar 'swift-footed' epithet employed by Homer for Achilles.[102]

Other poems reveal additional fresh information. 'The Beach' has often been assumed to refer to an unspecified Western Australian beach, and academics have argued for anywhere from Scarborough Beach down to Leighton in Fremantle, but once we recognise that

---

100 Splashed out on a bottle of warmish semi-sav, beef skewers, cheese and crackers, salad bits, and nibbles from the M&S Summer Selection. Found a spot, far away enough from the road to pretend we were in the English countryside, crammed in between the after-hours office workers and the girls sunbathing in their bras, tins of G&T perspiring by the magazines layered over their faces. I lit my foil barbie and poured myself a glass of wine. All around the field, like acne spots, were hundreds more of the same: everybody lighting their disposable barbecues.

101 What in sweet baby Jesus are those tiny foil fuckers? A foil baking tray full of charcoal is not a barbecue, it is an insult to my people. Almost a hate crime. Every supermarket I walk into, the aisles are full to the rafters with them – no wonder they can't play cricket and their soccer players fall over at the drop of a hat – they think a barbecue is disposable! An Aussie barbecue, a proper glorious wooden barbie, big as your car and covered in redback spiders, is a lifetime commitment, like a tattoo, or getting married, or having kids. Cheap, rainy-day, crumpet-scoffing, Queen-kissing bastards.

102 'Duckboard-harrier' was the trench name given to runners and messengers, after the long-distance runners of cross-country races, originally named after hares. Like Artie, I imagine, darting up to the sunbathers and barbecuing families, being shooed away by drunken shirtless louts, Em calling him back from halfway across the park. She was wearing an amazing rainbow-coloured sundress that swished around her knees in the grass. The skin on her chest was slick with sweat and Argon oil – she swears by the stuff. Artie jumped into my lap and licked my chin.

Well, isn't this a treat? She smiled as she sat down, as relaxed as I've seen her since the party. Amazing what a little sun can do for the spirit – why do we choose to live on this godforsaken wet puddle of an island?

Lewis wrote it in Lemnos, a reference to 'the south', which in most of the other poems is often correlated with a simplified means of referring to Australia, suddenly gains new significance.[103] A simple glance at a wartime map of Lemnos throws up many small beaches on the south of the island that could be the eponymous beach. The fact that indisputably supports this theory is the following line from the poem: '*behind the hills/the sun goes kipping*' which can only refer to the view of the sunset from a Lemnos beach, because, as any Western Australian sandgroper worth their salt will tell you: in the west, the sun sets over the sea.[104]

The far-fetched contrivances of earlier studies, with their Eastern States-centric mindsets and lack of geographical knowledge, led to the jumping-to of numerous conclusions, and assumed the group of poems written following Gallipoli contained references to, among others, the Western Front, Suez, Australia, or, in one memorably ridiculous journal article, a 'morbid fascination with the Bible'.[105]

---

103 Howard Greene, *Six Essays on the Australian Spirit*, p. 94. According to the 'instructions', once the 'barbecue' was fully ablaze, I should 'blow out the flames' and then proceed to cook the meat on the 'glowing coals'. I blew out the flames and thick sooty smoke enveloped us, like commandoes signalling for helicopter extraction. Artie started barking. I had sweat running down my back and dripping into my crack. Em fanned herself with one of those free magazines they hand out at tube stations. So hot.

104 Not hot-hot though, I said, thinking of home.

No, but you know. London hot.

London hot?

London thirty is hotter than Cape Town forty, swear to God.

How was work? I tried to fan the smoke away from us with my towel, Artie nipping at my heels, and succeeded in showering the dip with grass clippings. Em piled up a cracker with cheese and chutney and pretended not to notice.

It was fine. You know how hot it gets.

The Prof's office has air-conditioning and windows. The rest of us are housed in the Victorian-era basement, stuffed in like sardines with no windows, and, needless to say, no air-conditioning. Yeah, I knew.

105 L.L. Goodberry, 'The Christlike in the Unknown Digger', in *The Poetry and Literature Digest*, November 2007, Issue 45, Volume 34, pp. 46–58. Don't. Just don't.

But when we know Alan Lewis spent four months on the hospital island of Lemnos recovering from wounds before he was sent back to his regiment, the evidence for this extended period of recuperation becomes manifest throughout the poems.[106] Greene argues that 'based on the number of literary references in his poems, the Unknown Digger *must have* [my emphasis] studied the classics', which we know for a fact Alan Lewis did at The University of Western Australia.[107] All the available evidence points to one university-educated, Greek-myth reading, West Australian trooper being the author of these poems – and only Alan Lewis fits the bill.[108]

---

106 I placed the skewers onto the 'glowing coals' – grey and cracked, lumps of dried dog shit – and cut myself a wedge of brie. Em smiled at me across her plastic tumbler of wine.

Nice wine. She sounded tired. I noticed the smudged black outline of a FRAGILE stamp on her arm as she took another sip, the kind you'd stamp haphazardly on a box of wine glasses, or the male ego, or the concept of a British summer. Artie needed to pee, but we thought it best he didn't do it on the pale form of the heavily pregnant sunbather lying next to us, so Em took him for a lap of the park, while I kept an eye on the 'disposable BBQ' (I use the term oxymoronically, like the aforementioned 'British summer').

107 Greene, *Six Essays on the Australian Spirit*, p. 94. The skewers were burnt on one side, seared to the little metal grate with black tar and, trying to turn them, I accidentally touched the lava-like heat of the metal lining. My swearing woke the pregnant tanner, who gave me a dirty look, before taking a long swig from her third can of Pimm's and belching loudly.

108 Artie almost knocked me into the nuclear reactor as he bound back across the park and into my arms. I tried to protect him from touching the molten metal, and succeeded in knocking the open bottle of wine into the bowl of chips. Em lunged forward and saved the bottle before we lost too much, while Artie licked my ear. Fuck, sorry, I said. The heavily sunburnt pregnant lady tutted loudly. Em gave her The Look and the lady quickly turned away.

It's fine, she said, chips and wine – what's not to like?

'Crisps' over here, I said, gazing sadly at the blackened remains of the beef skewers. But we call them chips in Oz too. Two types: hot chips, or chips – that's all you need, right?

We smiled across the rug at each other, and the foolishness of the Brits. She piled another cracker high with brie and chutney.

How're the skewers? she said.

One had caught fire, filling the air with the acrid smell of burnt peppers as I tried to blow out the flame. Artie started barking in Em's lap, and wouldn't shut up until Em gave him a treat from her purse. Alistair's reading at this big conference next week – I nodded as she spoke, trying not to touch the sizzling, charred end of the skewer – in Paris.

That'll be nice, I said, the sad remains of what had once been a red onion disintegrating into ashes in the breeze as I tried to keep turning the skewers. Having the office to yourself for a couple of days.

Em didn't say anything for a while, and then when she did, her voice was slow and deliberate, like footsteps through broken glass: The Paris conference is a Really Big Deal.

I must have kept the bag of salad too close to the blistering heat of the barbie, because the salad leaves were starting to brown, and the fresh tomatoes were doing a passable impression of being sundried. Em took my hand and gave it a squeeze.

I carefully pulled the wooden sticks off the heat, suffering only minor third-degree burns in the process, and arranged them on our plates, alongside the wilted salad. We ate in silence for a minute.

I'm going to Paris, Em said, as I took a swig of wine.

Paris, France?

Matt, don't be like that.

I blinked. Something in my left eye twitched, sand under the eyelid, smoke from the barbecue. She wasn't smiling. I didn't think she was joking, but with South Africans you can never be sure. You're going to Paris?

Next week.

The skewers were inedible – bloody pink in the middle, gritty and black on the outside. Em gave some of hers to Artie, but he turned his nose up at it. Someone behind us was playing shitty rap music through the tinny speakers of their phone.

I bought another packet of crisps, I said, too quickly. Salt and vinegar. In the bag.

Em didn't move. I'm going to Paris, with Alistair.

I held back vomit in my mouth and forced myself to swallow bile. You can't go.

Excuse me?

You can't go.

Who the fuck are you to tell me what I can and can't do?

I pulled out the crisps, and in my haste to open them and get back to a semblance of normality, I ripped a long slit down the bag.

Are you crying? Em asked.

It's the smoke. The fucking barbecue.

I should go. Artie jumped up from where he'd been lying and growled at the smell coming from the burnt meat.

To Paris?

Now, she said, and stood up. But also to Paris.

Artie jumped up at her legs, his long nails leaving scratches on her skin.

Wait, don't leave. I'm sorry.

Small scatterings of cloud were beginning to pass in front of the sun, darkening the sky. The air chilled.

I messed up.

She didn't move. Artie whined by her feet. The shitty rap song finished and a shittier techno track started.

Please, I said, I bought marshmallows, and chocolate. I felt the grass under my calves reaching up and tickling tiny nails on my skin and wanted more than anything to scratch the skin until I drew blood. We can make s'mores.

Artie looked up at Em from the picnic rug with his huge wet eyes.

Artie says ok, we'll stay, she said, and sat back down.

Was it the s'mores?

More like the wine.

I smiled at her, and ruffled Artie's ears while he nipped at my burnt hand. I am sorry.

Don't ever tell me what I can and can't do, she said. My dad has been doing that since forever, and every ex-boyfriend I've ever had has tried. I will not be anyone's plaything.

Well, I said, not until tonight.

Oh hush, she said, and threw a soggy chip at my head. Artie was licking spilled wine off the picnic rug. Around us, people were gathering their bits and leaving. Em looked up at the clouds and shivered. I should have brought a jumper.

Come sit by the fire, I said, pulling the tray towards us. Fuckbastard McCunt! I pulled my hand back from the scorching tin. That's still hot, in case you were wondering.

The pregnant lady scoffed again and said, Really!, loud enough for us to hear. Em mock-laughed and asked if she could bum a cigarette. The look on the lady's face was priceless.

The first drops felt like spittle, and then we both looked up at the clouds and laughed, because of course, why wouldn't it rain tonight? Artie barked as the pregnant lady picked up her empty cans and ran across the park. The raindrops fell hot and heavy on our faces. We looked at each other and smiled, and I pulled another bottle of wine from the plastic bag. My place or yours? I said, as the rain fell harder, plastering my hair to my forehead, sizzling on the barbecue.

Mine, Em said, I've got a bathtub. She stood up and attempted to get Artie into his harness.

I kicked the foil tray into the plastic bag, which duly melted, hot coals tumbling out onto the grass. We both started laughing; silly, can't-stop-yourself laughing, at the stupidity of it.

That's what we get for trying to have a barbie in London, I said.

A braai, she said, in her gorgeous South African twang.

Please tell me you don't use disposable barbecues in Cape Town, too?

She gave me The Look, and we laughed some more, running across the park towards the tube station, Artie nipping at our heels.

Where the barbecue had been sitting was a perfect black rectangle of charred grass.

What a joke.

SOMEWHERE IN THE MIDDLE EAST. MAY 1917.

Each morning they wake to a new desert. Shifting dunes, like rolling waves, rearrange themselves in the dark.

They hate the dust more than they hate the Abduls. The Abduls are following orders, just as they follow theirs. The dust obeys no man. Every breath of wind, every movement of horse, digger or vehicle, envelops them in a white cloud. Dust is the one constant in their lives. It finds its way into everything: the bully beef, the sickly tea, the rare cups of black coffee, the water pulled from wells, the rarely-spied rum, baked into the bread they haggle from the villagers, their hair, their eyes, the stitching of their shirts, the sweat patch on their backs, the leather of the saddles, the wet corners of their Walers' eyes, the foamy flecks of spit by their mouths, the coarse hair of their manes, the roughness of their coats, their shit, their fodder, and the cracks of their saddle-sore arses, the peaks of their caps, the folds of a makeshift pillow, the waking hours, the writing hours, the eating hours, the downtime, the endless ride, the dreams at the end of the day.

They hunt the Turk, but they can still respect him.

They hate the dust.

~

My love, another day has dawned, red sunned and sandy, and I have opened my notebook to a page of your handwritten declarations. Half asleep, I thought perhaps you had visited me in the night and left a note on leaving. I hoped for your kiss on my cheek, a lingering scent, a hair, as proof, laid out upon my pillow. No such luck.

I write another letter I know you will never reply to. Another hopeful missive sent out into the world in the foolish belief that you might find it within yourself to forgive me. How many times must I ask for your compassion? I know, in the deepest recesses of my heart, that you felt the same strong feelings for me as I did for you. One cannot create those feelings. One cannot imagine them.

If I could, I would leave camp, ride out this morning and make my way back to you. Cross deserts, swim oceans. If I could, I would sit you down and explain. The life I left. The life I want. You would see that none of it matters anymore. There is nothing for me back there. There is only you. There is only us. I will spend ten years working my way back to you, avoiding the siren call of the south, avoiding the war, avoiding living, to feel what we had for one more day.

If I could, I would change it all. I would have told you on that first morning, through the pain, and let fate take its course. That is how confident I am in us. That is how confident I am in our love.

I cannot do this without you. I thought I knew love, I thought I knew purpose, I thought I knew the world. And then you entered my life, and I discovered a world ten thousand times larger than I imagined. Share it with me.

Yours, pleadingly.

Week two of R&R behind the lines, and this morning they've ridden into Tel el Fara, alongside men from every other regiment in the brigade. Some of them he hasn't seen since Egypt.

The stallholders hawk their cheap souvenirs in limited English. The smells of small-town life drift in the air. Animals and sweat. Raw meat. A woman walks down the road toward him, covered head to toe, her face peeking out, like a porthole on a ship. She keeps her eyes on the ground, doesn't respond to the whistles and calls from the men on horseback. As she passes him, she looks up, and for a second they lock eyes. Intense black pupils, judging him. Eyes like Nancy's. She melts into the crowd. As the roads converge, they meet more diggers, headed the same way. He barks a 'G'day' across the street to a fellow officer from the 8th, but he doesn't hear, walking on through the natives without a backward glance. They're all making their way to the same place anyway. Through the packed bazaar and down toward the murky waters of the nearby river.

As the stench of the river grows, the crowds drop off, until the soldiers are humping along alone. At the place, he orders the men to halt, and they slide from the saddle and stretch their legs. There is a wooden spar reserved for them, and two of the new recruits are press-ganged into acting as stewards, sorting out food and water for the horses while the rest of the men scatter, fanning out among the congregation, searching for mates. Kelly shakes her head in a long whinny as he hands the reins to the trooper. They'll need to be ready to ride at a moment's notice.

The horses sorted, he wanders among the crowd of assembled diggers, looking around for anyone he might know. Faces look familiar. Names elude him.

Right about now, Nancy would be doing her morning rounds, checking in on each of her patients, fluffing pillows, doling out pills and brightening the faces of the sick. Right about now, he would lean across and pinch her as she leant over the bed next to his, and she'd slap his hand away. To anyone watching, it might look perfunctory. To him, it would be as good as a kiss, enough to get him through the hours until she came around. In the hospital the days were measured in Nancy's clipped tones, her tutting and teasing, the touch of her icy fingers. He'd invent reasons to call her – pain in his legs, bad dreams, or terrible headaches. She knew, of course, but she'd roll him over nonetheless and massage the scarred muscles. Right about now, she'd catch his eye before she left, her steps echoing down the corridor.

The first event is a simple sprint, alongside the river, down and around the waiting men, finishing back where it started. The 10th volunteers four runners, three of the new recruits and one of the remaining Gallipoli veterans. He takes his place among the assembled crowd, watching the men line up, their bodies shaking with nervous excitement. The diggers around him yell encouragement, the crowd threatens to push forward. He wishes Nancy was holding his hand, like he's wished every day for the past year. She'd put up with the men's comments and give it back as hard in return. Nancy has a mouth on her like a drover, but English – his constant contradiction. He's learnt to drown out the noises around him, to focus inside, on memories of what he considers his new home: Lemnos with Nancy. He gets headaches when it's too loud, around the campfire at breakfast, on the beginning of a ride, when the men have the energy to talk, on days like today when the excitement of the unusual bubbles to the surface. He's learnt to excuse himself, to politely drop away, somewhere quieter, where he can hear himself think. Where his thoughts have room to bloom.

'You ain't running?' A hand claps him on the shoulder, pulling him back to the race; the crowd, the smell of the river. Nugget slaps him on the back and laughs, 'Al? Anyone home?'

'Sorry. Daydreaming.'

'I'll say.'

With a bang, the sprinters race down the track, the whooping and hollering of the crowd following their progress. The water in the river rolls by, dark brown and frothy.

'What're you thinking?' Nugget says.

That maybe he should find a way to injure himself, not too badly, but bad enough to put him out of action for a few months. A fall from Kelly. Enough time for him to make his way back to her, to put himself out of the firing line, maybe for good. A bullet through his hand. To give himself enough time with her to put things right. Running away, they'll say. Running towards something, he says to himself.

'Thinking of her.'

'You old softy.'

'Proper ro-fucking-mantic.'

'Rose is a lucky woman.'

He grimaces. The roar of the crowd is circling back to their position. Soon the runners will barrel around the corner, pushing for the line. The men behind him surge forward, knocking them, hands in the back and screaming by his ear. He can't hear what Nugget says next.

A young bloke from the 9th wins by a whisker, ahead of one of their boys. The runners flop, exhausted, into the dust, until the crowd rushes forward to lift them up. The winner is unceremoniously dunked in the brown sludge of the river, in his full kit.

Nugget turns back to him with a broad smile plastered on his leathery mug. 'I meant, what are you thinking you'll enter? You know the men will want to see you compete.'

'I don't know.'

'It's half the fun of a day like this,' Nugget says, giving him what he must think are puppy-dog eyes. 'Do it for the boys.'

He's written her letters, with dwindling regularity, for the last year. Through the Turkish attacks at Romani, through the shitshow of Magdhaba, and the failed charge at Rafa two weeks later. Early in the new year he even sent her a figurine, carved with his knife in his downtime, from the hard, dry wood they use for the campfires. It was meant to be her, peering down at her hands, but it looked more like a snowman, the body too round, the arms unrecognisable.

While the other men lounge in the sun, naked save for their slouch hats and the rifles by their sides, he can be found in his tent, poring over his papers. Every week, when the post rolls around, he has a letter from Rose, or Ma, or both. Every week, he sits down in the closest shade and forces out a reply, writing about the same events, asking after their health, promising to write more often. Every week, when the post catches them up, he waits for a letter from her and comes away disappointed.

Next up, an all-out sprint on horseback, with so many entrants they need to run five heats. The winners and runners-up advance to the final. Technically, he should be forbidding the men any exchange of money, and shutting down the entrepreneurs taking bets, but he turns a blind eye, preferring to maintain the peace. Silence is golden. He hovers about near the other officers, not talking, laughing when he should, answering their questions with as few words as possible; a grunt here, a nod. By the end of the day they'll have forgotten he was even there.

He enters himself in one of the heats. Not that he'd ever tell anyone, but he's quietly confident. Kelly might not be the fastest horse in the regiment, but no other trooper has a bond quite like theirs. Kelly feels like his last physical remnant of home, of Red, of a time before dust and sand and Turkish scouts. Of Rose, when it comes down to it. She'd been assigned to him in Egypt, a few weeks before the whole regiment was demounted and taught trench tactics. Before Alan and Red had fallen in with the mouthy Irishman, even. They'd spent enough time together on long marches, on endless parades, back and forth in front of one passing dignitary or another, to grow close. Kelly is his closest friend.

And Kelly was the first to greet him on his return from Lemnos, before Nugget or the Major, or any of the boys. She tossed her head and ran to him across the makeshift paddock the horses were being kept in. He tossed her the core of his apple, and like him, she ate the whole thing. He felt like he had to rebuild his friendships with everyone, except Kelly.

She can tell something is up as he walks her to the starting line – a ragged scratch in the dirt. She twists forward and back beneath him, champing, but soothes when he places a hand low down on her shoulder. He leans in close, whispers in her black ears. When the starting gun fires, she bursts forward, and he finds himself in the lead. He kicks his spurs into her flanks, pushing her forward, pulling away from the larger horses of the men from the 8th. Down the back straight, the bigger horses gain on him, and by the penultimate corner, he can feel the wind from their whips. As they slow past the bustling crowd and turn toward the final stretch, he thinks he hears Nugget's lilt above the other voices in the crowd.

'Ride 'er like she's Rose, Al.'

The men snigger.

But on the final corner, he finds he's too far out to make the turn. He's seen the other riders, in the earlier heats, push their horses up the bank, hoping the lighter sand there will hold. But he can't risk it. Not with Kelly. He'd never forgive himself. He slows, and gives her the space she needs. He finishes third, out of the running for the final, but not disappointed. The men clap him on the shoulder as he dismounts. Kelly stamps her feet, and gives him a look, like they could have won if they'd wanted. He pulls her head down and stares into her black eyes, bright against the white stripe that runs across her face.

'Alright, but I'd rather you didn't break a leg.'

She blows hot air into his face and shakes her head. He pats her fondly as he passes her to the steward.

Nugget appears from somewhere to his right, thumps him on the back, with sweat running from the blistered skin of his nose. He holds a small wad of notes and smiles like a fool.

'Close call,' Nugget says, waving the wad in his face, 'but thanks, Lieutenant!'

'You bet on me coming third?'

'No, mate. Just knew you wouldn't risk Kelly on a game, like.'

Nugget is smiling the shit-eating grin that has started its fair share of pub fights. Nugget swears it makes him look rakish. Alan hasn't told him it makes him look like a letch. 'So you knew I wouldn't win?'

Nugget slaps him hard on the shoulder. 'I bet on it!'

Nugget enters the sack race, which seems appropriate – the potato sack pulled nearly to his chin. He wins by six feet, that same idiot grin on his face, bounding through the dirt like a suntanned kangaroo. He collects winnings from no less than three men, earning himself more than a month's wages.

'How could you be sure you'd win?' Alan asks.

'I'm Irish,' Nugget winks, 'we know potatoes.'

They sit out the tug-of-war and the tent pegging, making their way back toward town for a bite to eat from one of the street-side stalls. After months of bully beef, every mouthful tastes vibrant and multicoloured. His stomach churns. They're about to head back when they pass what must be a local watering hole. A bearded Arab out front offers them tea. Nugget looks at him eagerly.

'I can't,' Alan says, 'some of us are still on duty.'

'C'mon, sir.' Nugget pulls the wad of notes from his pocket and heads inside. 'My shout.'

He follows reluctantly, but doesn't stop him.

Inside, they sit down at a table, and the Arab places two warm beers down in front of them. Already, there are flies milling on the surface. Across Sinai, they've become experts at whisking the flies out of their drink and gulping down the liquid. Any available water source buzzes with insects in seconds.

After a sip, he relaxes. He hasn't had a proper drink since their last bivouac outside one of the larger dusty cities. Back on Lemnos, when Nancy proclaimed him well enough to drink, but before the doctors had got around to sending him back, Nancy had snuck a bottle of red wine into the ward. She'd pulled the privacy screen around his bed and they'd passed the bottle between them, tasting hints of each other around the rim. Before Skyros, before he'd messed it all up. When returning to the regiment had seemed a fragile enough excuse for their private celebration – when he'd thought they might have a future beyond Brooke's grave and the sandy beaches.

'Where are you, Al?' Nugget has finished his beer, and orders them another round. He's drunk a few sips of his own warm mug.

'What do you mean?'

'I mean, you've been a bit off recently.' Nugget glances about the dishevelled room, eyeing up the carpets on the walls, the dirt in the air. 'Well, longer than that, even.'

Alan downs two thirds of his glass in one long gulp, placing the mug back on the table, avoiding the question.

'Not gonna lie, you've been a right moody bastard since Red.'

The Arab places two more beers down on the table and takes away the empty glasses. Alan raises his glass, offering up a wordless cheer. Nugget picks up his own glass, and they toast. Nugget doesn't look at him.

'Bad luck not to look when you toast,' he says, but Nugget ignores him.

'Sometimes I think they sent the wrong bloke back to Perth.' Nugget drinks, the dirty foam settling on his upper lip, the black dot of a fly struggling in his white moustache.

'What's that meant to mean?'

'Just saying.'

'You wish Red was here instead of me?'

Nugget doesn't say anything, just pushes the bowl of brown mush they're sharing towards his side of the table. A blur of flies rises as one from the bowl as it moves.

'You think it's my fault he was injured?'

Nugget looks up at him, surprise in his eyes. 'No. Red knew the odds. We're all playing the game until our turn.'

He feels stupid for saying anything. The Arab bustles around their table, spouting his guttural language. Nugget waves him off.

'What happened out there, Al?'

'What do you mean?'

'I mean, I see the way you wait for the post. I see you writing in your little book and never sending anything. I see you, Al.'

He's finished his second beer, and orders another round without checking with Nugget. He heads out the back of the bazaar to piss against a wall, the brown clay of the walls stained with the hot stream. The beers are on the table when he gets back, and Nugget glances at him expectantly.

'Nothing happened, Nug.'

'You know I don't believe you.'

He can see he is going to have to give him something – Nugget can be tenacious in his insistence, a pitbull gnawing on a bone. 'I suppose ...' Nugget is watching him intently. 'You ever read the Greek legends, Nug?'

'The fuck do you think?'

'Well, there's all these heroes, see, princes and warriors and whatnot.'

'Sure.' Nugget takes a long sip, but his eyes don't leave Alan's.

'And they're all written down in these old poems.'

'The *Oliad*, I know. What's your point?'

'I guess, I thought that's what it would be like. This. Right and wrong.' He motions around the room, from the dusty floor to the sweat stains on their uniforms, and sighs dramatically. 'But Red can't walk, and I'm so fucking sick of bully.'

'That's it?' Nugget eyes him across his glass, the beer at his lips.

'That's it,' he lies, and finishes his beer.

'You know anything you write in that little book, you can say to me, right?'

'Let's go.' He rises, his chair scraping as he stands.

'No secrets, Al.'

'Let's go.'

Nugget pays, and they walk back out into the street, turning back toward the river, the cheering of the diggers leading them forward. It's later than he thought. His legs are unsteady underneath him. The dark-skinned locals are watching him, judging. The beer has gone straight to his head.

'Nug, wait.' He says, and he's on his knees, spraying beer and chewed food into the dust. The burn of stomach acid. Spit dangling from his lips, and Nugget's hand on his back. He needs Nancy – the sweet smell of her hair, the cool touch of her hands. The flies settle on the sides of his mouth. Nugget helps him to his feet, but he brushes him off.

'I'm fine,' he says, head spinning.

'No, mate, you're not.'

~

My love. The last week has been spent in a rest camp behind the lines, recovering as best we can, tending to the horses and the men's spirits. It has been sorely needed. After a month on the line, one forgets what ordinary life is like – all that matters is keeping your horse alive and waking to the sound of the bugle.

I would have written sooner, but I spent the first two days sleeping, and the past three eating. I'm not sure you would recognise me anymore. In another time, I would have delighted in teasing you about returning home as dark as an Arab, smelling of horse, perpetually suntanned. You could keep me in the barn with the dogs, and let me out to run through the fields, and feed me bully beef through a hole in the wall.

Ma writes and tells me Red is doing well, though unable to walk without assistance or properly understand where he is. I have tried to write to him, but understand if my letters have gone unnoticed. Perhaps you could read them to him? I'm sure the sound of your voice would cheer him considerably.

I have had a dream recently, recurring, where I arrive home, and step off the boat in Fremantle to your waiting arms, the war a distant memory. I hope it proves foretelling, I don't believe the Jackos can withstand us much longer.

On Wednesday, we had a whole Brigade sports day in a small market town nearby. I can proudly state that the 10th outdid themselves in skill and panache, and were considered the eventual winners by all I spoke to afterward. Nugget performed valiantly, helping himself to a tidy share of winnings throughout. His finest moment may have come toward the end of the day, when he fell from his horse in a bout of horseback wrestling, and managed to break his fall in a large pile of fresh manure. A most splendid day was had by all.

I feel I am babbling, and would hardly be upset if you failed to make it this far. I have forgotten how to speak. Three pages of writing, you will despair, and not a word of it legible. Tomorrow we return to the line.

Yours, obediently.

~

They arrive back at camp late in the evening. The horses are tired and the men have lost all sense of decorum or propriety. It is like herding sheep, ordering one group of men to tend to the horses, another to fetch water, a third to start a fire. It's like graduation day at university, or the changing room before a grand final; the nervous excitement of children waiting expectantly for affirmation. He collapses into his bedroll long after night falls, and barely has time to dream before the bugle calls reveille and his tired eyes spring open once more.

They are to ride out at 0700 hours, after bathing in the river and forcing down a breakfast of Nugget's burnt porridge. As they are about to leave, a mail transport arrives from the depot, and he decides to let the men read before they ride off to their new coordinates.

There are two letters for him, one from Rose, and one in a cool, cream envelope in a scrawled hand he doesn't recognise. He holds the paper for a long time before he reads it, sensing her presence, imagining her sitting down to write it, between shifts, with the sun setting over the island out the dormitory window. She has been thinking of him. He has the proof in his hands.

Lieutenant Lewis, she writes. *I should have written you sooner.*

He can see the sun in her writing, the olive branches in the loops of her letters, the Greek heroes frolicking in the shallows of the blotted ink. He is in love with her handwriting, her thoughts, the image of her hands folding the paper and sliding it into the envelope, running her pink tongue over the seal, his name repeating in her head as she writes. He doesn't want to read any further, he doesn't need to.

I should have written when I first found out, but I was angry at you. I didn't want you to know. I am back in England, and against my better judgement, Father has persuaded me to write. You have an obligation, now. You have a reason to survive.

Her writing gets messier the further he reads, rattier, distracted. Like she can't bring herself to write what she's writing.

She writes, in a scrawl at the bottom of the page, *Her name is Harriet. She has your curls. She is your daughter.*

She signs off without warning, a bomb going off in the bottom right-hand corner, *Nancy*, and he closes the letter. When he stands to gather the men, his legs give out. He jumps in the saddle before his body can fall apart, and they ride further than they would normally. He doesn't want to stop. He doesn't want time to think.

~

The games have slowed down as they return to the river, though the competition between regiments turns fierce as the evening wears on. Rule-keeping grows notably lax. At one point, he is forced to break up a fight between two close friends, barracking for different men in the final of the horseback wrestling. As the horses wheel in the dirt, the crowd blurs, messy around the edges – breaking off into small groups of friends, troopers napping in the sun, bottles of wine passed around right under his nose, knowing Lieutenant Lewis won't say a thing.

In one corner of the field a large group of men stand in a rough circle, distracted by something on the ground. He saunters over, and pushes through the fringe to discover the entertainment. A small, round arena has been constructed, dug into the ground, walls made from shirts, bridles, whatever is hanging around. Two wicker baskets are overturned on opposite sides of the shallow pit.

'Alright, sir, is there a problem?' A trooper he doesn't know stands in the circle, holds his slouch hat in his hands, full of ripped and faded notes.

'No problem. Just curious.'

'Yes, sir. Thanks.'

The man nods and passes the hat around the crowd, and when all bets have been placed, steps out of the ring. The men hush in anticipation. He hasn't moved. The men beside him hold their breath as one as the trooper places a hand over each basket.

Nugget is at his right shoulder. He doesn't know how long he's been standing there, or if he's been talking, if he's expected to respond. Nugget's got a queer look about him, eyeing him up.

'Didn't think this'd be up your alley, Al.'

'What is it?'

A smile floods Nugget's face.

'Legs or Tails?'

'What does that mean?'

The trooper lifts the baskets simultaneously. A large desert scorpion twitches where the right basket had been. From the left basket scurries forth the largest spider he's ever seen.

'Tarantula,' whispers Nugget, 'as dead cert as you can get.'

He looks at the two animals. The tarantula is larger, but covered in a soft fuzz. The scorpion has huge pincers and a deadly looking spiked tail. Its body is ridged and armoured, metallic looking. It is three times the size of the scorpions back home.

'No way. The scorpion has to win, surely.'

Nugget looks across at him, a smile spreading across his face.

'Care to make it interesting?'

He looks back at the animals. The tarantula attempts to climb over a shirt to safety, but one of the troopers pokes it back with a long stick. The scorpion scuttles forward.

'Sure.' He never bets, hasn't his whole life. Never joined in on the long card games aboard the *Mashobra*, never throws away his pay in the local towns. Lieutenant Lewis sits and watches. Stays silent. You're gambling with your life, Rose had said when he told her he'd signed up, but it hadn't seemed like a wager then. It was justified. Nancy had loved to stalk the ward throwing out cigarette boxes, telling them they were more likely to be killed by rotting teeth and disease than the bombs and bullets of the Turks. Easy for her to say, from the safety of the hospital. She's not putting her life in any danger. He's never gambled. Not with money, at least. But then he's never been offered such a guaranteed result. He can picture the scorpion stinging the spider repeatedly between the eyes from a safe distance, emerging unscathed. 'One month's wages, and loser tends both horses.'

Nugget breathes out.

'Too much?' Alan teases.

'Ah, fuck it. Bring it on.' Nugget spits into his hand and they shake.

The animals are circling each other in the makeshift pit, sizing each other up. Lightning fast, the scorpion shoots forward, crushing one of the tarantula's legs in a pincer, tearing the furry limb off with an audible crunch, and then retreating. The spider staggers for a second or two, then regains balance. The scorpion discards the leg.

He glances across at Nugget and smiles. There's a dark patch of sweat blooming on the back of Nugget's shirt.

The scorpion shoots forward again, and grabs another of the furry legs in a jagged pincer. The spider wriggles, threatening to throw the scorpion onto its back through sheer size. The hooked tail extends back, and once, twice, three times, the venomous barb stabs into the gleaming black eyes.

It's all over. He whoops with joy into the night sky, surprising himself with his enthusiasm. He doesn't know if he's happier to be right, or for Nugget to be wrong.

He's expecting the tarantula to topple over, curl up with its legs in the air, but it doesn't. Quicker than he can catch, the spider is hovering over the scorpion's armoured abdomen, bobbing up and down multiple times, long fangs dripping. Then silence, both animals unmoving.

The spider limps away. Injured, but alive. Which is more than he can say for the scorpion. The spider's fangs have made short work of the hard armour on its back, ripping through the thick body, revealing a dark, greyish ooze. The tail continues to twitch for another thirty seconds.

'No rush on those winnings, mate,' says Nugget as he pushes in for a closer look at the carnage, 'but my horse likes carrots. And he can be a right impatient lout.'

Alan hadn't realised he was holding his breath. The air tastes old.

They release the tarantula back into the scrub before returning to camp.

CHAPTER 5: Further original evidence from the campaign in the Middle East demonstrating an Alan Lewis authorship of the Unknown Digger poems: The Lost Years as a source for contiguous postulation.

Past studies of the Unknown Digger's poetry have assumed his death came relatively early in the timeline of the war, either on the fields of the Western Front, or during the campaign in the Middle East (some arguing for a moment during the defence of the Suez Canal in 1916, and others arguing for a later date, around the first unsuccessful attack on Gaza in March 1917).[109] Certainly, no previous academic has argued, as I am about to do, that the Unknown Digger survived as long as Alan Lewis, who died in September 1918, a full year after even the most far-fetched theories.[110] How can we consider Alan

---

109 See Susan Freedland, Max Whitlock, Howard Greene, et al. All are worth considering, though there is still no general consensus. Em's off to Paris tomorrow, catching the Eurostar early in the morning, so I went round to hers tonight to say bye. I'm not allowed pets in my apartment, so Artie is staying with Em's friend Sam. For the first time since we bought him we had the place to ourselves. Em made dinner (roast chicken, asparagus and lemon, side salad) and we finished a bottle of wine.

Want me to stay? I said, when the credits on the terrible Johnny Depp film rolled. I've got a tute tomorrow, but my boss is away. I did an over-the-top wink and smiled, but Em missed it.

Nah, you should go.

Ouch.

She gave me a plastic bag of leftovers, and ushered me to the door. I felt like a sheep in a sheepdog trial.

110 For far-fetched, see Whitlock or Goodberry, or me, hoping to stay the night. Hey, I said as I was leaving, it'll be fine. You'll be fine.

I know.

If you feel uncomfortable, say something.

I will.

And call me if anything happens. She rolled her eyes at me. Anything, ok? I pulled her into a bear hug. If I can get to Sloane Square at four in the morning, I can get to Paris.

Why do you have to do that? Her voice was all scratchy as she pulled away.

Do what?

I told you to drop it.

Lewis the rightful author of the poems, if his death comes so much later than previous academics have theorised? To understand how Lewis's death works as yet another factor in proving his authorship, we must first examine the existing theories.[111]

In her otherwise excellent *The Mystery of the Unknown Digger*, Susan Freedland works her way through the poems with a fine-tooth comb, searching for clues as to their authorship, context, themes, allusions and wider meaning.[112] According to Freedland, the final poem written by the Unknown Digger contains obvious references to the Suez conflict, and, she writes, 'since there are no more poems written after this one, it seems probable the Unknown Digger was killed in the skirmishes surrounding the defence of Suez'.[113] Hers is an intensive, judiciously observed argument, reinforced by readily discernible substantiation. She is, regrettably, wrong.

Freedland argues that the singularly identifiable contextual clues in the final Unknown Digger poem 'Bully Beef', the humorous ode to the basic ration that fed most of the men fighting on the frontline throughout the war, point to the author being stationed in or around the Suez area at the time of his death. The pivotal lines, for her, occur during the fourth stanza:

---

111 She gave me a quick peck on the cheek and said she'd try and message if she could, and then started to shut the door on me. Hey, I said, I love you.
I know, she said, as she closed the door. And then, I love you, too.

112 Freedland, *The Mystery of the Unknown Digger*. An invaluable aid to my own research, if only to prove that the established theories are easily debunked. Had an interesting email from Jennifer Hayden recently, while I'm on the subject: *Hey Matt, it's nothing personal. Keep doing good work, and I'm sure you'll do great things in the future. J.* Not entirely sure what that means. Em hasn't called or messaged yet, but I assume they got into the hotel ok – they've got adjoining rooms, so I told Em to make sure the door between them is kept locked at all times. It's not that I'm worried about her, Em knows how to handle herself, it's more that I don't know what I can do to help from over here. I feel completely neutered.

113 Freedland, *The Mystery of the Unknown Digger*, p. 204. Had an email from Max Whitlock, of all people, that simply read: *Now you know how I feel. Sucks, doesn't it?* Poor guy seems to have completely lost it. No idea what he's on about, but then I never really understood his argument anyway. Still not convinced he knows what emails are.

Float me down the sea toward the sun –
Put a fork in me, cobber. I'm done.[114]

Freedland argues that '*float me down the sea*' must 'refer to the Suez Canal, where the Light Horse regiments were fighting at the time. As the Unknown Digger's final poem, it follows that the man died in the defence'.[115] One can hardly deny that this theory plays into my hypothesis: Lewis returned to his regiment at Suez, and was certainly, as his letters home show – after several years away from family and loved ones – extremely tired of the whole ordeal and ready to return to Australia. However, as is common knowledge, Lewis lived for almost two more years. Freedland must be incorrect somewhere in her assumption.[116]

Howard Greene believes that 'the evidence suggests' that there were several poems written after the defence of Suez, and after 'Bully Beef', which would prove that the Unknown Digger was alive longer than Freedland's stated date.[117] Greene identifies the final poem

---

114 Cooked myself steak and oven chips – still no word from Em, but I knew she'd be super busy minding the Prof. I'm not worried. Figured I'd get some more work done, so went online to read the latest issue of *Australian Literary Journal*, and nearly threw up my dinner. Jennifer Hayden has stitched me up, royally.

115 'Those Who Would Be King: The Next Steps in Identifying the Unknown Digger', by Jennifer Hayden in the most recent issue of *Australian Literary Journal* (Issue 6, Volume 70, April 2019), is a 60-page condemnation of everything I am currently killing myself to achieve. Outright attacks against my working thesis, mentions of me and Alan Lewis, by name, along with repudiations of my last article, my current work and future job prospects, and even my honours thesis back in Perth. Complete radio silence from Paris.

116 Fuuuucccccckkkkkk.

117 I've called Em sixteen times, left ten voicemails, and sent about thirty messages. She's still not answering. I don't know what to do. Do I email Jennifer and ask her to retract her comments? Do I need to respond somehow, with my own article? I keep hearing her question over and over in my head: 'The very idea of Alan Lewis as the Unknown Digger is laughable – who should we nominate next, Ned Kelly? Or Skippy?' (p. 33) Where the fuck is Em?

written by the Unknown Digger as 'Percute Velociter'.[118] Hayden hypothesised that 'Percute Velociter' was written around the end of 1915, while the Unknown Digger was stationed in Gallipoli, because of its placement within the manuscript, surrounded by other poems more implicitly referencing the actions of the Gallipoli campaign.[119] Greene argues, however, that 'it was actually written around the beginning of 1917, after the Anzac charge at Rafa, two weeks after the final decisive victory in the defence of the Suez Canal'.[120]

---

118 Message from Em, finally: *Sorry, Matt – big day & bigger night. Don't take JH personally. You rock. Speak 2moro? Xxx* And then one of those smiley faces with the heart eyes emojis, which we all know doesn't mean anything concrete. Don't take it personally, when my last ten years work is being eviscerated on an international scene? Em's message came in at about 3am, so I woke up to it, but she hasn't replied to my new messages. I couldn't eat anything this morning – the very thought of vegemite on toast made me feel sick. Em's probably eating Parisian croissants and European delicacies with her big sunglasses on, sipping espresso.

119 'Alan Lewis was a remarkable soldier, and certainly a brave man, but nothing in his military record or civilian life points towards a career in the literary arts: unfinished degrees, unremarkable letters home, and a penchant for volunteering himself and his men for extra duties do not equate to literary heroism' and 'the Victoria Cross is not the same thing as the Nobel Prize in Literature' and 'poetry can come from unexpected quarters, and appear in the most undistinguished of forms, but unfortunately for Matthew Denton, the idea of Alan Lewis writing the poems I discovered in 1995 is absurd' and 'I'd be amused by Denton's claim if I wasn't so saddened by the fact that he seems genuinely convinced by his inaccuracies': Jennifer Hayden and the remains of my academic career, ladies and gentlemen (pp. 1, 2, 4–60, etc.).

120 Greene, *Six Essays on the Australian Spirit*, p. 213. Em called and helped me get some perspective.

Don't listen to it, she said. Don't read it, don't respond to it, don't worry about it.

I feel sick, I said.

I didn't tell her about the half a bottle of cheap red wine I'd bought from the offie and started drinking at ten o'clock. Or the three packets of Polish pretzels.

Ali says it'll all blow over and once you publish and prove her wrong, she'll be biting her tongue.

'Percute Velociter' is a fairly simple – by the Unknown Digger's standards – sonnet, calling on soldiers and '*all men in love's trenches*' to pursue love without delay, quite literally, to strike, and strike swiftly.[121] Greene argues that 'Percute Velociter' was written toward the end of 1916, while the Light Horse rode across the biblical sands of the Sinai, following the disastrous retreat at Gallipoli and the battles of the Suez Defence. Greene's evidence for the later writing of 'Percute Velociter' amounts to two vital lines: in the fifth line of the sonnet, '*farewell, our valiant lies*', which Greene argues must be a reflection on the events of Gallipoli, rather than a contemporaneous exclamation, and in the seventh line of the poem, which ends: '*bring them back to us, the harbour cries*' which Greene argues – rather effectively, it must be said – is a reference to the Egyptian harbour of Port Said, an important battleground in the defence of the Suez Canal.[122] The cunning wordplay in the poem equates the anthropomorphised 'harbour cries' into the historical location of Port Said.

Greene argues that the Unknown Digger was still alive and writing in Christmas 1916 and into 1917, but died in May 1917. His estimate

---

How's Paris? I rolled over on my bed. I miss you, you know.

I have to go, Matt. I could hear someone laughing in the background. She hung up.

121 Greene, *Six Essays on the Australian Spirit*, p. 215. I emailed Jennifer Hayden: *What the Ken Oath, Jennifer? You couldn't have told me you disagreed with my findings after one of the 52 separate emails I sent you for corrections and advice? What's with the personal attacks? I can't believe I thought we were friends! What made you such a turn-dog? Get regimentally reduced.*

Probably a mistake to send it from my uni account but I made sure I didn't swear, so it wouldn't get flagged up by the filters.

122 Taking Greene's findings into account, 'Percute Velociter' becomes a socio-political statement on the foolishness of war and the absurdity of 'The Long Ride' through the Sinai toward Jerusalem. Definitely a mistake to send it from my uni account. I've been locked out of my emails, and told to schedule a 'Progression Evaluation' with my consulting supervisor. That's the Prof, when he gets back from Paris. Fucking perfect.

And the offie has sold out of the cheap wine. And the Polish pretzels. And ice-cream.

is the latest date in a long line of hypothetical dates. And yet, we know only too well that Alan Lewis died on the fields of Har Megiddo in September 1918. Either Freedland, Greene, Whitlock et al., who have analysed the poems within an inch of their lives, are incorrect in their assumptions, or my theory is wrong. So here I find I must part ways with contemporary theoretical assumptions, and plunge headfirst into the lonely world of conjecture.

Freedland and Greene both came to their conclusions for the death of the Unknown Digger by inferring that the final poem in the collection 'must have been written around the time of his death.'[123] Freedland argues that 'nothing but death would stop a wordsmith of the Unknown Digger's ability and prodigious output from continuing to write'.[124] In fact, all historiographical theories about the Unknown Digger's death come about because 'the literary world has always assumed the order in which Hayden found the poems is the order in which they were written'.[125] But if we disregard the presumed timeline

---

123 Haven't spoken to Em again since this morning, but I have heard back from the Prof, so how does that work? They get back late tomorrow night, and my 'Progression Evaluation' is scheduled for Friday afternoon. How many messages is too many messages to send to one phone? I must have sent about fifty to Em in the space of twelve hours. I'm trying to hold back on sending any more – don't want to freak her out. I miss Artie. I'm convinced something happened. She's never this quiet. I badly need a hug. I might stop writing for a little while – the thought of Alan in the desert, the smell of dead horses, the sand getting in everywhere, the dark shadowy huts and the spark of a match ... Everything about this thesis is making me feel sick.

124 Death, or, I don't know – a war, maybe? Riding nonstop across the desert for three years, fighting an invisible enemy, missing the love of your life, maybe? Being told your thesis, the thing you've been working on for the past ten years or more of your life, is 'laughable', maybe? Sitting at your desk late at night, waiting and waiting for your phone to light up with the comforting purr of a message, as it gets later and later, your head drooping onto your chest, your thoughts running ragged, the darkness taking over. Blood. Anger. Betrayal. Love.

Maybe?

125 Greene, *Six Essays on the Australian Spirit*, p. 77. Em didn't want me to meet them at the station, so I waited until she was home, and then headed

of written poems – if neither 'Bully Beef' nor 'Percute Velociter' were the last poem the Unknown Digger wrote – then all options remain on the table, and Alan Lewis remains as logical a candidate as any other.

If we examine Lewis and the 10th Light Horse's movements through 1917 and 1918, we notice parallels with the poetic themes and imagery of many of the Unknown Digger poems. On 9th December 1917, the Turkish army surrendered Jerusalem to the Allies. It was the 10th Light Horse who were the first troops to pass through the city and accept their surrender. Leading the column was Lieutenant Alan Lewis. In a letter home from the period, Lewis wrote:

> *Leading the men through those ancient streets, I felt like both victor and vanquished. Gallant crusader and unholy infidel. It is a strange feeling to know you are walking through the most significant moment of your life.*[126]

---

around to surprise her with a box of chocolates and some flowers. She opened the door in her bathrobe, tiredness in dark rings under her eyes, her bags thrown in a heap by the window.

Matt, she said, I'm tired. Can I see you tomorrow?

I've got my meeting with the Prof, tomorrow, and I'm scared. I need you.

You'll be fine. Ali said they might need to give you a slap on the wrist, but nothing will come of it.

Immediately the tension in my shoulders relaxed and I smiled. I overthink everything.

Well, celebrate with me?

I have to sleep, Matt.

Of course. Everything is fine, she's just sleepy.

I let her sleep.

126 Arrived at the Prof's office early to see Em for a few minutes, but she wasn't at her desk. Come on in, Matt, the Prof called out, and I could tell something was wrong. First up, he was wearing black socks and a proper tie, unlike his normal pink shirt and messy hair combination. Second, he had a printout of my email to Jennifer Hayden on his desk. And he wasn't smiling. He sat me down on the squeaky chair Em says they use to torture undergrads – every time you so much as shift your weight, it lets out a long whiny squeak.

Look, Matt. As your friend, I have to be straight with you.

Here Lewis makes a reference to the seasoned campaigners, riding alongside him in the saddle for many years. In 'Shearing Season', the shearers celebrate with an ice-cold beer after '*a long/bloody crusade*'.[127] In 'Caught and Disembowled', the captain of the cricket team recalls leading his team out for the latest season as '*boys/But now look at 'em*', and after a particularly long slog in the field late on the fifth day of a Test, even calls them '*veterans of the game*'.[128]

I fumbled awkwardly in my seat, and the chair squeaked. As my friend? Something had happened with him and Em. I knew it. He was unable to control himself, and Em paid the price, and now I'd have to kill him. Well, shit.

It's not good. He sighed a long, fatherly sigh. We have to let you go.

I didn't breathe. Didn't nod. Didn't move an inch. The chair creaked. Let me go?

Obviously this isn't coming from me. I fought hard for you, but the higher-ups have made their decision, and there's nothing I can do. You can finish up your tutes next week, and then we have to part ways.

I mumbled something pathetic, like, But my book?

Finish it, Matt. Prove them wrong.

I can't ... I ran out of words. He didn't mention Em.

I believe in you. He shook his head and wouldn't meet my eyes. But you've dug your own grave, I don't know what got into you.

127 I'm sorry, Matt, the Prof said, in his pathetic, Colin Firth–miserableness.

128 Two forty-five on a Friday afternoon. Boom. It all came sliding down, like the first strip of wallpaper we put up however many months ago. Not enough glue. We slapped it up on the wall and stood back to watch, and the tessellating triangles all smooshed together and widened out as the whole sheet slid down, rolls of paper piling up on top of each other until it grew too heavy and fell and spattered the carpet with wallpaper-glue constellations. The sky out the Prof's window was that particular London afternoon smudge of orange, where the sun is lowering itself behind the smog and the clouds are backlit, and there are chubby birds flitting above and hopping back and forth on the windowsill, but they're not like the birds in Australia, these fat London pigeons – they're not sun-kissed and windswept like the seagulls back home, these gluttonous London filth-bags – and as the smear of sky collapses the birds stop chattering and slide from the air, and dissolve into the grey concrete wall, and your tongue turns to liquid in your mouth, your thesis slipping away into dark oblivion, and

The similarities are too frequent to dispel: surely even Jennifer can see that?

Assuming the Unknown Digger kept writing up until his death in September 1918, it is a simple matter of rethinking the order of the poems. Forget Hayden's assumed chronology, and look where the evidence points: 'Assault on a Machine Gun Nest' is not one of the earliest poems, but rather a cryptic reference to the Battle of Es Salt, written as late as May 1918. 'Mate & His Pack' wasn't written on the evening of the regiment's disembarkation for Gallipoli, readying for the battle to come, but rather is a reflection of the nomadic lifestyle of the 10th Light Horse and their long journey across the desert toward Damascus. With a little rearranging, the poems of the Unknown Digger fit perfectly into the timeline of Alan Lewis's military record, up to and including his final, fated days in the fields of Har Megiddo. The final, conclusive evidence for Alan Lewis's authorship can be found in one of the Unknown Digger's most famous poems, 'Ken Oath', a poem that I am convinced is the final Unknown Digger poem, written only days, even hours, before his tragic death in Har Megiddo. 'Ken Oath' is often the first poem young Australians learn in primary school. This humorous, tragic, bittersweet ode to mates everywhere contains many immortal lines, which are regularly shouted out at sports games and graduation ceremonies, and used as dedications and epitaphs. The crucial point that proves to me that this poem was written by Alan Lewis in Har Megiddo is the final stanza, when the tired boys arrive at the bar after a long day in the bush, and are greeted by the publican, sorrowfully proclaiming that the pub has run out of beer. I ask, what better approximation of Armageddon could any Australian possibly hope to produce?[129]

---

all the background noise of the university, the students thundering through the corridors behind you, the hum of computers, the papers on the desk, turn black and white and then the black seeps away until there is only white oblivion in your periphery. You sit there, wings broken, wondering how you ever had the confidence to jump off the ground and into the sky.

The Prof is shaking his head, but you swear there is a smile in his eyes.

129 The Prof walked me out of his office and told me to take the rest of the day off, said he'd take my afternoon tutorial. Em still wasn't at her desk. My bag, I said, and ran back to the office to pick it up. My eyes fell on the email

How heavy, exactly, is a rifle, with the bayonet attached? I've researched it, of course, but the numbers, when you read them on the page, don't mean a lot. I tried to approximate the weight, using an old broom handle, and some of my downstairs neighbours' dumbbell weights, but they kept sliding down the pole, and I had to keep rearranging them, and the gravitas of the situation was ruined. So I went down to the Imperial War Museum and asked to hold a replica, for research purposes, and stood out on the grass, with the polite man in charge of First World War weaponry watching me, and held it to my shoulder and walked ten metres up the gravel driveway and ten metres back, and aimed it at the tip of the dome, but then the polite man asked for it back, and I immediately forgot how heavy it had been in my arms.

It's not until you lose it that you start to question its weight.

And it's not until you've held the wood and metal, cradled it in your arms, or lugged it through mud and blood and soil for days on end, that you understand the heavy-baby weight of it, the load of it, the way it becomes an extension of your own body, an extra limb that follows, turns where you turn, jumps when you jump, or pushes back into you, against your shoulder, with the force of the bullet discharged from the barrel, the ease with which the long elegant weight of the bayonet slides through the air and into the body lying before you with the lightest of caresses, rolling forward and slicing through skin the way you would reach out and touch someone's face in darkness, your fingers light as sundust, glittery through the air onto their eyelids, their nose, their full lips, the gentle curve of their cheek. The butterfly flutter of their eyelashes.

But instead of feeling the unmistakable features that make up the face you know, you find a different nose, foreign lips, and you find you are holding a stranger in your hands, and with the ease of a stolen kiss and the simple roll of the wrists that slices open a belly, you rock your weight forward, into your palms, into your thumbs, and pushing back, you crush your nails into the wet sheaths of the stranger's eye sockets, until all you feel is damp slop against the

---

printouts on the Prof's desk, and without overthinking it, I picked them up and stuffed them into my satchel. Grabbed the pile of torn papers from his bin as well, because the top one was an email from Em, signed off with three kisses. xxx

darkness in front of you, and the rifle in your hands, your bloody thumbs, come away so easily, so lightly, from the body before you that was once a living person that you wonder, for a breath, if you did anything at all, or if all it took was your presence, your being here in this moment, holding this weight in your hands, this constant pull toward the warm welcoming earth beneath your feet, this solidity of wood and metal, this ache in your muscles, this extension of your arms, this living part of you that leaves you wondering if all it took was you being here in this specific place at this specific time for what happened to have happened as it happened.[130]

---

130 I've been looking for the wrong proof.

SOMEWHERE IN THE MIDDLE EAST. JANUARY 1918.

First clue is a drop in pressure, the sudden headache, the horses throwing their heads back. Over the horizon they see the sandstorm approaching, like a wave of dark water rolling in from out the back, breaking across the plain. No time to avoid it. Barely time to pull scarves across mouths, to button shirts, to lean down and calm the horses. The sunlight withers. They are thrown into sudden night. Against exposed skin, the sand tears, flicks, pierces – tiny pinpricks of pain – goosebumps, pins and needles. The air is thick and sharp, peppering their uniforms, spraying dust.

He ducks his head, squints, but he can't see more than a foot in front of Kelly's ears. The horses scream, closing their eyes. Blinded, they walk through the storm. He pulls his hat lower and breathes in dust. He tastes the bitter, alkaline powder on his tongue, coating his throat. It's in his ears, up his nose, in the pores of his skin.

Kelly grunts, turning her head back toward him, but he pushes her on, into the maelstrom, through the gritty air. He reaches a hand forward to rub her mane, and a vivid blue spark jumps from her matted hair into his palm. He pulls back in pain, flexing his fingers.

As fast as it arrives, it is gone again, blowing across the plains and through the scrub, back the way they came. The air left behind is empty and thin. He pulls the scarf down from his mouth and takes a sip from his canteen. His saliva is thick and white. He pours a little water onto his face and neck, and looks around. The men have separated in the storm, gone walkabout in all directions. They turn and ride back towards him, their faces flawlessly divided above the bridge of the nose into dark and light; burnt and raw.

He wipes the grime from his eyes and tastes chalky bitterness. Kelly snorts, and wiggles her ears.

'All right, girl. Almost there,' he lies.

~

My love.

The dust devils have been through camp and upended everything, tearing out tents and riling up the horses. The willy-willies pick up all sorts and fling them, whirling, into the sky. Each afternoon I pray for the Freo Doctor, and each night I lie awake with the bugs, and hate this place. Only exhaustion brings me sleep.

One of the new boys has a ritual he performs each night, a particular kiss, on a particular photograph, a muttered goodnight to the stars. We make fun of him, of course, call him sentimental and soft. Then we lie awake and worry while he sleeps soundly. I wish I had a photograph of you to keep me company. Would that be possible; do you think?

The locals have tired of us. They used to clamour for our good favour, offering the 'Billjims' the best products, dusting off the gold plates, the silver, for our arrival. We have lost our novelty. I miss Red. If he was marching with us, the children would gather in small groups and point. I would pay them in chocolate to point and snigger, teach them to say Ginger or Sunburn and then laugh at his shock. My tent is eerie quiet – strange what you can grow accustomed to.

It feels about time to leave – we are fidgety and nervous, even Kelly has been temperamental lately, she almost threw me off yesterday. Other than that, the days have passed in their usual monotony – sand and meal and sleep and ride and meal and sand, repeat, ad nauseam. Add sunstroke. Add poisoned wells and invisible assailants.

Add missing you to that list.

Apologies for the scribble, apologies for the dark. Light me up with stories of your own. I need your touch.

Yours, longingly.

He dreams of Gallipoli. They all do. Sometimes he'll scream himself awake, drenched, the harsh canvas of his bedroll sticking to his back. He'll peel himself off the mattress and crawl outside with a saddle blanket wrapped around his shoulders, and sleep out under the stars. He won't be alone. Two or three of them will sit in a circle, sharing cigarettes and tall tales, waiting for reveille.

He hates the dreams. He hates dreaming them. He hates the control they have over him, so he prefers to lie awake. He refuses to sleep, preferring the endless tiredness to their hold. He thinks himself weak, and like the thousand men sleeping around him, pretends nothing is wrong, refuses to discuss it, picks himself up and spits out the dust and carries on carrying on. The night echoes with their cries.

He hates the way the trench is different in the dream. He hates the paper cut-out way it dissolves to thin lines in his peripheral. He hates the way the pocket watch in his hand weighs down his arm, the way the clock hands flicker, like fireflies, backwards and forward. Hours passing by like heartbeats. Minutes stretching into eternity.

He rolls over and looks at the lump across the tent, listening to the steady in and out. His watch says ten minutes to three – ten more minutes of precious sleep until the bugle sounds reveille. He sighs, sits up and tugs his boots on in the dark. Out into the coolness of the night air, the brightness of the moon shocking his half-closed eyes. The sound of boots in sand has become his life, the quiet murmur of the horses, the gentle familiar sounds of the night.

Kelly has her usual spot at the far end of camp, down past the saddles laid out before each mount in preparation for the new day. He trails his hand along the picket line the horses are tethered to; each morning the men brush them down, feed them, talk to them. They say what they can't say to each other. What he can't say to anyone else. Not to Rose, not to Red or Nugget. Not to Nancy. The horses nod, and shake their heads, and laugh their whinnied laughs at all their insecurities. The horses listen.

Kelly waits for him, pawing at the ground, gouging deep ruts in the dirt. Her eyes lamplight-huge in the moonlight, knowing which nights he'll sleep, which nights he'll toss and turn and kick in the dark. He takes her head in his hands, pulls her close and whispers in her ear. He pops the bridle over her head and she gives him one of her slow winks, the playful glint in her eye more sheepdog than horse. Her tongue is sandpapery in his palm as she nibbles on the sugar cube he's saved for her.

He throws the saddle onto her back, and fastens the buckles, pulled close to her, the smell of home and the farm in the hard muscle of her shoulder. The coarse hair of her coat is firm against his temple, down her neck, the thick black mane like matted, wet beach hair. In the dark, only the white line across her eyes is visible, peering at him like her namesake, ready for mischief and adventure, swivelling to meet him then turning towards the open desert; pleading, hopeful. He walks her toward the camp gates as the bugle begins to call. From the surrounding tents, he hears the murmuring and grunts of his men. Heads poke from under tarpaulins. Somewhere across camp someone calls out for the bugler to 'shut the fuck up'.

He hooks his boot into the stirrup, pushing off the ground with his right leg and throwing himself up and onto Kelly's back. He's spent more time in the saddle than his own bed recently, riding from camp to camp – new orders sending them first one way, then the other. The horses are exhausted, and the men are grumpy, and all he can offer is the promise of a nearby bed, the dream of sleep, hot food and fresh water. He trots up and down the lanes of tents, calling for the members of first patrol to be in their saddles in five minutes. The horses grow restless. They've lost weight, ribs jutting from sagging skin. The endless heat, the dry arid air, the constant film of dust. He's watched horses eat their own shit, rolling their fodder around in the dirt and eating sand in their hunger. They must wait until the regiment returns to camp for the evening before getting their allotted two buckets of water, which sometimes takes hours to find. Once the horses have been fed and watered the men can worry about themselves, and fall asleep exhausted under the stars.

Kelly never complains. She never bucks and fights like some of the other horses, never drops her head and refuses to meet his eye. He knows where she'll be each morning, and she trusts him to find food, to bring her water, to brush her down at the end of a march. She walks him back toward the camp gate to wait.

Slowly, like wildflowers blooming, men ride up from the darkness. First come the new recruits, the ones still eager to impress him, trying to curry his favour. Next are the post-Gallipoli recruits, the ones who made up the numbers while he recovered in Lemnos. He doesn't know them. He doesn't care. Last of all, laughing among themselves, grizzled and leathery, come the Gallipoli veterans. They make him wait. If any of the others tried to do the same, he would play the officer card, spit flecking from his lips, but he allows the Gallipoli vets this one concession. They know he won't say anything. He has become his father. He accepts that. There are worse fates.

He's aware of the way the men talk about him. Silent. Shell-shocked. The stranger leading them. He tries not to think about it. It's easier if he doesn't remember names, or stories, or faces. Bookworm, they say. Loner. It's easier if he doesn't make friends.

Kelly shuffles her feet in nervous expectation, dancing her own little Kelly foxtrot, and he holds an open palm on her neck to calm her, while the men form up around him.

When they're assembled, they ride.

He loses himself in the rhythm of the hooves, the repeated *takatuk, takatuk* of metal horseshoes thudding into the hard earth. Nancy. Her mock disapproval, the faces she made when she didn't think he was watching. He pulls himself lower, closer to Kelly's neck as her strides lengthen, the music of the ride changing. Remembers the way Nancy's eyebrows relaxed, her natural frown, giving her a look of righteous indignation even as she let loose with a tirade of filth worthy of some of the oldest hands in the regiment.

The men fan out behind him as they race across the plain.

To make her sigh, to hear the little tutting noise she'd make when his jokes fell flat, the trim edges of her smile. The ground races beneath Kelly's feet. And the child. His child, he has to keep reminding himself. She sent him a blurred photograph on her first birthday. Two black eyes peering into the lens, peering out at him. Judging. He kicks his heels in harder, pushes Kelly to speed up. Faster, away from it all. The men behind race to keep up. He sends her half his pay packet each month, all he can afford, but she writes every few weeks. Sometimes he pretends he can read love in her words. Sometimes he can't bring himself to open the letter. He can't get a feel for the baby. For his baby.

Kelly is foaming at the mouth, sweat on her haunches, each ragged breath a burst of frost. He can hear one of the troopers behind him yelling, begging him to stop. He pushes them harder.

They are flying.

The sand streams by beneath, like he could be ten thousand miles up and the tiny pebbles huge boulders, the brown brush vast forests. High up above him a black spot circles in the ever-brightening sky.

He slows Kelly to a trot, then a walk, then halts entirely, her nostrils flared large, her flanks steaming in the dawn. The men pull in on either side, and he points a gloved finger up at the dot. Kelly stamps her feet like a petulant child. The drone is in his ears, a summer evening croak of mosquitoes and crickets, of flies in his room buzzing by his eyes. Slowly, the plane climbs. They watch for a minute, as it cuts through the wisps of pinking morning cloud, spinning, turning, banking, climbing higher and higher until it wings away, off in the direction of the Allied lines. He sits for a moment, perched in the saddle, listening for a return, but the hum of the engine fades, and all he can hear is Kelly's sniffle of impatience, his own breath, the thump of his heartbeat in his ears.

'One of ours?' says one of the post-Gallipoli recruits.

'Must be. We control the sky.' He spurs Kelly forward, but slower, as they approach the Turkish lines.

The sparse plain and the thick brush remind him of home, the arid fields where the spinifex grows, where the bleached bones of dead cattle are picked clean by the weather. Home. And Rose. Sending him tedious letters. Patiently waiting for his return. Each letter professing her love, renewed. He's not sure he believes in love anymore.

Love is being unable to tell someone you no longer love them.

Love is hating yourself for falling for someone new.

Love is hating someone for loving you.

He writes to her like he would write to the family of a dead trooper. Opens each new letter with disdain, numb boredom and the bitter taste of self-loathing on his tongue. But still he doesn't say anything, can't bring himself to write the truth.

One of the recruits whistles, and he glances up. Off to his right, a small plume of smoke outlined against the smudge of morning sky. He would have missed it, deep in thoughts of the past. He's still asleep. Wake up, Al, get a grip.

They dismount, leave the horses with a volunteer behind the crest of a hill, and scramble closer for a better look. There's not a lot of cover. He drops to the ground and pushes forward on his hands and knees among the scrub. The rest of the men do the same.

Turkish scouts, cooking breakfast over a small fire. They should know better, but it's bitterly cold. He doesn't blame them.

One of the Turks drifts away from the camp, close to their hiding spot, and lowers his pants, crouching in the brush. Alan motions for two of the men to bring him in. Silence, but for the grunting of the Turk. From their camp, the stagnant air carries the oblivious chatter of the Turkish scouts. The grunting stops.

The two troopers drag him over with his pants around his ankles, bayonet held against his throat, brown smears down his skinny legs. Alan tells him to pull up his pants. There's a whispered interrogation, nervous looks toward the Turkish lines, cold seeping into their kit from the earth. In a few hours, the earth will be baked and dry. For now, they freeze.

When they're done, they face a dilemma. They can't take the Turk back with them, and they can't set him free without alerting the scouts to their presence. They must destroy the evidence. Grim job, but orders are orders.

'Go get the horses ready,' Alan says, pulling out his knife. The Turk's eyes widen. They've stuffed part of a shirt into his mouth, but he can whimper, can still squirm. Alan holds his knife against the bare skin of his throat, and the noise stops. 'Sorry, mate.'

Always the same dream. The morning of The Nek. The same stretch of trench. The same gnarled pine tree on the horizon. The same blurred faces of the men around him, the men he signed up alongside. Men he knows from home, their faces like old shoes, comfortable and worn. The pocket watch at the end of his right arm. The whistle between his lips. The pistol in his left hand. The sun, imminent.

Some nights, he dreams he is back on Lemnos – sun in his eyes and the cool touch of seawater drawing him down into the dark, pulling him, down, further down, until he can't breathe. Suffocating, his eyes bulging in his head. The crush of bodies on his chest, drowning in blood.

On the good nights, he won't remember his dreams, will wake to the bugle call refreshed. He can't remember the last good night.

The troopers are waiting to ride as he scrambles back to the horses. He nods to them, job done, and throws himself onto Kelly's back. They race back the way they've come, putting distance between themselves and the Jacko camp. Then they can slow down, and reassess. Already, the sky is lighter, the day warming up. The Turk told them what he knew – it's been a successful morning.

The cool air disperses as the temperature rises, and the heat settles back on them like an old coat. It weighs on his shoulders, saps the strength from his arms. Kelly shakes her head as the flies find her wet muzzle and turns to eye him up. She sticks her long tongue out the side of her mouth like Dad's kelpies panting.

'Alright, girl.'

He leans forward and runs his hand through her mane. Turning to the men, he orders them back to camp.

The campsite is a roar of activity as they ride back in – the smell of the billy on the fire, shorts hung on makeshift lines, the other horses already fed and watered. He pops a feedbag over Kelly's head and asks the trooper on detail to give her some extra care. He pats her rump as he leaves, but she ignores him, engrossed in the feedbag, tail swishing to keep away the flies.

After debriefing with the Major, he heads back to his tent, passing groups of laughing, jockeying troopers lying shirtless in the morning sun, mixing burnt offerings in their mess tins. He passes a group of men walking back the way he came, off to swim in the cold waters of the nearby creek. No-one salutes, but some of the older boys, his original Mena crew, give him a quick nod. All of them wear khaki shirts and slouch hats as per orders, but are naked from the waist down, thick dark hairs on their upper legs and groins. They laugh among themselves as they disappear behind him. Once he might have found comfort in the sound.

Back at their tent, Nugget sits by a stuttering fire, a mess tin perched over the coals. The men from the surrounding tents lounge around listening as he rabbits on. Alan catches his eye before popping into the tent to take off his spurs and change shirts. When he re-emerges there's a tin plate of hot food and a mug of tea waiting for him, the flies already congregating on the surface. He grunts a quick thank you and tucks in. He hadn't realised he was hungry.

'Anything to report, Lewis?' One of the new officers asks, white foam on his cheeks and a razor in his hand. Alan catches his eye in the reflection of the pocket mirror he's hung from the front of his tent. He hasn't shaved for weeks, thick tufts of hair on his cheeks. He can't remember when he stopped caring.

He chews a chunk of gristle and mutters between mouthfuls.

'Not much doing. Interrogated an Abdul scout – we're about three clicks south of their main force. A biplane, but I think it was one of ours.'

'Clear skies. Perfect weather for a recce.'

One of the other fresh recruits screws up his face in protest. His hair is orange and the skin on his nose is peeling. 'It's bloody freezing – there was frost on my bedroll this morning.'

'Mate. You don't know what freezing is. Back on Anzac,' Nugget pours the last dregs of tea onto the hot ashes and the coals spit and crackle by his boots, 'back on Anzac, it freezed so hard you couldn't blow a candle out. You had to knock the flame off with a stick.'

The ginger kid tilts his head, squints his eyes.

'Ain't that the truth, Al?' Nugget peers up at him.

Alan laughs. 'You ever get to uni, might be worth starting with some basic science.'

His stomach rumbles uncomfortably, growling in pain. He drops his plate and mutters a quick apology, running half-stooped to the wooden shack housing the latrines. He can smell them half a field away. As he clatters open the wooden door a cloud of flies rises from the dark holes in the bench. When his eyes adjust, he can make out three other men hunched forward, drained of colour, the whites of their eyes obscured by the swarms of flies. The flies land on his lips, tickle his ears, crawl close to the wet corners of his eyes.

He barely has his shorts around his ankles before he relieves himself, his skin clammy and wet. His stomach settles and he relaxes, until he realises he's forgotten bog paper. He risks a sideways glance at the men next to him, but the looks on their faces tell him they won't be sharing.

There are two letters in his shirt pocket.

Rose's latest. The one she wrote because his mother didn't have the strength. Tom has fallen at Passchendaele. I'm so sorry, Al, she says. She writes on thin cream paper, smelling faintly of banksia and the smoke from the hearth, her writing looped and floral. He holds the pages up to his nose, breathes her in, forgets the flies and the stench and the humid heat.

The other is from Nancy, who has started to write more often now, hoping to build a relationship after her year of silence. It's about the baby, cute descriptions of the way she toddles around like a tiny drunk. When it's all over, she says near the end, we will find a place in the country and make this work. I want to make this work, she writes on hard white paper, unscented. What she means is she wants his money.

The white paper is rough as guts, and the sand that has found its way between his cheeks tears his arse. It leaves his skin pink and raw, but it does the job. His stomach gurgles once more as he knocks his way back out into the light and breathes in the sweet smell of a thousand men living together, the fresh air of a thousand Walers and all their farm smells. Slowly, wincing with each step, he winds his way back to his tent.

~

Always the same dream. The last minutes of night. The pine tree. Standing on the firing step, at the lip of the trench, peering down at the watch in his hand. Playing at being an officer. One moment the watch hands are spinning wildly, back and forth, close to his eyes so his breath fogs up the glass, and next his arms are longer than they've ever been before; so he can't make out the minutes, his breath catching in his chest. All he'll hear is the tickatick of the hands, the spinning cogs whirring and each second passing with a click that shakes the trench walls. Then it's time, and the whistle in his hand won't reach his mouth, can't make the journey from his side in time. He blows a dead, silent blast, cold metal scratching on his teeth. The eyes of the men around him are hardening. Peering. Thinking, who is this boy, leading me to my death?

~

Mate,

Nugget's getting on my nerves, bless him. Truth be told, it's all getting on my nerves. Bloody sand and the same old routine every day. None of it is the same without you.

The girls in Cairo miss you. If that fuckin' shell hadn't had your number, I wouldn't be surprised if you weren't shacked up with one or more of them by now. For some reason I can picture you with a harem.

You wouldn't put up with any lip from the new boys. You always knew what to say, what to make light of, when to put the foot down. Don't get a big head up you when I say I looked to you for some of that stuff. Lord knows you were no good when the bill came.

I wish I was brave enough to send this.

~

The tent is quiet for a half hour, and he finds himself writing yet another letter he doesn't have the guts to send. His notebook is full of them. Half written. Scratched out. Dead before their time.

He re-reads the first letter from Nancy, for the thousandth time.

I was angry at you. I didn't want you to know. You have an obligation, now. You have a reason to survive. Her name is Harriet. She has your curls. She is your daughter.

He tries to feel something for the baby, some form of ownership of the letters on the page and the person they embody. The words are thin and distant. He writes because he is expected to, because he misses Nancy's curves, her schoolmarm mouth.

Nugget's voice arrives a full half-minute before his body, announcing his approach and giving Alan time to fold the paper in half and stuff it in his pack. He looks up as the wiry Irishman enters the tent and skips his way over to his bedroll. No sooner has his backside hit the material, then he's back up like a jack rabbit, making his way over to the makeshift desk.

'Bit of a sauna in here, Lewey. Mind if I crack open the French doors?'

Without waiting for a reply Nugget crosses to the entrance and pulls back the material, twirling the long drapes around the side posts. Alan squints; the whiteness of the sand sears into his brain and everything is a bright haze.

But it's not worth fighting Nugget on this. He grunts. A throwaway sort of back-of-the-throat noise. Half-hearted. Nugget looks at him. Can read his silences like he reads the odds on the horses in the regimental races.

'What's up with you then?'

'Nothing.'

'It's always nothing.'

'Well, this time it really is.' He smiles, and the rough skin on his lip breaks. How long has it been?

Nugget inclines his head like he's accepting this as a reasonable response, then asks again.

'Missing your woman?'

'Women. Plural. Bars. The beaches back home. Grass.'

'Ain't that the truth.'

They sit in the sticky air for a while, not talking. Then Nugget pipes back up, as he always does. 'You know, there's a pretty young bint in the local town ...'

'Get out of it, Nug.'

'I'm just saying, you're only human.'

'Shut up.'

'Rose wouldn't need to know. No-one would need to know.'

'Shut up, Nug. Listen.'

He holds his breath. Nugget does the same. For a moment, there's nothing but the sound of horses whinnying at the other end of the camp, and then, faint at first, the mosquito buzz. They stare at each other like dumbstruck mullets, gasping for air. He watches as Nugget's pupils widen, staring back at him, watches the words being formed by his mouth, but all he can hear is the mechanical roar of the engine, all he can hear is the tinny rattle of his own voice, lost somewhere on the journey between his chest and his mouth, the whispering cry.

'The horses.'

Nugget sprints out into the light with his shirt unbuttoned, running down the row of tents, screaming to the men. When Alan closes his eyes all he can see is the bright haze on his eyelids.

The machine gun begins firing as he exits the tent, and finishes by the time he's at the end of the row, turning the corner, racing across the camp alongside the other men who have cottoned on. Then come the screams. Up ahead he sees Nugget fall to his knees in the sand by the dark form of a dropped horse. A few of the men have their rifles out, taking pot shots at the plane as it finishes its dive and climbs, machine guns steaming. Already it is tiny in the vast space of the sky, a dot receding into the distance, back the way it came.

The screams are human. Like children. The mother on Cottesloe Beach who'd lost her son in the wash of waves when he was little more than a child himself. The screams like The Nek. Like Lemnos – the sound of the surgeons on the hospital ships taking off limbs. The animal noise of frightened creatures. Mouths filled with blood. Gurgles.

He looks down the line at the horses, the blood-drenched sand, the reins torn off in terror, the few who missed the rain of bullets standing tall over the twitching bodies of those on the ground alongside. His feet move of their own accord. The trooper on steward duty managed to let twenty or thirty horses loose; they fan out across the plain, knowing the danger, running for their lives. Two injured Walers, exit wounds like huge craters in their thighs, have jerked loose and are stumbling toward the tents. A trooper grabs the reins, soothes the startled creatures and lowers them to the ground. Alan hears the soft murmur of whispered comforts.

Kelly sits on the ground like a giant puppy. She swings her head around at his approach, her eyes huge and terrified. Purple veins swim in her milky whites. All around her, the ground is shot up, sharp pebbles in her mane and a thin sheen of white sand on her flank that clouds off when he rubs his hand along her side. She's breathing rapidly, rabidly, spit dripping from her lower lip, teeth exposed. He moves alongside and quietens her, breathes in time with her. Running his hand down her mane, his fingers knot in the thick hair.

'Easy, girl.'

The bullet has entered at the base of her neck, in the thick muscle of her shoulders, and crossed her body diagonally, down through her chest and exiting through her stomach on the opposite side. She tries to raise herself, back onto her feet, but he wraps his arms around her muscled neck, pulls her close and whispers soothing words in her ears. He takes a quick look at the wound, and gags. The immensity of her ribs, each bone thick like a table leg. The writhing red snakes of her insides, the drip of thick dark blood. He sits down next to her back legs, the puddle growing by his thigh, bits of pebble floating in the stagnant dark pool.

His hands shake with the uncontrollable tic of adrenalin, and he struggles to get into his own pocket: the tiny corner of a cube of sugar, the letter from Rose he couldn't bring himself to destroy. He holds the cube under Kelly's mouth, and a long glob of spit drips into his palm, dissolving the sugar, but she slips a leathery tongue onto his skin. The edges of her tongue are white, and blood mixes with her spit. Pink drops patter, raining the dirt below while her teeth grind the cube. He unfolds the letter, thick scarlet smudges on the ink. Tom is dead, and he couldn't find the courage needed to kill a lone Turk. Kelly coughs like the smokers in the morning.

A gunshot from somewhere close by, and he swings his head. Nugget walks down the picket line, silencing those horses too injured to survive. 'Brave unto the last', like he writes home in the letters to the families. He raises himself off the ground, sand sticking to his red palm, and tries to wipe the muddy sludge off on his shorts. He leaves a long red streak down Kelly's back as he strokes her, the blood fading into her coat.

Nugget reaches the end of the line and stares at him across Kelly's bulk. He shakes his head. Nugget turns the pistol in his hand, offers it to him across the night sky of her back, handle first. He nods, and Nugget leaves him to it. No need for words.

He misses home. His proper home, the one he pretends he has forgotten. He misses the smell of gumtrees and the cackle of kookaburras in the dawn light.

There are two bullets in the chamber.

He weighs the pistol in his hand. This war is not for him. It would be quick, cold metal on his temple, and the simple click of the trigger. Or on the roof of his mouth, like that English officer on Gallipoli, blowing out the back of his head in a pink cloud. A quick release. Falling on his sword like the Greek heroes he once idolised. He could find his way back home, safer then, as a memory.

Kelly's wild eye follows him, the flicker of a wink, then it rolls back until all he can see is whites, her tongue lolling from her mouth. A baby's whimper. The white strip across her eyes is brown with blood and sweat and dust. A thick gobbet of pink snot stalactites from the darkness of her muzzle. She's gone feral, a wild brumby galloping alone across the Kosciusko plains she can't even remember anymore. Time to take her home.

'I'm sorry.'

His hand moves in slow motion, through the water at Cottesloe, remembering, and strokes the side of her face, while he practises, placing the barrel against her forehead. He mimes pulling the trigger, and lets the gun fall. He let the Turkish scout scramble free, unable to plunge the knife into the soft skin of his neck. Unable to do what was necessary. Their scouting party had probably followed them back to camp, unobserved, and sent the plane. He leans forward and places his forehead against hers, like the Maori boys taught them, and pulls back. She looks him in the eye, saying, do it, you coward. Be brave for once. Please.

'Thank you.'

He pulls the trigger.

The noise is enormous, filling his ears, ringing through his teeth, kicking his brain about in his head. He closes his eyes and waits for the spasms to subside.

Kelly screams; the end screams, wandering lost in a field of agony. Her head thrashes in his arms ragdoll loose. She throws her neck back, trying to pull her body up but lacking the strength. Her back legs kick out, throwing sand and showering them with powdery dust.

All he's succeeded in doing is blowing her left eye and ear off. Thick stringy links of pink sinew and skin hang down the side of her head. Dots of blood splay out across the black canvas of her back. She falls onto her left-hand side, hiding the cavity of her eye socket in the dirt. He can't bring himself to look down at the creature twisting by his feet. The wild beast, the fallen soldier.

The sky is perfect clear above them, blue like children draw the sky, and clean. Kelly's right eye peers up and through him.

He places a sandy boot on her muzzle to keep her from moving, and fires the second bullet through her brain.

CHAPTER 6: Conclusive evidence of a physical relationship between my girlfriend and her boss, who also happens to be my boss: Analysis of the primary sources, secondary confirmation and just how fucked are we?

It has taken me a few days to get my head around it; the idea that Em might not have been 100% truthful with me during our relationship – accepting the realisation that I might be wrong about certain fundamental aspects of my life, understanding that various basic tenets of my London existence would very likely have to change – but the evidence speaks for itself. And, as in all things, I have reviewed the evidence and come to a balanced and impartial conclusion.

Basically, I'm fucked.[131]

My initial evidence was purely circumstantial: I walked out of the Prof's office after they fired me, and Em still wasn't at her desk. I stumbled across the litter-strewn square out the front of the English and Social Sciences Building, in a daze, and happened to pull out my phone. Em had sent me a message: '*I've had to run across to the Admin Centre, but let me know how it goes! xx*', which I must have received sitting in the Prof's office while he mumbled his platitudes and pretended to care. And yet, I know full well from multiple personal experiences, and as evidenced in this thesis, that 'there's no reception in [Em and the Prof's] office'.[132] Maybe it was a lucky quirk of fate, maybe the message came through before I arrived at the office, and I hadn't seen it before I went in. But then I looked at the time stamp, which said it had been sent at 14:42, right

131 Messaged Em and said we needed to talk.

She messaged back: *Ali told me, I'm sorry. [Sad face emoji] Silver linings: you'll have time to finish your book? [Shrugging emoji] Out to dinner with Sam tonight, but you could come round tomorrow night? xx [Heart emoji]*

132 Matthew L. Denton, *Identifying the Unknown Digger: Conclusive Evidence for the Composition of the Unknown Digger Poems by Lieutenant Alan Lewis, VC* (soon to be published as a handsome hardback, just as soon as I can find a publisher willing to take a chance on me, despite what Jennifer might think, despite everything), Chapter 2, footnote 46. I paid good money for those tickets and we missed the whole show thanks to her stupid office and its 'lack of signal'.

as the Prof was explaining how hard he had fought for me to stay. Random happenstance, or first microscopic crack? Let us examine the further evidence.

There is a large amount of anecdotal evidence for a possible relationship between my girlfriend and my disgustingly British supervising mentor: the countless nights spent working late on what exactly – teaching rotas, introductions to books, university courses? No-one else that I know works until eight or nine o'clock each night.[133] No-one else messages at five or six o'clock, the official time that they are contractually paid until, when they should be packing up their desk and heading home, just as I'm getting the pasta on or the chicken marinated for what would be a perfectly timed dinner, and says '*Sorry, Matt, [something] has come up, it's going to be another late one. I'll be home as soon as I can. xxx*' And sure, the somethings that came up with regularly scheduled timing might all have been actual, provable somethingses (Deputy Head of Linguistics calling in sick a day before the exam period / booked guest dropping out of appearance on late-night live TV show and a certain supervising professor being asked to cover / that one time when the photocopier wouldn't stop beeping, etc.) but that doesn't get anyone off the hook – I'm calling bullshit on the whole thing.

The emails I swiped from the Prof's desk were unhelpful in my search for evidence:

1. A printout of my late-night ramble at and toward Jennifer Hayden.
2. An email from the Dean of Studies asking for the Prof's thoughts on the 'severity of punishment bringing such disrepute on our esteemed establishment might warrant'.

---

133 One of the many things Jennifer Hayden found fault with in my thesis proposal – the idea that an active lieutenant like Alan Lewis would have the personal time available to write eighty-odd world-class poems over the course of a five-year campaign, alongside all of his official capacities, his letter writing and his well-documented passion for joining the other troopers in a game of cricket or football. Which I would counter with my own observations over the four years I've lived and worked in London forcing myself to write and love and grow with Em: if you love doing it, you will find the time.

3. A touchingly sincere email from Jennifer Hayden herself asking the university to forget about my email, citing the 'pressures of academic discourse' and the 'exciting findings such evident passion for the field might yield with a little firmer guidance'.
4. The second page of each of the aforementioned emails, asking the user to be mindful of wasting paper, and only printing out emails if 'essential'.

Though one could, and one will, proceed to argue that the Prof's sincere promises about fighting against the bureaucracy for me to stay, and trying to reduce the severity of my punishment, look like utter crap in the light of these emails, one will hold back from wielding such childish accusations in light of provable evidence. More likely the Pommy git pushed for me to be removed to get me out of the way and allow his blossoming romance with my girlfriend the space it needs to grow into something more substantial.

I am painfully aware that my 'evidence', so far, amounts to nothing but conjecture and far-fetched contrivances, proof of a far deeper well of insecurity in my own self-confidence more so than confirmation of any wrongdoing on Em's behalf.[134] But we would need more space than this thesis has to offer were we to delve into those depths. I will admit that I began to doubt my own reasoning around this point – Jennifer got to me, and Max Whitlock and Nicholas Curtin-Kneeling, all crowding into my head and throwing their doubts at me. But Alan faced far worse, and made something of it, so I took a close look at the emails I found in the Prof's bin – torn in half, covered in mayonnaise and coffee, destined to be destroyed. A confirmation email for the hotel stay in Paris, sent from Em's work account to the Prof's for authorisation:

> *Hey Ali – all booked, confirmation attached. Close to the conference centre like you asked, but off the main street. Good reviews online. Easy taxi from the airport. Em xxx*[135]

134 But I can't help thinking about the way our own relationship started, and how Dan must have felt when the inevitable blow was dealt, and whether we are, indeed, destined to repeat history.

135 There's a part of me that feels so dirty for reading Em's emails. My heart

Signed off with three x's, one more than is universally accepted as appropriate for emails between work colleagues, reminiscent of the lurid, promising neon lights of Soho bookstores and adult toy shops. Have scoured my own messages from Em and found a high correlation between instances of three or more x's at the end of a message and occurrences of physical intimacy during the course of the next twenty-four hours. Or am I reading too much into it?

And, just as I'm about to throw the email back into my own trash and curse myself for being so suspicious, I look over the confirmation from the hotel: one booking confirmed.

One room, one king-sized bed.

Well, fuck.

Unless that's just the confirmation for the Prof's room, and there's a separate confirmation for Em's room, I think, clutching at the flimsiest of straws, hoping against hope that the erratic beating of my heart is the precursor of a heart attack, please, or an aneurism, anything that'll drop me dead in my tracks rather than face the awful truth I know I have to face.

So I send Em the message, and we make plans for tomorrow night, and I see the rest of tonight opening up with a depressing reliability before me: sitting at my desk shuddering and crying for an hour or so, finishing a bottle of wine, arguing with myself all evening like a shell-shocked veteran trying to convince myself I'm wrong, finishing a second bottle of wine, more crying, more arguing, a sad, solitary wank in the shower, followed by more crying and arguing, et cetera ad infinitum. Spread out in front of me on the desk are my years of research into the Unknown Digger and Alan Lewis, the fruit of thousands of hours of hard work to prove that the man

---

pounding away in my chest like it's about to break free, and not knowing whether I want to find something that confirms my suspicions, and kills me, or not find anything, and understand that the only weak link in mine and Em's relationship is me, and my jealousy, and the ever-present knot of doubt in my gut.

And another part that says, Well, what would Alan do? You think he'd run away and give up on something he'd been fighting so hard for, or do you think he'd head back into that darkness, not knowing what might happen, not caring that it might be the end, but willing, always, to fight?

And a third, quieter part that whispers, Yes, but you are no Alan Lewis.

I believe wrote a bunch of Aussie poems actually did, and it's like I haven't learnt anything from them. Like I've been so busy analysing the rhyme schemes and syllabic structures I haven't been paying attention to what they say. What would Alan do? He'd charge back into the fray, he wouldn't give up, no matter the odds.

I call Sam, and ask her where she's meeting Em for dinner, and please, please, I say, I just want to speak to her, that's all.

And then Sam says, But Matt, we don't have plans? I thought Em was with you?

When did she stop calling him Alistair, and start calling him Ali?

~

Alan Lewis sacrificed his life in that Turkish village so that I could travel halfway across the world on a whim, so that I could pursue my dreams wherever they happened to take me, so the entire population of Australia, including his descendants and friends and fellow soldiers, could live in a world free of fear. He ran into that dark hut three times to save his mate, and anyone else he could find. The explosion that killed him may have torn apart his body, leaving no trace of his physical existence, but through his poetry he has lived on, and given Australia and its people new life.

And in the spirit of Alan Lewis, tonight I headed once more into Em's dark-windowed apartment, knowing full well that whatever happened, some part of me was never going to re-emerge.

She opened the door with her back to me, distracted by something Artie was doing in the kitchen, laughing. Hey, she said as I walked in, and I realised this was going to be harder than anything I had ever done before in my life, including leaving Perth.

We need to talk, I said. My voice trembled, and Em turned around and looked at me properly for the first time.

Are you crying?

No. Although I could at any moment.

You want a glass of wine?

No. Artie ran and jumped up at me, then lay on his back waiting for a tummy scratch. I sat down on the kitchen floor and tousled his fur. Em fussed in the kitchen, telling me all about her day, explaining the new tutorial the Prof has her planning for once I'm gone, about how good it was to see Sam again last night, how she wants to make a habit of it, how they want to join a yoga class together.

I know about you and Alistair.

I focussed all my attention on Artie's tiny puppy feet.

Silence from the kitchen.

I know you shared a room in Paris, and I know you lied about working late, and I know you weren't with Sam last night because I called her.

I spoke too fast, trying to get it all out before she had a chance to explain herself. To her credit she didn't interrupt – just nodded and pulled her hair back from her face and put her hand on the table like maybe she needed help to stay standing.

I finally looked up from Artie and we stared at each other for a minute, neither of us speaking.

I know you're in love with him, I managed. QED. I didn't know that at all, but sometimes it pays to make an educated guess, and then backtrack and prove the point with the benefit of hindsight. She choked back her words so I knew I was onto something. There's a point you get to in all research, in testing out any theory, where the pieces start clicking together in your head, where every fact you find and every possibility you can think of matches up with what you're putting forward and you get that heart-filling warmth where you know you couldn't possibly be wrong. I felt that back in Australia, on my first research trip to Canberra and the national archives – the first time I laid eyes on the original Unknown Digger poems, and my mind flew to Alan Lewis and everything I knew about him, and suddenly every hurried line of poetry in the collection in front of my eyes made sense.

I felt something similar in Em's kitchen, my hand in Artie's fur, my gaze fixed on Em's unblinking eyes. A different heat, maybe, but the same fluttering of the heart, the same sweaty-palmed, standing-on-the-edge-of-a-cliff nausea that could either end in glorious flight or a broken body dashed on the rocks of knowledge a thousand feet below. Not sure which option I really wanted at that moment. Not sure I know now.

I'm sorry. She whispered, like if she broke it quietly to me she could ease the truth between my ribs like the Turkish blade that killed Trooper 'Nugget' McRae.

And how quickly that wonderful moment of clarity dissipates, clearing the space for months or years of relentless questioning. We went to the pub with friends a few months back, when I was blissfully ignorant and Em was still my beautiful, lying future-wife. We had all been drinking, and someone started talking about the movies they'd loved as kids, and soon we were all reminiscing about the terrible, brilliant eighties blockbusters we'd been raised on. Someone couldn't remember the name of that actor, with the shock of red hair and the squint, who appeared in all the best worst movies of our generation, so I pulled out my phone.

I looked it up, brought up his website, his acting credits, his entire career. Found out he's a shoe salesman now, doing a bit of convention work on the side. And we all smiled and nodded and fell into silence.

Nice going, Matt, Em said, that night in the pub. I ruined it with my need to get to the bottom of everything, my insatiable need to be right. Still doing it now.

Em was crying, silent tears streaming down her face, and Artie could tell something was up because he'd gone completely silent and stopped wriggling.

I never, ever meant to hurt you, she said. Her voice sounded strange. You have to know that. She took a step towards me and then thought better of it and stayed where she was.

But you did.

But I did. And I'm so sorry. I ... she trailed off, unsure what to say, probably trying to come up with a placating lie, some way to ease her guilt. I wanted to tell you, I promise.

But you didn't.

But I didn't. I couldn't. You were so happy.

We were so happy, I tried to reply, but the words were mangled in my throat, and suddenly there was snot dangling from my nose and my eyes were itchy.

You were so happy. She sat down at the kitchen table and Artie jumped out of my hands and crossed the room, his tail wagging. And I didn't want to be the one to destroy that.

I bought you Artie.

Don't, she raised her voice and Artie's tail stopped mid-wag. Don't do that.

I thought you were happy.

I know (and what I wouldn't give for my own dynamite explosion to blow up her flat at that moment, as she so effortlessly laid my own ignorance out before me), and I was. Sometimes. I'm sorry.

You said.

It wasn't meant to happen. At some point we became, I dunno, closer, than we had been, than we should have been. And then it just felt right, and to Ali's credit–

No. I surprised myself with the loudness of my voice. Artie ran back over to me to lick my fingers.

I did this, I know. I'm sorry. But you have to know, it was never planned. Swear. I never wanted to hurt you. And I am so sorry you found out like this. I was going to tell you, but then the Jennifer Hayden article came out. And everything at work.

She paused for half a minute to get up and turn off the oven, then walked back to the table, looking out past me toward the couch and the TV and the backyard and the purplish bruise of sky visible through the back window. I never wanted to hurt you.

That's it? I said. At some point I must have moved to the couch, because that's where I was sitting. Em was standing by the kitchen table. I played with Artie in my lap, trying not to look at her, but watching what she was doing. She turned an apple over and over in her hands, throwing it up, catching it, spinning it in her palm. Graceful movements, like a dancer.

That's what I wanted to say.

I didn't say anything for a long time, and neither did she. We let the minutes slip over us like rain, waiting for a break in the clouds.

Do you love him?

Artie had his teeth around my finger, and he bit down harder as I wiggled. A minute passed.

I do.

How long? I refused to cry.

We only slept together in Paris.

How long have you been in love?

Longer than that.

Thank you for your honesty.

Thank you for understanding.

It was all so clean. Disinfected. Like a hospital. Like the kitchen where I cooked last week and the couch we fucked on and the bed we fell asleep in every other night had all been bleached or burnt or sprayed with chemicals, and any remaining trace of us, any of our happiness or passion or love, had been wiped clean.

I said I should go.

What, now now? She looked around the kitchen, at the oven and the delicious smell coming from it, at her plates and her cutlery, her chipped mugs. Her painted walls, like they would be enough, and then back to me. I nodded. She walked me to the door and kissed my cheek. She stayed there, with her arms around me, her mouth by my ear, breathing like she'd run a marathon, squeezing me tightly, like she could keep all the love from gushing out of the gaping hole in my chest where my heart had once been.

I said, I don't trust anything you say.

That's fair, she said. I lied to you. Past tense, like she's stopped now.

Did you ever love me?

I still love you.

~

All this time – every initial thought that led to this thesis, every word I've typed late at night, every research session in the Imperial War Museum's archive, every dead end and possible breakthrough, every half rhyme and enjambed line, every unnamed soldier's death and forgotten battle – I've wondered: If it came down to it, would I have the presence of mind, the courage and the bravery to do what Alan Lewis did, that fateful day in the fields of Har Megiddo?

At every setback and stumble, and there have been a few, I've asked myself: What would Alan Lewis do? Like even after all this time, he would have the answers.

But Alan Lewis is dead.

So the real question is: What would Matt Denton do, when faced with his own Armageddon? And now I know.

I'd run away, like all miserable cowards, to the ends of the earth, to hide my shame.

I caught the next train to Brighton.

ARMAGEDDON. SEPTEMBER 1918.

At the front of the column, he's the most exposed.

The cobbled streets echo the clopping of the horses down the narrow lanes. Dust on the rim of his slouch hat. Worn leather beneath white knuckles. They pass windows, flung open, the inhabitants of the city watching them ride by from the shadows. No parade. No celebration. Dark-eyed children scamper in their wake. He glances up at the centuries-old stone, runs his hand along the dark sun-stained wall as he rides past. Eyes open for danger. Alert, muscles tensed.

The Turkish garrison has been abandoned, the rooms emptied, shutters knocking in the breeze. The dust dances in long beams of sunlight. Someone has left a letter, unfinished.

The column stretches out behind him, like the long trail of sheep brought into pasture. The heads of the horses droop like the men's shoulders. Rifles slung across backs. Flies skitting by their ears.

His arms are dark with sun, rangy and muscled. His men follow where he leads. He keeps his eyes forward, scanning the buildings, silently watching. Never looking back. He can't allow himself, bottles it all up inside, plasters a smile on his face and cracks black jokes like the rest of them. All the while staring straight ahead, ignoring the tiny splits in the walls of the buildings, the long scars of the many wars, like his, that have marched through this city like his men straggling behind.

He leads the way through the streets, the worn point of the Allied advance. His men haven't slept in days, their horses need water. The war keeps asking them for more. He's not sure he has more to give.

He rides on.

~

My love,

It's been years now, surely, that we have been riding, passing the same watering hole, the same small tangle of buildings that calls itself a village, the same bleached bones of the horse that never made it home. I am in a foul mood.

I fear the war has made me a cynic.

The men have grown battle-hardened, sharp and angular. I hardly recognise them. I received another letter from Ma. Dad's illness has taken a turn for the worse, and it doesn't look like he'll make it through to harvest. What happened to the world we left four years ago? What will we return to? Will Australia even remember us?

There's a man in the first patrol: Gordon, a sunken sort of bloke, small eyes and a shaggy toothbrush. Can't say I care for him. Quietish, so you never know what he's thinking. Wouldn't draw sniper fire, if you catch my drift. Got his missus back home, and a little one, growing bigger every day. Gets a parcel now and then. Like any of us, he's trying to avoid cashing in his ticket.

Yesterday they brought round the mail. Haven't had it for a while, riding scout. Gordon got his. I didn't read it myself, but word spread quick. The little one was swept off the rocks at Point Peron. They didn't find the body for two days. I'm sorry, his wife wrote, but the local banker has been my pillar, here when I needed him, and we are to wed.

The war has found infinite forms to take a life. I've put Gordon on round-the-clock watch. When I catch my share of metal, I hope you will find a new bed to warm. I wouldn't blame you. Mine has grown cold and callous. I forget what your skin feels like.

The saddle grates. The dust blinds. It's too late for me.

Yours, despairingly.

They ride into the village at daybreak, making good time, following the trail of the Jackos where it meanders through the gully. He eases his horse into a trot, flicking his eyes around the huts, watching for movement. Dark earth. Dust hangs in the air. The Turks were here. His horse breathes like a smoker. His thighs ache – riding for three solid hours, keeping touch with the Jacko outriders, following in the column's wake.

He dismounts, and leads his horse over to the well, ties her to the wooden strut while he pulls up the bucket dangling on the nearby rope. Nugget is by his shoulder, startling him, and he drops the rope, the precious water splashing back into the darkness.

'Steady, mate,' says Nugget, yellow teeth pulled back in a smile. He's always fucking smiling, is Nugget. Nothing – not the sand or the Turks or the other men – nothing fazes Nugget. Not even Alan, the darkness weighing on his chest, growing heavier each day. The sickness, eating away at him. The ever-present fear. Nugget has stood by him through it all. Held his hand through the dark times and carried him in the darker still. Always smiling. Nugget should make him feel safe, but all he does is make him feel inadequate. How small he feels in comparison to the tiny Irishman.

He hates Nugget a little bit.

'What're you so chipper about?' he snarls.

'Word is the Turks are about to surrender.'

'And you believe it?'

'I'm an optimist, Al, you know that.'

He pulls the full bucket up to the rim of the well, and hauls it onto the stones. Nugget dips a leathery hand into the cool water and runs it through the bristles of his hair, then flicks the last few drops at Alan. 'Smile, you sullen bastard.'

Alan grunts. It's easy to smile when you don't have to think. When the health and wellbeing of an entire regiment doesn't weigh on you with every step. When there aren't people relying on you, or looking up to you. Judging you. Easier to smile when you don't have a child and a woman taking everything from you, secrets eating away at the hard muscle of your shoulders, a home that doesn't feel like home anymore. Easy to smile when you are brave.

Nugget scoops his open palms into the bucket, and raises the water to his chapped lips. Alan slaps his hands away before he can drink, the water spilling on the hot stones.

'Smell it first, Nug.'

Nugget smells his hands, and gags. The water that drips down through the dust from his forehead is tinged a reddish-brown.

In the darkness of the well, they can't tell what is floating in the water, but they can smell it. The retreating Turks have ensured no-one else can use this one. The horses will have to wait for a drink.

'I'm a realist,' Alan says, as they remount.

Har Megiddo, they call it, the flat plains outside Damascus where it was written that the final battle for the souls of mankind would take place. The Turks had vowed to make one last stand here, but the pace of the Light Horse outstripped their slow infantry, and only two days ago they'd captured another thousand dishevelled prisoners. Not bad blokes, mind, those Jackos. Fighting for the wrong side. Born in the wrong place.

Alan gave all his cigarettes away at the first village they passed through in a foolish bout of charity, and they haven't seen another delivery for weeks. Some of the men have taken to chewing tobacco like the locals, walking around camp dribbling great streams of black spit from between their teeth. He would line these troopers up before a firing squad and wipe them off the face of the earth, given the chance. The little puddles of black bubbling spit repulse him.

It all annoys him now. Men laughing. The crackle of the fire in the evening, the smell of billy tea in the early hours. He is sick of the eternal jokes. The constant bickering. The weight of the pistol on his hip aggravates him, he wants to throw it behind him in the sand. He wants to rip off his uniform and feel regular clothes against his skin. The stench of the horses makes his stomach roil. He's gone through four horses in the past month, riding them until they break, tripping them in the hidden potholes of the desert, walking back to camp with the bridle and saddle. He hasn't bothered to name this one. A strong back and good pace off the line, the ability to outrun a Turkish charge – that's all he asks.

The brass have no idea what they are doing, changing plans midway through a march. Johnny Turk disappears into the landscape as they approach.

The dark red wound on his leg is festering, it rubs against the leather of the saddle and never heals. His coughing is constant. Each morning he spits dark sandy gunk from the back of his throat into the sand.

There are few pleasures keeping him going. There were the five seconds of bliss the first cigarette brought each morning, but he has lost those along with the cigarettes. The swig of a bottle, when he can get it, eases the long afternoons into night. And there are the sunsets that bathe the marching column in a red haze, like the Illawarra tree back at university bursting into fiery blooms each summer, his forgotten memories of home.

Another village, another day. Another dusty street, another faceless enemy. Just him and Nugget, out ahead of the main body of the troop, as usual. He glances around at the brown earth of the houses, distrust in the dark clay, baked hard in the sun. Like pots in a kiln. Hiding things. He dismounts, and lets his reins drop, knowing his horse won't stray far.

Nugget dismounts behind him and leads both their horses over to a trough of brackish water. He checks it before letting them drink. He's whistling, the same Irish jig he's been whistling day in and day out since his mother popped him out.

'Don't you know any other songs?' Alan says, pacing over to the closest doorway and peering into the gloom.

'Sure I do,' Nugget says, and keeps whistling the same tune.

Alan imagines eyes in the darkness, watching his movements. Somewhere down the road the shrill cry of metal on stone, a knife being sharpened on a whetstone. The horses drink noisily.

He pulls out his own canteen and drinks, the cool water dripping down his chin. He is made of straw, dried in the sun, ready to snap and twist and shear off at the slightest gust. His shirt is worn thin enough to see through, his boots encase his feet in a sauna of sweat and pebbles.

'Reckon they passed through here?' Nugget says.

No sign of life in the street. No noises. The place is a ghost town. Birds circle above, waiting to pick their corpses clean.

'Follow me,' he says, ducking into the doorway.

'The rest of 'em will be here in half a –' Nugget's words fade behind him as he creeps further into the room. His feet are walking on the soft plushness of carpet, and he can make out bundles of fabric in the corner of the room, sleeping mats, potential hiding places. There is a wooden door at the back of the room, and he hears Rose's familiar laughter, the loud, unashamed howl. His revolver is shaking in his hand and he doesn't remember pulling it out.

Alan pushes through the door, and surprises two women, laughing as they cook. The thick smell of spices, meat and vegetables – proper cooking – floors him. His mouth fills with saliva. The women stop what they are doing at the sight of him, and uncertainty clouds his mind.

Behind his back, the door swings open and Nugget bowls him over.

'G'day, ladies,' he says.

The women don't move. Nugget reaches across and lowers Alan's hand, pointing the barrel of the revolver away from them. For a second he's not sure where he is – one of the women has Nancy's black hair, gleaming in the dusk. He can't speak.

Nugget speaks for him. 'Sorry to barge in like this.' He places his hand on Alan's shoulder, and pulls him back toward the door. There's a window at the back of the room, and through it the sun is setting, dropping over the rim of the earth, dissolving into an endless dark night. Nancy doesn't love him. Never did. Though he's not sure he loved her. He's not sure he's ever loved. All the certainties in his life have left him with the cigarettes, with the sun, with Rose and his brothers and the dead.

'Anything else, Al?' Nugget is saying.

He's back in the room. The women stare at him. Nugget turns his body, and holds him by his shoulders, his face large in the shadows. 'You ok?'

He nods, unsure what it is he is agreeing to – Nugget tips his hat to the women and opens the door to usher him out. On a shelf behind the women there's a dusty brown bottle of liquid. Whiskey? Arak? He walks forward. The women jabber at him in their Arabic, clawing at his shirt, but he pushes through them. He can't read the bottle, but he unstoppers the cork and it smells alcoholic, so he walks back to the door. Nugget cocks his head.

'I'm taking this.'

Nugget doesn't reply, for once.

The women prattle on; he walks out the door and leaves Nugget to deal with them. He shoves the bottle deep into his pack.

Nugget emerges from the doorway, tucking a small wad of notes back into his trousers.

'The fuck was that about?' he asks Alan.

'You can do the questioning, I do the requisitioning.'

'Right,' Nugget mounts his horse, 'but there's no need to be a bastard about it.'

Alan doesn't respond. He is a product of his environment – he wanted the bottle, so he took it. He deserves a little compensation. And once again, Nugget broadcasts his inadequacies to the world.

'They don't deserve our pity, Nugget.'

'They don't deserve our hatred, either.'

He doesn't know how to respond to that, so he rides ahead, pushing his horse faster down the narrow streets. As they reach the outskirts of town, Nugget rides up on his right side.

'What are you doing, Al?'

He doesn't say anything, because he doesn't know the answer.

Nugget starts to whistle.

His pencil lies snapped in half at the bottom of his pack. The last one. He fishes the snubby end out and tries to write, but feels stupid, his fingers huge. Maybe one of the other boys will have a spare. He turns around to ask Red, but it's Nugget's bedroll on the other side of the tent. Red is back home relearning the alphabet.

He must have dozed off in the heat of the afternoon. He finished the bottle of arak he requisitioned from the house and then woke up dry-mouthed on his bedroll. He's halfway to Damascus, on the opposite side of the world to Red and his family. He was trying to write a letter home to Ma. Dad is coughing up long red streaks in his hanky. Rose told him as much in her last letter. She's been helping Ma with the nursing. Almost moved herself in. They don't need him.

Tomorrow they leave for the next city, the next parched brown toy town, the next day of saddle sores and chapped lips. He tries not to think about it. Flies buzz around his wet eyes. He's stopped caring enough to wave them off. He's hanging on by a thin thread.

His water canteen lies on his bedroll like a drowsy girlfriend. Fucking Nancy, taking him for a fool. Or Rose, perhaps, in a different world. Lost in the tumbled dunes of sweat-stained material. Waiting for another man to return home. Someone he will never be. He's given up writing to both of them. Their letters arrive and he can't muster the energy to read them. He throws them in the bottom of his pack, and hopes they'll vanish. They peer out at him, accusing, each time he opens it.

Nugget will be back soon. Bounding in and making noise, forcing conversation for too long, pushing him too far. He'll snap, and Nugget will joke about needing his beauty sleep. They'll sleep for three hours before waking for another patrol. So it goes.

Should be time for a quick cigarette before the patrol returns.

Nugget's half of the tent is a mess of uniform parts and papers, tawdry postcards and souvenirs for his family. He's sure there is half a pack around somewhere, Nugget is good for one or two. As long as he doesn't sneak too many, Nugget doesn't need to know.

The letter is tucked into the back of Nugget's bedroll. He notices when it slips out and flutters to the floor. It's the same heavy white envelope she always uses, the same scrawled, rushed hand. For half a moment he wonders why Nancy is writing to Nugget, but then he notices the letter is addressed to him. It's one of the ones he threw into his pack unopened – he never would have noticed it was missing.

It is open. Nancy writes about Harriet, about the tantrums she throws when put to bed. She asks after the next paycheck, says she needs it to pay for Harriet's clothes. She says her father might have a job for him when the war finishes.

Nugget knows and hasn't mentioned it. Hasn't told anyone. He contemplates confronting the Irishman about it, but knows he doesn't have the heart. As late as Lemnos he thought he might be one of those men who discovered in themselves a certain fortitude in times of great need. He imagined that he might be special, but all these years later he's resigned to the fact that nothing special is headed his way.

He should confront Nugget about the letter, but he stays silent, like his father before him, like the war has taught him. He replaces the letter in Nugget's bedroll, and then lies down on his own. He stares at the canvas ceiling. When Nugget crashes his way back inside, he pretends to be asleep. Silent in the corner.

This village is larger than the last. Clay pottery houses. Long reams of black material flying from clotheslines. In the centre square there's a well, an abandoned market, an eerie silence. He wipes the thick layer of dust from below his eyes, wets his lips, glances around the deserted street.

'Where're the natives?' Nugget asks.

'Something's up.' He dismounts, ties his horse to a nearby post. Nugget slides from his horse, stretches his legs and peers into the dark doorway next to him.

'Shady fuckers.' Nugget smiles his lopsided Irishman grin.

Alan pulls back his cheeks and stretches his lips wide, the tight dry skin at the side of his mouth cracking and splitting. He's falling apart, covered in sores, aching all over, wound tight like a child's toy. He's forgotten how to smile. He pulls his revolver from his holster and checks the chamber.

'What's that for, big fella? Fancying yourself another requisitioning, eh?' Nugget pours water from his canteen through his hair and down his face. The dust turns to clay, painting dark streaks down his cheeks. In a street close by something bleats, a part-human cry, cut short. The backs of Alan's legs are carved wood after many hours in the saddle. He hasn't relaxed in years.

A gunshot nearby. The large compound at the end of the road. They race towards it. He cocks his revolver, and Nugget attaches the bayonet to his rifle.

It's some sort of meeting hall, large and empty. They can hear Arab gobbledegook somewhere near the back. They reach a long corridor, and the noise is all around them. Nugget heads left. He takes right. His palm, holding the pistol, is slick with sweat.

He kicks through a door and emerges into a long room, dappled in sunlight, the walls hung with faded carpets. Eyes turn to meet him: two women, three bearded natives, two tiny children on his right, and at the back of the room, silhouetted in the window, a Turk holding a pistol, shouting. He fires before he has taken the time to aim, and the woman closest to him drops, screaming, to the floor. His second bullet catches the Turk, who slumps backward against the wall. His third bullet kills one of the bearded men – another Abdul in disguise. They're all the enemy. Another bearded man turns, yelling at him in his guttural tongue, fear in his eyes, and it is too easy to pull the trigger to shut him up. The bullet slams into his face and pulverises the soft flesh. The second woman is screaming. Alan fires two bullets into her. The screaming stops. The last man raises his hands. Alan drops him with a bullet in the stomach. Each bullet rings through the room, a kookaburra laugh echoing in the bush. The children are screaming on his right. The revolver is heavy, pulling his arm down. He struggles to pull the trigger. Clicks from the barrel. He keeps pulling the trigger as the room falls silent, as the voice in his head tells him he is safe. He has forgotten to breathe. The air tastes liquid, thick and clean when he swallows.

He looks down at the two children, who have stopped crying, glancing up at him like he is the terrible monster from his childhood stories.

'What?!' he screams, but the children gawp. He reloads his revolver and looms over their tiny bodies. He cocks the hammer.

Someone barrels into him, knocking him into the carpeted wall. He fires the pistol, two shots, quickly, but his assailant is holding his gun hand away, pointing it into the ceiling. A meaty hand wraps around his neck and knocks his head back twice against the wall. The revolver falls from his fingers and clatters to the floor.

'It's me, Al.' Nugget's eyes are in his face, his breath sticky and hot.

Alan breathes steadily, his gaze clears, his heartbeat settles. He's surprised to find himself in the same room, the same dusty street out the window, Nugget's hand around his neck, his toes grazing the ground.

'I'm fine, Nug.' He's not fine. He can't do it anymore. 'Sorry.'

Nugget lowers him back to the floor, bends down and picks up the revolver, hands it back to Alan handle first. The children are huddled by the wall.

'Fuckinell.' Nugget whistles out. Alan's hands are shaking from the adrenalin. There was a boy on Gallipoli who couldn't stop laughing while they waited in the dawn light for the order to charge. One of the other men hit him hard in the jaw, and the boy had gone down, and Alan had looked away. For the good of the regiment, he remembers, and starts to giggle.

Nugget looks at him. Little judgmental bastard – look then, what does he care. All Alan wants to do is sleep for a hundred years with the mozzies buzzing past his ears and the screen door knocking back and forth, his parents sitting out on the veranda talking in low voices, his brothers snoring in the next room. Fuck Nugget. Fuck the Jackos. Fuck 'em all.

'Get the bloody kids out of here,' Nugget says, and Alan nods automatically. He kneels in front of the children, a boy and a girl, and flashes a split-lip smile. The girl starts to cry. Alan scoops her up in his left arm, the young boy in his right. The boy twitches in his arms, his feet kicking, but Alan pulls him in tighter.

Back out the door, through the corridors, into the street. He puts them down by the horses.

'Go! Get out of here!' he yells as he runs back inside.

Nugget is kneeling over one of the women, holding her hand in his, murmuring low under his breath. Alan can't hear what he's saying. Nugget crosses himself. Alan does the same, though he's never believed in a God. Not now, especially. God is the gaping red bullet wound in the brown hair of the second woman, lying on the floor before him.

The Turk is dead. Alan nudges the body with his foot to make sure. He looks stupidly young. Younger than Alan. His cheeks are shiny and smooth. The bullet hole is a too-tiny puncture by his left temple.

'You see anyone else out there?' Nugget looks over at him, the bayonet over his shoulder glinting.

Alan shrugs.

'Did you check?' They both glance over at the second door as it clatters open and a second Turkish soldier runs at them, a wicked curved blade in his hand. Nugget doesn't have time to react, rising to his feet as the Jacko falls into him. They roll across the carpet, the blade flashing. It's like they're moving underwater, the slow toss of arms and legs, the heaviness of the room around them. The Jacko emerges on top, the knife facing down, his wrists held in Nugget's arms. The blade lowers inch by inch toward Nugget's chest. Nugget who knows everything. Nugget, his one friend.

Alan doesn't move. He watches the knife-edge scratch Nugget's shirt as the Jacko leans his weight forward.

The Irishman grunts in pain.

The back of the Jacko's neck is smudged with dirt.

'Al.' Nugget screams, a child's voice. The blade pushes through his ribs with a loud crack.

A long sigh emerges from Nugget's lips, the sliver of metal driving into the buttery white skin of his chest as Alan raises his revolver and fires. The first bullet hits the Jacko in the left arm, and he releases the knife and turns to Alan with a look of surprise. The second bullet thunders into his chest. He staggers back against the wall, sliding to earth with a thud and lying silent. The third bullet makes his body dance, a puppet pulled to life for an instant by impatient hands.

He crouches and shakes Nugget's shoulder, and the eyelids flutter. The man looking up looks much older than Nugget. The elaborate strapping of the handle protrudes from his chest, a gleaming stone embedded in the butt of the knife. It's beautiful, in a way.

Nugget tries to speak, but the words evaporate in the room. Alan crouches closer, until he can feel hot breath on his ear. 'Get. Out.' Nugget closes his eyes. 'Explosives.' The word comes out as a long hiss. 'Getthefuckout.'

He grabs Nugget under the arms and drags his body free, free of the room with all its smells and colours, free of the darkness and out into the fading light of the street. He sits him up next to a water trough. The two children watch by his side. He looks up and they cringe from his glance. He reaches a hand into the trough and wipes Nugget's face with the water. Nugget licks the cool water from his lips, so he holds a palm under his mouth and tries to get him to drink. The water splutters down his chin. His breath comes in ragged chunks.

'The whole place is rigged. Al. Dynamite in the other room.' Nugget nods his head toward the well and the empty square, and Alan notices the black fuse running the length of the road, darting off into doorways of the houses. No wonder it's deserted.

Nugget lifts his head back up and fixes Alan with a look. Alan can't hold his gaze. Nugget knows.

'That baby needs a father,' Nugget whispers, each word agony. Nugget knows his true character. Knows his every weakness and disappointment. 'Don't be scared, Al.'

Alan can't breathe. He killed them. All of them.

'You don't have to be scared.'

Nugget reaches a weak hand inside his shirt and pulls out a small bundle of papers, wrapped with a thin leather strap. He pushes them toward him. He's shaking his head, but Nugget is insistent. Continues to believe in him.

'I killed them all, Nug.'

'No mate, I killed them.' Nugget coughs and dirty brown blood stains his pale lips. 'Save yourself. Please, do this for me.'

He takes the bundle of papers from Nugget's hand. Nugget pulls him closer and tries to speak. His lips move, but no sound comes out. Alan turns his head and holds his ear by Nugget's mouth, but all he can hear is the wheeze of breath, the whimper of pain. A croak, disappearing.

A noise to his left – the kids, watching this all play out with shock on their faces. He gestures towards the kids to leave, run, get out of it. They don't move. He stands and takes a step towards them and they stagger back. He roars, and runs at them, and they scream and scatter up the street.

He walks back to Nugget. The sky has turned purple, orange, rose. The sky is on fire.

'I'll try, Nug. I promise.'

But when he looks down, Nugget is dead.

In the square, a Waler appears, followed by another, and another. The rest of the troop, the boys, his mates. A teenager he doesn't recognise turns into the street, trying to control his mount.

'Get the horses out of here,' Alan screams at him, 'the whole town is rigged.'

He has left his revolver inside, by the bodies.

'Get everyone out!'

The whole building could blow at any moment, erasing everything. He can feel it all rolling off him – responsibilities, expectations, orders. A weight lifts from his shoulders.

It's easy once you give up. Nothing matters.

He doesn't look to see if the boy has listened, just ducks back into the compound. The bodies of the women, the men, the Turks. He steps over them gingerly, pushes through the door at the back and finds the stack of dynamite, the long black fuse. He takes Nugget's bayonet from his fallen rifle and cuts, giving himself enough time to make his peace.

His whole body feels lighter now he's decided.

Nugget died thinking he was still capable of change. And maybe this isn't what he had in mind, but it's an end, the only end available.

A candle burns in the back room. He holds the fuse in the flame. It lights with a spark, crawling along the wire faster than he'd anticipated. He runs back into the main room. Bloody footprints on the carpets. The oppressive silence of death. He places the dynamite in the middle of the room and sits beside the body of the woman, glances down at her stony eyes and asks for forgiveness. He's sure of himself for the first time in a long time. He breathes easily.

The fuse grows shorter.
The long black cloth billows on the line outside.

The first explosion shakes the earth, and the horses scatter, rearing up in panic. The men soothe them in low voices as the second detonation goes off. They cautiously pick their way toward the billowing column of smoke ripping its way across the sky, scything the watercolour-palette sunset in two.

CONCLUSION: Final thoughts on the legitimacy of Alan Lewis's legacy, the importance of a unified theory of authorship, and acknowledgements.

When I set out to write this thesis, I thought I knew all there was to know about Alan Lewis, the Australian experience of the First World War, and what it might take to prove, finally, and without doubt, that the author commonly referred to as the Unknown Digger was a man already revered among the Australian populace for his bravery and the sacrifices he made for his country. I wouldn't say I was foolish for my belief in the concrete corporeality of these objectives, but I certainly wasn't prepared for the journey I would be led on by these words. Like Alan Lewis and the Anzacs, I started out a foolhardy young man, eagerly heading out from the relative safety of the beautiful city of Perth, into the dangerous unknown of the academic world. Like Alan Lewis and the Anzacs, I have seen things too horrible to describe, and witnessed horrors unimaginable.[136]

I began this dissertation by marvelling at the astounding candour of the Unknown Digger poems, the spine-tingling electricity conveyed

---

136 Fuck Brighton.

Fuck the half-arsed pebble beach and the dirty bogan jetty. Fuck the too-bright sun and cheap plastic sunnies. Fuck the midget waves and the piss-weak summer breeze blowing in off the freezing water. Fuck the fat dickheads pouring penny after penny into those crappy Royal-Show coin games and fuck their sugar-addicted crackhead offspring running past your knees, wiping snot and fairy floss on your jeans, laughing like hyenas. Fuck the stodgy fried fish and the too-thick chips. Fuck mushy peas. Fuck the row after row of knock-off leather coats and hippy-dippy bric-a-brac-crap blocking the way down lanes of namby-pamby vegan cafes, rammed with more fat motherfucking London couples walking fucking-hand-in-obese-hand, buying shitty gardening gloves embroidered with disease-ridden foxes, pushing their cackling little demon spawn in their ridiculous four-wheel-drive prams. Fuck the maze of jewellery stores and tattoo parlours that lead to nowhere. Fuck the Taj Mahal–looking Lego castle they call the Pavilion. Fuck the jokes and the buskers and the groups of teenagers sniggering to themselves, lying with their tits out on the grass, drinking cheap cans of ethanolic cider. Fuck their laughter, fuck their smiles, fuck their youthful skin and their tight young-people arses. Fuck their happiness. Fuck their goddamn self-righteous optimism, and fuck fucking Brighton.

by their imagery, and the astonishing way they succinctly capture the collective idealisation of a national identity. I end with my astonishment doubled.[137] Finding myself at the conclusion of this thesis, alone in a Brighton hotel room, subsisting on chocolate bars and four-packs of cheap beer, I hope I have done enough to have convinced my readers of the truth. I have learnt all there is to know about the Unknown Digger, have delved deep into the critical and analytical investigation of his poems, have worn myself out with all-day research binges and countless sleepless nights studying every aspect of his gilded words, and at this point – friendless, peerless, loveless and pantsless – I fear there is nothing more I can do. I implore you: read Jennifer Hayden's stirring and, undeniably, compelling take-down of my work in *Australian Literary Journal*, and then make up your own mind.[138] For me, there is only one man capable of placing those beautiful words down on those yellowed pieces of paper.

In the previous chapters, I have proved, conclusively, that Alan Lewis is the Unknown Digger using a thorough critical analysis of his

---

137 I wanted to stand on a wet pier in the rain while waves, twenty-foot tall, pounded the concrete, spraying saltwater over my windswept hair. I wanted dark clouds, ripe with rain, to cover every inch of visible sky, and thunder to break like guns in battle. I wanted dogs whimpering under couches and children crying for their parents. I wanted rain running down my face and mixing with my tears. I wanted to taste the saltwater of home with my collar turned up against the wind, artfully displaying my tormented soul to the world.

The guy at the front desk when I checked in said, Australian, huh? You must have brought the weather with you!

Fuck him too.

138 I made my way down to what they call the beach here, and then walked further along the coast away from the screaming of the crowds and the smell of waffle cones, until I was alone. The water was a dark concrete grey, crashing in heavy waves onto the slippery pebbles. Out on the horizon stood the skeletal husk of the old burnt pier – a warning, maybe, to anyone hoping to escape from London to the wilds of Brighton, that inevitably, we all must die, and that even when your girlfriend says she loves you and you talk about marriage like it will definitely happen in the future, she's probably banging your boss on a work trip to Paris.

I'm so angry, at everything.

I'm so tired of being angry.

poems, intimate knowledge of his letters home, a detailed account of his service history and the importance of his time spent on Lemnos recovering from his wounds, and a completely new way of understanding the poems in relation to his much-later-than-theorised death. While certain personal aspects of my research may be considered irrelevant to the final product, I stand proud of my accomplishments. After publication, there will inevitably come concentrated attacks on my results, my argument, my method of discovery, probably my academic tone and certainly my unconventional writing style, but at this point I find I don't really give two shits either way. This is the end result of my findings. This is my reality.[139]

~

There's a great little comedic poem written by an anonymous digger at the end of the war, entitled 'Andy MacNoon', which academics

---

139 The beach back home is wide open and inviting, stretching up the coast to the white tower of Scarborough and down past the dinosaur shapes of Fremantle's cranes. I know the beach back home, know the best place to throw my towel, the parking spots that will always be free, the areas where the reef hides beneath the sand but you'll still stub your toes. I know on the overcast days, what we call shark weather, you'll only see the diehard surfers, the retirees doing their daily swim and tourists in the water. I know on sunny days the sand will be too hot to stand on, and only digging your feet into the coolness of the sand a few centimetres down will save you from doing an awkward dash across the beach. I know the searing pain of diving headfirst into a stinger. I know the hangover-curing cold of a morning-after swim. I know once you dive under that first wave and into an underwater world that nothing, not girlfriends or rival academics or long-dead soldiers, can disturb the pure, clear, cleansing wash of a good swim.

I sat down on the pebbles and pulled off my shoes and socks. I wasn't wearing boardies, or anything resembling bathers, and taking off my T-shirt the wind whipped across my skin like knives, and I began to doubt the wisdom of my plan, but by that point I'd taken off my jeans, and I figured there was no turning back.

I walked slowly down the beach, careful to place my feet on the smoothest pebbles I could see, until the sting of water on my toes brought tears to my eyes.

Nothing to it, I thought, and walked in.

originally believed could be another Unknown Digger poem – a line of thought that was rapidly rescinded following another Jennifer Hayden broadside – that I've always dreamed of putting in the acknowledgements section of my finished thesis.

I didn't think it would end like this, but maybe that just makes the poem more relevant:

> *I couldn't have made it through this s--t,*
> *Without you lawless b-----ds,*
> *'Coz who'd've shot the d----d Abduls*
> *If we'd all f-----g scarpered?!*[140]

And so I find I must acknowledge the following for their hand in creating the manuscript you find in your hands: Dr Patrick Rossen at The University of Western Australia, for urging me to continue with my initial idea and share my idea with the world, inspiring me to settle in London (the mecca of academic study, he said, forgetting to mention the grime and the rain and the adulterous girlfriends) and even setting me up with an interview with the Prof; my third girlfriend, Meg Fallon, for breaking my heart and giving me the impetus to leave Perth; Nicholas Curtin-Kneeling, despite his derision, and all my colleagues

---

140 From *The Bonzer Book of First World War Poetry,* Noelle Miller, ed., Allum & Alexandra Publishing, Sydney, 2002. The beach at Gallipoli, from what little I saw of it, perched high in the stands over the length of a long April night – from the disappearing outcrops of rock as the sun dropped behind us, the sound of the waves slapping onto the beach that supported us through the dark as countless politicians, school groups and military men, Australian and Kiwi and Turkish, kept us entertained through the wee hours of the morn, to the thin white lips of foam that pushed up the beach, tinged orange in the first rays of morning light as the Last Post rang out from the rocky scrubland surrounding us – was far more reminiscent of the beaches back home than the cold, wet beaches of England.

I think about the men streaming up the beach on that first morning, hearts hammering in their chests, the numbing cold of the water seeping into their skin as they plunged their boots into the shallows, the bullets whizzing past their heads, the fear of imminent death and, rising out of the icy Brighton sea, finding my feet on the pebbled floor, wiping the cold water from my stinging eyes, running a shaking hand through my hair, gasping for breath, like I've been shot myself, I think I understand.

at FWWWAC (sorry for the tackle, Dr Richards, but I'm Australian – we don't do things by halves); Professor and Head of English Literature Studies Alistair Fitzwilliam-Harding, for teaching me the value of loss, the importance of perseverance, and the danger of thinking ridiculous British stereotypes could never be a serious threat; my parents, for their unwavering support and unlimited pecuniary assistance; Jennifer Hayden, for teaching me that not every friend can be relied upon in the trenches, and that not every enemy wears a foreign uniform; my grandfathers, who both fought for their country, so that I might be here today; and the manufacturers of every tiny, ridiculous excuse for a 'disposable BBQ' in the world, for convincing me that the British are no more civilised or cultured than the island of criminals I happily call home.

And finally to Alan, who taught me the meaning of sacrifice.[141]

And to Em, who taught me the true meaning of sacrifice.[142]

---

141 I stumble out of the waves in my underwear. There are no dead mates floating by me in the shallows, no bullets taking chunks out of the beach by my feet, no cannons thundering shells into the cafes and bars of the seafront boulevard before me, no grey warships floating in the water behind. No near-year-long stay on the beach confronting me, no dysentery or typhoid looming on the horizon, no years of life in the saddle to come.

I thought I knew everything Alan went through, and I used to think, if it came down to it, if World War Three started up and even the academics were enlisted and they made a regiment up of the leading lights in Australian literary academia, I'd be at the forefront of the vanguard, broadsword in hand (it's already an insane proposition, don't question the choice of weaponry) charging headfirst into the fray.

But now, after everything, I don't know. I don't think I'm that person.

142 And I'm ok with that. The men of Lewis's generation, the Anzacs, and my grandparents' generation, and even those of my parents' generation, are a different breed. I can live with it. I couldn't pull the trigger if my life depended on it. I couldn't hate Em any more than I could hunt down the Prof and punch in his smug English teeth any more than I could confront Jennifer Hayden face to face. I feel condemned to sit here, cold and wet, on a windy Brighton beach, and keep watching, keep writing, keep fighting in my own, non-spectacular, non-bloody way.

We can't all be Alan Lewis. We can't all be Unknown Diggers. We're not all Jennifer Haydenses.

We don't all get the girl.

Where to from here? The world of the Unknown Digger is suddenly open and exciting once more. The eventual publication of this work will spread the knowledge that these poems were created by Alan Lewis, and will produce extensive opportunity for studies into the true significance, the actual contextual background and the real meanings of these renowned poems. I look forward to engaging with my colleagues in the academic world on an equal basis for a long time to come.[143]

If we have learnt anything from this, I hope that it is the following: that our military heroes are capable of writing the most beautiful poetry, and our greatest poets can be the heroes we looked up to all along. I truly believe that all of us, from the lowliest trooper to the highest-ranking general, have everything we need inside of us to be poets. And that all of us, students and lovers and academics and Australians, poets one and all, can be that hero when the time comes. Don't let anyone tell you otherwise.[144]

Maybe I would fight in that war, but not at the front of the charge. I'd be somewhere towards the back, making notes. I'm ok with that.

143 I struggled into the warmth of my shirt and hoodie, and then realised that my jeans must have blown away while I was in the water. The sun had disappeared behind a looming evening of cloud, and I shivered, tucking my legs up under my hoodie and wrapping my arms around my knees. I pulled my phone out and looked at the long list of messages, and then, in an act of unrivalled stupidity that I envisioned to be epically cinematic, threw it into the waves. I didn't throw it hard enough, and instead it shattered into pieces on the rocks before sinking into the shallows.

The water helped clear my head. Like the water at Cottesloe Beach does after a big night – the world's best hangover cure. It would be so easy to run away, buy a plane ticket back home and throw myself into the ocean and sun, but I can't bring myself to let him down like that.

Maybe there is a little Alan Lewis in me after all.

144 When I get back to London, I'll start looking for new openings in UK universities. Bound to be something, as they can't get enough of us Aussies. Even if it takes me another ten years, working away, avoiding the siren call of the south, avoiding living, I will prove that Alan Lewis wrote these poems.

Might start with Scotland, I'm thinking. Not many South Africans in Scotland, and fewer English twats.

HOME.

IT'S to be hoped that we hear no more about 'the Mother Country' from misguided people who hold that tortured land up as an example of united socialism. The British election figures prove beyond all doubt that at least half the entire population there opposes socialism; but for the peculiar distribution of seats and methods of voting the people would have thrown the socialists right out.
– R.H.G., Boddington.

The train is pulling into the station, and he doesn't have time to read the rest of the letters to the editor, or the reviews. He hates reading about the world that has passed him by, but he reads anyway. Can't look away. Out the carriage window he knows the streets they'll be passing like he never left, the oval and the schoolhouse, the track leading to the beach, the dogs running wild down the main street. He keeps reading.

... his new collection BUSH POETRY:
''ALF a mo', bloke,' says the cobber, 'what's your blinkin' rush?
Billy's almost boiled, an' the damper's lookin' lush,
You can kip 'ere for the night, if you ain't got nowt to be,
Ain't nowhere 'alf as luvvly as a bed beneath the trees.'
I look down at the cobber, splayed out in the evenin' light,
An' it pains me to admit it, but y'know what? B-----d's right

He leaves the paper tucked into the back of the seat for someone else to read on their way back to Perth. The town is different, but nothing has changed. The cream paint of the station peels like sunburn, cars putter down the side streets. Seagulls call, and the smell of salt and seaweed rolls up the road that leads to the beach. Everything is smaller than it once was.

The station hand takes down his bag, and looks him straight in the eye and says thank you, sir, as he drops his last coin into his hand, and doesn't recognise him. He doesn't recognise himself any more. He's grown his beard long, flecks of grey in his hair, his eyes hooded. He's tired all the time. He stinks too, cooped up on the train like cattle. He doesn't remember a time when he wasn't moving, from one place to another, one life to another, one lie to another. One dream to another. Cases and bags. Back alleys and halfway homes. A new name. A new story. He's convinced himself this is a life.

He carries his bag on his shoulder and walks down from the station toward the sea. The schoolyard, empty now. The grocers. The police station, unattended, like the empty towns in Har Megiddo, in another life. The street he's walking down seems flimsy, make-believe: a film set, a cowboy town from one of the Hollywood films he'll sit and watch, hour after hour, to get out of the rain. He hasn't eaten in two days. His stomach swears at him. His shoes are an old married couple, bickering away, falling apart at the seams. A young woman walking up the street toward him changes sides to avoid walking past. He lowers his eyes.

As he passes the grocers he swipes an apple from the display and keeps walking before anyone challenges him. If you act confident, nine times out of ten, they won't bother you. He walks down the hill, chewing away, trying to stay in the shade of the gums that line the perimeter of the park. He's not sure where he's going, but then he hasn't for a long time, not since he stopped following orders. He bites through the core, swallows the pips, licks his fingers. It hasn't killed him yet.

Walking for the sake of walking. Walking in circles. Walking through another town where the locals eye him up and wonder if he's worth the trouble. Not for the first time, he wishes he had a horse. A hardy little Waler. A place in the bush. A bit of land. Someone waiting for him.

He read about it a few years after, once the rest of the diggers had been sent home and they could immortalise the bloody campaign in books and newspapers like what they'd done was some sort of glorious crusade. Once the bodies had grown cold. Once the nightmares had become his only friends. After Damascus, and Jerusalem, and Armageddon, once the Turks had surrendered and Fritz had given up, and the world was put back together like a broken vase. Once the orders came in that the Light Horse was set to return home.

Without their horses.

There was never a contingency plan for the horses. Too expensive to relocate back home, for all but the very highest ranking. Too many to consider. Too disposable. They were sold off, in their hundreds, to marketplaces, to farmers and chieftains and nomads and recent enemies. For riding and farming and slaughtering and tanning. For their hair, for their bones, for their meat.

In the bars, he heard talk of diggers taking their closest mates for one final ride in the desert, and returning with saddle and bridle. Tall tales of broken legs and rocky ground. The Light Horse had returned to Australia tens of thousands short, the final cost felt more keenly than the casualties at The Nek, at Suez, at the failed Gaza attack.

But by that time he was long dead and immortalised as Lieutenant Alan Lewis, VC, a stranger he had never met, a thousand times removed from the murderer he had turned out to be. Once word of his commission came around he knew his old life was over and he could never return. It was easier then. Getting away had been the easy part. Running away he could handle. A tactical retreat, they had once called it. From life.

He had thought that killing himself would solve his problems, and in a funny way, it had. But sitting in that room, surrounded by bodies, reliving every mistake he'd ever made, the fuse disappearing before his eyes, he had come to accept what he'd always known. He didn't have the courage to kill himself.

He wasn't brave enough to die.

He jumped out the window before the explosion tore the building in two, and disguised himself in strips of long black cloth fluttering in the breeze, wrapping the material around his body until his eyes were all that could be seen, like he'd seen the women do before. When the crowd gathered to watch, emerging from the surrounding desert like wildflowers in spring, he mixed with the other women and vanished into their midst, like a drop of blood into the ocean. The diggers shouted, their rifles pointed at the crowd, until they dispersed.

Part of him never left Har Megiddo. Part of him died there. In every flash of fear he catches in a stranger's eye, he recognises the faces of the women. The bearded men crumpling beneath his bullets haunt his sleep. Around every corner, scampering children fall silent until he passes, like they can smell it on him, like he is the evil their parents warned them about. Maybe he is.

On the road that curves around the park, he walks past an older man, who is missing an arm, his moustache trimmed, akubra shading his face from the sun.

'Where is everyone?' he asks.

The man smiles and points back through town. 'Probably at the cricket. New around here?'

He nods, and then shakes his head.

The man removes his hat, and holds it with the stump of his arm and the fingers of his remaining hand. 'It's a special Anzac Day match.' The remaining fabric in the sleeve has been sewn back up under the stump, where it wobbles back and forth each time the man moves. 'Bit of two-up afterward if you're keen.'

'Thanks,' Alan says, then surprises himself by adding, 'I might be.'

'No worries.'

The cricket oval, and the pavilion, lie over the hill, on the other side of town. He could walk it with his eyes closed.

Half the town must be watching, the seats in the pavilion crammed full of suited men, women in their lace fanning themselves, children running riot on the grass banks. He tries to slow his breathing. He's not a fan of large crowds.

He knocks at the door of the groundskeeper's shed, away from the eyes of the crowd. When he pushes inside, the mowers and the heavy rollers look used, but he finds cobwebs growing in the corners. Decent spot to spend the night, once the crowds have departed. He throws his bag down on the rickety table. He doesn't own a lot. A few bits of clothing, half a pencil, a blanket for when it gets cold.

He leaves his bag inside a rusting toolbox. Carrying it makes him look like an outsider. The years of practice have taught him well. They don't glance twice at you if you're a local. But if you want to keep it, carry it on you. Never hide what you can't leave behind. In most places, they'll run him out of town soon enough. Most places, he's passing through.

Marybrook High are batting. Three for ninety-two. He finds a spot on the grass and lies back, watches a few overs. The young bowler has a good action, the ball coming close to the outside edge each time he sprints in. Beside him on the grass the children scream and laugh, playing their own game around the bearded stranger in their midst, cheering each time the definitive *tok* of bat on ball heralds a boundary.

Half an hour later, the next bowler makes the breakthrough – the ball catches a thin edge and the wicketkeeper jumps up in a loud appeal as soon as the ball is in his gloves. The umpire holds up his left hand to signal the wicket. His hand is warped and scarred, missing fingers. Drinks are called, and he watches the umpire limp over to his mate and chat, a wide white hat shading his face. From the crowd by the pavilion a small woman strides into the middle of the ground carrying two glasses of liquid. From his spot on the grass he recognises the gentle roll of her hips, the gold sheen of her hair. She stops by the umpires and offers them each a drink, waiting as they drain the glasses. Before she leaves, she stands on tiptoe and kisses the taller umpire, the gangly one with the mangled finger and the limp. She smiles as she walks off the ground.

Play resumes. He slumbers in the sun. He could camp on the beach and work odd jobs and make a bit of money, or head north and work the cattle drives, lose himself in the dust. In time, he might feel welcome. His stomach grumbles.

After a few years attempting to lose his past in the steamy cities of the East, he made his way to England, and tried his hand at odd jobs. He caught the steam trains up and down the length of the country, searching. He wasn't sure what he was looking for. He slept under bridges with the other searchers, in barns, in open fields under the stars. They slept in groups, the wanderers, like they were back in the camps, huddled for warmth. He painted fences and built houses, rounded up sheep and shovelled coal. For a year he led a normal life in a small village, running the post office, drinking late into the night in the pub with Roland who'd survived the Somme and kept pace with his warm ales. One night he woke screaming at the darkness, the Thompsons from next door banging on his front door to check that he was alright, and he knew it was time to leave.

He was skirting them, unconsciously at first, but then methodically – circling the town where they lived, dropping closer and closer with every visit, like the big bombers circled the munitions dumps – spurred on by a demand for closure. It wasn't that he was avoiding them, or was scared of what seeing them might do to him, it was that he was scared of what he might do to them.

Winter came, and snow, and the work dried up, and he caught a cold from sitting in the rain. He snivelled and sneezed and made his way into their little town. He slept in the church shed, the snow piled up around the door, until the vicar found him, feverish and frozen. The vicar tried to take him straight to the local hospital, but he imagined her pulling back the curtains and refused. He said he'd prefer to die than spend another night in one of those death factories. The vicar prayed for him, like that would help.

Once he was back on his feet, he offered the local publican his services for the winter. She already had a man for odd jobs, she said, but they did need someone new in the kitchens, if he was up to it, if he kept himself clean and didn't drink, like the last fellow. No bully beef, no biscuits, he said, and took the job. The kitchen was warm. He slept in front of the stove like a big, hairy dog.

And then one day, as he stood outside the pub in the snow smoking his last cigarette, he saw them. They walked across the road toward him, holding hands, approaching the church and the station. She looked the same – a bit rounder maybe, and pinker. Or sharper maybe, pointier. Her nose held high and her heels clipping through the snow and the angles of her face a millimetre off. He ducked his head but she didn't look his way, her attention on the girl.

The girl's shoes barely left a trace on the snow, and two thick coats trebled her size. A scarf wound up tight around her head so all he could see was a pink nose. Like she was being protected from more than the cold. Nothing changed in him – no sense of ownership, no paternal urge. After all, it was only her word that the girl was his.

And he was surprised to find he wasn't angry at them either. They were strangers to him, and nothing more. As they walked up the road, a man came walking down it. Older than him, ruddy-cheeked and barrel-chested. The girl ran forward to meet him, and he picked her up and spun her into his arms.

He could hear her giggles over the noise of the pub. The three of them disappeared up the hill. He threw his cigarette into the imprint of the child's shoe in the snow, and left town without a word, melting into the white.

~

In the heat of the midday sun, he walks down to the beach, to the empty sand and the gentle lapping waves and the endless blue of sea and sky. He strips off and the water burns, cold and cleansing. The scars on his back sting. He takes the time to wash his socks, leaving them to dry on the hot sand. His feet are white and bony.

He ducks under the waves and holds his breath until he has no choice but to kick up. Tiny air bubbles stick in his beard. His ribs jut from his chest like a scrawny dingo. His hair sticks up on the back of his head as it dries. His nose runs clean with salty water.

Out the back, beyond the small crests of white foam, he convinces himself he can make out the telltale grey triangle of fin. He swims back into shore, lifting his arms with long, heavy strokes, slow kicks, deep breathing. When he can stand, he pushes back up the beach with his fingertips trailing the water by his side.

He puts his thin shirt back on wet, the material clinging to his bones. His face dries tight with salt in the midday sun.

A young family passes him as he leaves, small children squealing in delight. A teenage girl, who must be about her age now, chats with excitement to her father.

He nods as they pass, and the father returns his gaze.

The family heads past him toward the beach.

'Be careful, think I saw a fin,' he turns and calls, but they're already halfway down the beach.

After the second war, when they'd killed off another generation of young men and destroyed another set of dreams, he left Europe. He paid for his fare and caught the boat back home, alongside families heading off to new lives, other survivors. No more running away, he lied to himself.

Perth was greyer, muted and concrete. The sand on the beach wasn't as white as he remembered. He slept by the river, watching the rowing boats skim past at dawn. The makeshift huts from his years of study, a lifetime before, had been transformed into an office block. He made his way to the university, a huge expanse of beautiful new limestone buildings swarming the bay he had cycled around as a different man. He watched the ducks swim across the pond, the peacocks amble across the lawn. He was walking through someone else's memories.

Inside the library, he made his way down to the deserted bottom floor, the shelves bulging under the weight of old books and forgotten manuscripts. In a corner stack he searched the names until he reached the M's. From inside his battered bag he pulled the small bundle of papers Nugget had left him. The leather strap was worn, the outer pages ripped and yellowed. He'd lost half a dozen pages in a freak downpour one summer in England. But the rest he'd kept safe throughout the years. He'd never had the strength to read it.

But he'd never left it behind. It was all he had left to do. Something he could do for Nugget, finally. It wouldn't change anything, but it might bring him a little peace. He was getting better at finding peace.

He reached up to the higher shelves, and wedged the bundle behind a weighty set of leather dictionaries. His fingers left long lines in the dust.

'There you go, mate,' he said in a whisper, 'you made it.'

As he's walking back into town, sand in his socks, his shirt already dry, he notices a young police constable marching down the main street. The officer crosses the road and walks right up to where Alan waits in the shade of the trees on the edge of the park.

'G'day, old-timer. Mind if I ask you a few questions?' Frowning at Alan as he looks him up and down. That didn't take long.

'Do you have somewhere to be tonight?' the officer says. 'Somewhere to sleep?'

Alan shakes his head.

'Friends, you're staying with?'

He shakes his head again.

'Any reason to be here?'

'I'm only passing through,' he says. 'I won't be any trouble.'

'Where are you headed, then?'

'Home.'

'Where's that then?'

He pauses before answering, weighing up his options, glancing back the way he's come, the sand and the chatter of the gulls and the pull of the dark waves.

'Long way from here.'

The constable nods, considering this, and then, with a grunt, walks away. As he crosses the street, he turns back, giving Alan one final glare, as if to say 'I'll be watching'.

As Alan looks around the park, he notices the monument they've erected in the corner, like a miniature Gothic church made from rough granite, rising to a triangular point in the cloudless sky. He walks over for a closer look. Someone's left a wreath of red poppies by the base of the memorial, but the sun has bleached the flowers pink, and spiders have made webs among the folds.

The inscription carved on marble inserts: *In Honour of the Men and Women of This District Who Volunteered for Service.* On the other side a long list of names, *In Memoriam.*

The Heroic Dead, it says, above his old name.

Lewis A., VC.

No-one could possibly live up to that name, to those stories.

To those lies.

He spends a long time standing in front of the stone, unable to move his leaden feet. Staring up at the legacy some other version of himself has left behind. Over the hill he can hear the cricket game, the hubbub of voices, the occasional cheer or groan as the batsman dispatches the ball with a crisp *tok* all around the field.

The names of the real heroes, long dead, tower above him. The spiked point of granite pierces the brilliant blue.

Each time the batsman hits the ball the sound carries over the yellowing grass, like the thud of his heart in his chest.

Tok.

Tok.

Tok.

ACKNOWLEDGEMENTS

In striving to be authentic to the time period, some of the terms used by the soldiers in this novel are derogatory, though at the time they were terms of common use. No offence is intended in their use.

While the stories in this novel are entirely fictional, some of the books and articles referenced in Matt's thesis are not, so I would like to acknowledge the following, specifically, for my research purposes as much as Matt's: 'On Rupert Brooke' by Frances Cornford reproduced with the permission of the trustees of the Frances Crofts Cornford Will Trust; *The Moods of Ginger Mick* by C.J. Dennis, Angus & Robertson, Sydney, 1916; 'R.H.G. of Boddington' quote from *The Daily News*, Monday 13th March 1950, p. 5, accessed via Trove, trove.nla.gov.au; *Gallipoli to Tripoli: History of the 10th Light Horse Regiment AIF 1914–1919* by Ian Gill and Neville Browning, Hesperian Press, Carlisle, 2012; *The Price of Valour* by John Hamilton, Pan Macmillan, Sydney, 2012; *Devils on Horses: In the Words of the Anzacs in the Middle East 1916–19* by Terry Kinloch, Exisle Publishing, Auckland, 2007; and *The Penguin Book of First World War Poetry* edited by George Walter, Penguin Classics, Sydney, 2007.

Likewise, without the following books, neither Alan's nor Matt's stories would exist: *Harold's Diary* by Ian H. Reece, self-published, Toowong, 2005 (with thanks to Jessica Reece); *During the War I Rode A Horse: A Cheeky Story of the 10th Australian Light Horse 1914–1919* by Lyle Vincent Murphy, AuthorHouse, Bloomington, 2011; *Great Anzac Stories* by Graham Seal, Allen & Unwin, Sydney, 2013; and *Somewhere in France* by Allan M. Nixon, The Five Mile Press, Fitzroy, 1989.

Thanks also to Jonathan Myerson, Clare Allan, Anthony Cartwright, Kate Worsley and Evie Wyld for their guidance during the first draft of this novel. Massive thanks to Amelia, Amy, David,

Jon, Kathleen, Mahvesh, Molly, Remy, Scarlet, Tansy, Tina and Zehra for all the workshops and critiques, and inspiring me with their own wonderful writing.

Thanks to Fremantle Press and the Fogarty Foundation for shortlisting and publishing this novel, and especially to Georgia Richter for making sense of the beast. Sorry for all the footnotes.

Thanks to my crazy, creative family and friends. To my parents, for raising us to make art. To my grandparents, who served their countries so that we can enjoy the lives we do. And to Kate, who has been with me every step of the way. This book wouldn't exist without you.

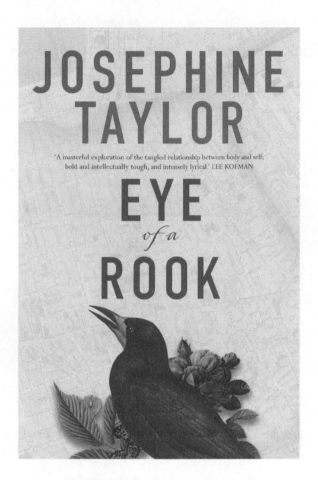

First published 2021 by
FREMANTLE PRESS

Fremantle Press Inc. trading as Fremantle Press
25 Quarry Street, Fremantle WA 6160
(PO Box 158, North Fremantle WA 6159)
www.fremantlepress.com.au

Cover images Shutterstock and iStock.
Printed by McPherson's Printing, Victoria, Australia.
Designed by Nada Backovic, nadabackovic.com.

A catalogue record for this book is available from the National Library of Australia

ISBN 9781925816341 (paperback)
ISBN 9781925816358 (ebook)

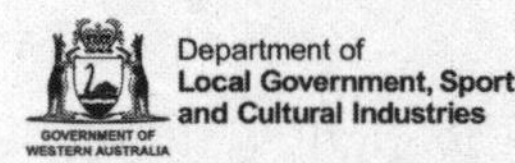

Fremantle Press is supported by the State Government through the Department of Local Government, Sport and Cultural Industries.

Publication of this title was assisted by the Commonwealth Government through the Australia Council, its arts funding and advisory body.